P9-DJU-335

"WE DON'T THINK ALIKE,"

Justin Forbes said with an ironic smile. "But don't take offense."

Meghan O'Brien had to laugh. "Oh, that's big of you."

"But I figure the more we get to be together, the closer in thinking we'll become."

"Do you really?" Meghan asked. "And which one of us is going to give in?" She lifted her chin in mock defiance.

"Neither—or both. We'll see. At least we like the same foods," Justin said, a teasing reminder of the night he had declared they were made for each other.

His fingertip gently brushed Meghan's chin, and Meghan's pulse heightened in response. "If we work at it, I think we might find we have some other appetites in common." The glint in Justin's eye left no doubt as to his meaning....

ABOUT THE AUTHOR

Eleni Carr is on the move again. She and her
husband have lived in California, Long Island and
Virginia, and they're now considering a home in
the south—somewhere near water so they can own
a boat! *Till There Was You*, Ms Carr's third
Superromance, reflects her desire to explore life to
the fullest. She has created some surprising role
reversals to show that a hero can be a sensitive
care giver. The results are thought provoking and
very uplifting.

Books by Eleni Carr

HARLEQUIN SUPERROMANCE
245—THE FOREVER BOND
289—MORE THAN EVER

Don't miss any of our special offers. Write to us at the
following address for information on our newest releases.

Harlequin Reader Service
901 Fuhrmann Blvd., P.O. Box 1397, Buffalo, NY 14240
Canadian address: P.O. Box 603,
Fort Erie, Ont. L2A 5X3

Eleni Carr

TILL THERE WAS YOU

Harlequin Books

TORONTO • NEW YORK • LONDON
AMSTERDAM • PARIS • SYDNEY • HAMBURG
STOCKHOLM • ATHENS • TOKYO • MILAN

Published June 1988

First printing April 1988

ISBN 0-373-70313-9

Copyright © 1988 by Helen Maragakes. All rights reserved.
Except for use in any review, the reproduction or utilization
of this work in whole or in part in any form by any electronic,
mechanical or other means, now known or hereafter invented,
including xerography, photocopying and recording,
or in any information storage or retrieval system, is forbidden without
the permission of the publisher, Harlequin Enterprises Limited,
225 Duncan Mill Road, Don Mills, Ontario, Canada M3B 3K9.

All the characters in this book have no existence outside the
imagination of the author and have no relation whatsoever to
anyone bearing the same name or names. They are not even
distantly inspired by any individual known or unknown to the
author, and all incidents are pure invention.

® are Trademarks registered in the United States Patent and
Trademark Office and in other countries.

Printed in U.S.A.

CHAPTER ONE

MEGHAN WASN'T GOING to let him bother her. With those long, sinewy legs, he could pass her easily if he wanted to. Obviously, he didn't want to.

Meghan O'Brien always started her Tuesday afternoon workout at the health club with a two-mile jog around the indoor track. She had no intention of letting this man with his muscular torso and provocative smile interfere. She had noticed him at the club before. He had an uncanny faculty for showing up to use the same facility just when she was there.

Coincidence? Meghan doubted it. If he was trying to dog her, it wouldn't be difficult. She had a set routine for each of the days she came to the club. Today it was a two-mile jog, a half hour on the Nautilus equipment, an aerobics class, then a short break before her tennis game with Stacy.

Meghan accelerated her pace, and when her raven-haired companion did the same, she shot him a dark look. He answered with a disarming smile. "Jogging's a good way to start a workout," he commented. Meghan didn't respond.

She was usually successful in ignoring or repelling advances from the male patrons of the Alexandria Health Club, but she had a feeling that this man would be difficult to deter.

"Actually, I prefer running out of doors," he said.

"Then why don't you?" she asked oversweetly.

He grinned. "Sometimes, I prefer the indoor scenery." He gave her lithe figure a leisurely appraisal. Meghan braced herself for a come-on, but he surprised her. "See you," he said, gave a short wave and forged ahead.

She couldn't help noticing that there was grace as well as strength in the way he moved. The track was only one fifth of a mile around so he passed her twice before she finished her course. Each time he smiled, but she kept her gaze straight ahead.

Meghan finished, noted her time on her program sheet and headed for the exercise equipment. Methodically, she went through her usual progression of bicycling, leg strengthening, and chest expansion, following up with some stretching exercises on a floor mat. Meghan noticed that there were very few people using the machines and her running companion wasn't among them. Maybe he'd quit early today. It was almost five, the time when the club started getting busy. Meghan usually arranged her appointments so that she could come to the club before the rush at least two afternoons a week. Lester Patterson, the senior member of the law firm where Meghan worked, didn't mind. Compensatory time off, Lester called it, since Meghan often met with clients during the evening hours.

The participants in the aerobics class were assembling on the far side of the huge open area, so Meghan strolled over. Individual mats were strewn around the gym floor, which doubled as the basketball court. Fritzi, the instructor, was setting up her music and microphone. It was too bad the aerobics class couldn't be held in a separate room. Often, the men waiting to use the basketball court at six o'clock became leering spectators. Fritzi occasionally cajoled a few into joining in, but most of the guys preferred watching the women.

The class was about to start. Meghan looked around for her friend Stacy. Stacy Tolliver was the law firm's paralegal assistant and Meghan's frequent companion here at the club. Stacy wasn't into jogging or exercise machines, but she loved the aerobics classes and her twice-a-week tennis game with Meghan. There she was, coming out of the women's locker room in an electric blue leotard and tights.

"Hi," Meghan said. "New outfit?"

Stacy nodded. "Does it make me look svelte?" Chubby, blond and curvy, Stacy was constantly striving for thinness, or the illusion of it.

"It looks great," Meghan said, giving her friend an affectionate smile, "but why do you need a whole wardrobe of leotards?"

Stacy surveyed her appraisingly. "If I was shaped like you, I wouldn't. But in case you haven't noticed, I'm not five seven with a willowy figure that's marvelous in a tight black leotard. I'd be a washout in plain black, but on you it looks good. It's that rusty hair and green eyes."

Appearing businesslike and attractive in her professional capacity was important to Meghan, but she gave little thought to how she looked here at the club. Without make-up, and with her tawny hair freed from its usual neatness, she exuded a vibrancy that she kept subdued during her workday.

"All right, ladies. Let's get going," Fritzi called. She started the music. "Any of you gentlemen care to join us?" she asked, addressing the men on the sidelines. A young athletic type accepted the invitation but the half dozen others stayed put. Another man joined the viewers.

"There he is," Stacy whispered excitedly.

"Who?"

"Justin Forbes. The guy who's got the hots for you."

"Don't exaggerate."

"Come on. He keeps following you around."

"How do you know his name?"

"I asked Perry."

"You didn't!" Perry was the assistant manager and kept close tabs on all the members. He also prided himself on the many romances that had their beginnings at the Alexandria Club.

"I thought you'd be curious," Stacy said innocently.

"I'm not." That wasn't quite true. Meghan derived a certain satisfaction from being able to affix a name to the man whose attention was disturbing her.

Fritzi started the class and Meghan tried to concentrate on the instructor's voice as she led them through the routine. "Now, arms outstretched, and bend to the right, one two, that's the way, five six, keep on going, nine ten. Good. Straighten. Now reverse and stretch, one two..."

Meghan didn't have to think. Her body was limber and she could easily duplicate what Fritzi was doing without listening much to the words. She kept herself from glancing toward the sidelines where Justin Forbes was standing, but she was well aware of his eyes on her. Justin Forbes...a strong name. It suited him. Or at least it went with his appearance; she knew nothing about the man himself. But that wasn't entirely true. She knew he was interested in her and that his approach was not typical. He wasn't heavy-handed with a here-I-am-you-lucky-woman attitude, nor did he come on with the slick line of a singles-bar regular. He was biding his time, waiting. For what?

"Now bend from the waist, one two. Come on, Gladys, you can do it. Seven eight, that's the way. Reach, reach..."

At the end of the class, Stacy and Meghan started for the locker room. "He's looking," Stacy whispered.

"So?"

"You could say hello."

"No, I couldn't." Meghan chose instead to stare him down, but it didn't phase Justin a bit. He met her look with a broad smile.

Stacy gave an audible sigh. "Now there's a smile you could die from."

She had a point. The man's smile was affable, curious, admiring, slightly mocking and very sexy—a potent combination.

The two women showered and changed into tennis whites and went to the club's coffee shop for their refreshment break. Meghan decided on an English muffin and a cup of tea and sat at their usual table next to the huge window wall that overlooked the exercise floor. The men had started playing basketball and Meghan's eyes picked out the dark head and darting form of Justin Forbes. She knew little about the game, but he seemed skillful and was certainly enjoying himself.

At one point, he glanced up, but Meghan couldn't be sure he saw her. Since he apparently had her schedule memorized, he probably knew she was there, just as he knew she was playing tennis in a half hour. Justin Forbes didn't have a regular game, but he always seemed to show up at the courts at that time, sometimes catching a game with someone, sometimes just hanging around to watch.

Stacy set down her tray and Meghan was surprised at the double cheeseburger and chocolate brownie. "We never eat heavy before tennis," Meghan reminded her.

"I know, but I had to skip lunch and I'm famished."

"We could eat after we play."

"I'd never make it through the game."

But at five to six, when they got up to leave, Stacy moaned. "You were right about the cheeseburger," she said. "I feel kinda sick."

"You probably just ate too fast. It'll pass."

"I don't think so. Everything I ate is sitting here—" she rubbed her solar plexus "—in one big blob."

"We don't have to play," said Meghan.

"I'll be okay. I just won't run around too much."

But she wasn't okay. When Stacy missed a gentle lob that Meghan had carefully directed to her forehand, Meghan called a halt. "Stacy, you're beginning to look green. You'd better quit."

"I guess you're right, Meghan. I'm sorry."

"No sweat. Want me to take you home?"

"No. Tony's supposed to pick me up at seven. I'll give him a call to come early." She started off the court, then turned. "Hey, I could check if Rod's free. He might want a game." Rod was the tennis pro at the club. When he had free time, he enjoyed playing for fun.

"Why not? I'll stick around and practice my serve for a while." Meghan had played with Rod before and relished the challenge.

It was, however, a different kind of challenge that was offered.

Meghan didn't notice him until he was directly behind her. She had just tossed the ball and brought her racket back when she heard the words, "Not high enough."

Distracted, she followed through feebly and her ball didn't clear the net.

"Your toss isn't high enough," Justin Forbes observed mildly.

"It would've cleared if you hadn't sneaked up on me."

"Sorry. But you really will do better with a higher toss."

"I'm not in the mood for a lesson, thank you anyway."

"How about a game, then?"

"As a matter of fact, I'm waiting for Rod."

"He's tied up. I told your friend that I'm available." He smiled. "She told me to come ahead."

I'll just bet she did, Meghan thought. "I really don't think so, Mr. Forbes." Oh damn! She let it slip that she knew his name. Would he think she'd gone out of her way to learn it?

"Why not?" he asked. "Hey, I promise I'll go easy on you."

"Oh, will you now?" Meghan felt her temper rise. Justin Forbes had watched her play, but he had never seen her at her best. Stacy was a competent player, but Meghan had to adjust her usual hard-hitting style when she played with her. Only on the rare occasions that she played with Rod had she been able to let loose. She couldn't resist Justin Forbes's challenge. "Okay then," she said. "Let's have a game. But no going easy."

Meghan noticed there was a definite arch to Justin's brows as he raised them at her words. All his facial contours were pronounced—aquiline nose, sharply etched mouth, high cheekbones, eyes set wide apart. Nothing wishy- washy there. Perhaps his lower lip was too wide, but the fullness, curved that way as he smiled at her, suggested sensuality, not softness.

"You're on, Meghan O'Brien," he said.

It turned out that they were well matched. Justin had the power and strength, but Meghan's years of competitive playing in high school and college helped her make up in skill what she lacked in brawn.

He had a blockbuster of a serve and a swift, powerful forehand that Meghan couldn't always return. But Justin's eyes were often on her, not on the ball, and she could surprise him by placing a shot where he least expected it. Going into the third set, they were tied and Meghan played with heightened fervor. She felt she could win. Her concentration was better than his, but that damned smile seemed to indicate that he was having a better time. His smile actually broadened when she won the last set and the game.

"You *are* good," he said with sincere admiration.

Why couldn't he have been a sore loser as she had expected? She found herself returning his smile.

"Have I been hustled by a pro?" he asked cheerfully.

"Hardly."

"You play like one, like you've got to win."

"That's the whole idea, isn't it?"

"Not always." They started to walk out, and he pointed to a group of four older players just as a gray-haired woman hit a high, wafting ball. "Look at that foursome. They don't care about the score. They're just having fun."

"There are all kinds of fun. I like winning."

Justin cocked his head and looked at her quizzically. "I've watched you play with your friend. You're not cut-throat with her."

Meghan had to laugh. "I guess Stacy doesn't bring out the competitiveness in me."

"And I do?"

"Apparently. Does it bother you?"

"On the tennis court, no."

"Well, I don't think we have to worry about anything else."

"Don't we?" he asked with a raised brow. When she turned away, he caught her arm. "Look, why don't we celebrate your victory with dinner tonight?"

"A tennis win is hardly cause for a celebration."

"It'll do, for now."

"Thank you, but no."

"Other plans?"

He was certainly persistent. She could cut him down by telling him it was none of his business. She could, but didn't. It was that ingratiating smile of his. "I have work to do," she said.

"A drink?"

"No."

"Just coffee then?"

"I can't. I've got to go. Thanks for the game."

"My pleasure." He reached for her hand and the strength and warmth of his fingers closing over hers came as a surprise. There was no need for the gesture. It wasn't a handshake exactly, and the way he held on made it an intimate contact. Flustered, but covering with a cool smile, Meghan pulled away. "Can we do it again sometime?" he asked.

It took her a second to realize he meant the tennis game. "We'll see," was her noncommittal reply, and she hurried off to the locker room.

JUSTIN WATCHED HER RETREAT, for that's how he saw her action, a retreat. But why? Her turndown had been cool and emphatic. He continued to watch as she stopped at the front desk to say something to the receptionist. With an unconsciously graceful gesture, Meghan raised her hand to push her hair back from her neck. She was beautiful—shapely long legs, a slender body, those green eyes and vibrant hair. But it was more than Meghan O'Brien's looks that attracted him.

He was intrigued by this woman who brought such fiery passion to a simple competitive game and then withdrew into a cool shell at a personal overture. She had ignored or discouraged his previous attempts to be friendly. At least he'd managed to get to first base this time. And she probably meant to keep him there, he thought wryly.

Justin wasn't used to being rejected and this, too, intrigued him. Bachelors in their early thirties were a prized commodity in any metropolitan area, and Alexandria, Virginia was no exception. But it wasn't the challenge of the chase that interested him. He'd gotten over that long ago. To Justin, chase and conquest could be as boring as submissive admiration, an opinion not widely held among his male acquaintances who still liked to play that game.

In Meghan O'Brien, Justin sensed a complex woman of strength and discipline and passion. And pain, too. She aroused his curiosity—and his desire.

MEGHAN USUALLY had a feeling of accomplishment when she finished a workout at the Alexandria Club. Keeping fit and trim was part of her routine. Unlike some women whose initial burst of enthusiasm for exercise was followed by a slackening of purpose, Meghan stuck to the program mapped out for her. The club as a social center wasn't what appealed to her. The single men there were mostly macho types who hit on any woman who looked good in a leotard. She had assumed that Justin Forbes was in that category, but he seemed to show more finesse than the others. Not that it made much difference. Subtle or crude, he just wasn't her type.

So why did she feel so unsettled? Maybe ten minutes in the sauna would drain it all out of her. Meghan stripped, wrapped a towel around herself and went into the sauna chamber. With relief, she saw that no one else was there. She could never understand why some women tried to make conversation in this hot, dense atmosphere. Very soon, Meghan's body became as liquid as the air. The towel slid from her. She closed her eyes, letting all conscious thought evaporate.

The bracing shower afterward brought her back to reality. Her skin tingled as she rubbed herself dry, and she wondered fleetingly at the unusual sensuous pleasure she felt. Because of the encounter with Justin Forbes? But that was ridiculous. They'd hardly exchanged a dozen sentences. Of course, physical attraction didn't depend on conversation as a stimulus, but then Meghan had always distrusted that kind of magnetism.

As a child, she couldn't understand how her mother could continue to sleep with a man who abused her. But Tim O'Brien was a handsome rogue, charmingly seductive when he wanted to be. Her mother hadn't the strength of will to resist. Meghan was determined never to display such weakness.

MEGHAN'S SUPPER came from the salad bar at her local supermarket, rounded off with a cold chicken leg left over from last night's meal. She seldom cooked for herself. It was so much easier to pick something up and nibble while she tackled the work she often brought home. Work was by far her highest priority.

Meghan hadn't set out to specialize in women's issues; it had just happened. Her reputation for taking on hard-to-win cases and battling through to victorious decisions for her clients made her sought after for that kind of work. Her staid colleagues in the prestigious Alexandria law firm didn't always approve of her choice of clients and her hard-hitting courtroom tactics, but that didn't slow her down. They were all men. Meghan refused to be daunted by male disapproval just as she was not swayed by male admiration.

She was still at the table in the alcove of her cramped kitchen when the telephone rang. She barely had to stretch to reach the wall phone. One good thing about living in this small apartment was that practically everything was within arm's reach.

"Meghan, it's Stacy."

"I was going to call you. How are you feeling?"

"Much better. Tony got me some fizzy tablets that fixed me right up. He just left."

"Tony's a sweet guy."

"Yeah, sure. Now tell me all."

"All what?"

"You know what I mean. Justin Forbes."

"I almost think you planned the whole thing."

Stacy was indignant. "One does not plan on getting indigestion."

"Not that part."

"Could I help it if he happened to be there when I told Rod you were looking for a game and Rod happened to be tied up and Justin happened to volunteer and—"

"All right," Meghan said with a laugh. "So it just *happened*."

"And then what?" Stacy was avid for details.

"And then nothing. We played tennis. I beat him."

Stacy gasped. "You didn't."

"It took some doing. He's pretty good."

"You shouldn't have tried so hard."

"I hope you don't mean what I think you mean," said Meghan. "Women don't hold back for fear of bruising a man's ego. Those days are over."

"Maybe," Stacy said doubtfully, "but you don't want to be too independent."

"There's no such thing in my book."

"I know. I know. And then what?"

"Well, I took a sauna, showered, picked up some salad, came home and ate it. What else do you want to know?"

"Don't tease. What about Justin Forbes? Didn't he ask you out?"

"He mentioned dinner or a drink. I wasn't interested."

Stacy groaned. "I'd kill for a man like that, and she says she's not interested."

"You've got Tony; count your blessings. They don't come any nicer than that."

Meghan's praise was sincere. Tony Nicoletti was a CPA with an office in their building and as sweet and gentle a man as Meghan had ever met.

"Sure, but that's not your type," Stacy reminded her.

They said goodbye and Meghan replaced the receiver pensively. Before he met Stacy, Tony had been interested in Meghan, but she had turned him down. The episode was so unimportant in Meghan's mind that she had almost forgotten about it. Yet here she was extolling his virtues. If sweet and gentle was what she prized, why couldn't she drum up any romantic interest in such men?

On the other end of the scale was the type that repelled her, the aggressive male who flaunted his masculinity and strength. Her father had been like that. An Irish rogue, sinfully handsome, charming when sober, funny and rambunctious with a couple of drinks in him, but dangerous and brutal when he had drunk too much.

Meghan couldn't stem the flood of painful memories. For years, Meghan's mother had covered up for her husband, but as he became increasingly violent, she couldn't explain away her bruises. At first, Meghan had cooperated in her mother's attempts to shield her from the truth; the child didn't want to see what was going on. When she was twelve, she couldn't pretend any longer and refused to be shielded. She learned she could stop her father from hitting her mother by stepping between them, intimidating him with the shame of his conduct.

Her mother, wanting to believe her husband's promises to reform, kept accepting his contrite apologies, but Meghan couldn't. Not time after time. Finally, Elizabeth O'Brien gave up, took her teenage daughter and moved to Washington, where she had relatives.

Rationally, Meghan knew that her mother's untimely death a few years later wasn't directly attributable to her husband's abuse, but emotions weren't always rational. Meghan still blamed the father she hadn't seen in fifteen years. When her mother died, Meghan had burned all the pictures of her handsome father, but she couldn't burn away the memory of him.

Stacy was the only friend to whom Meghan had mentioned this part of her childhood. Playing amateur psychologist, Stacy had suggested that Meghan unconsciously blamed all men who reminded her of her father, all tall, muscular, handsome men with easy charm and ready smiles.

Like Justin Forbes?

To herself, Meghan conceded that she felt a protective mechanism come into play with such men. Their natural attributes drew susceptible women who didn't mind taking a dependent role. Meghan was not that kind of woman.

Was Justin Forbes that kind of man?

CHAPTER TWO

"MY NAME IS STELLA CRANSHAW. I've just got to see you."

Meghan wondered why Phyllis hadn't handled the request for an appointment. "Let me transfer you back to the secretary," Meghan said. "She'll give you an appointment."

"No, please. She already told me you were busy all day."

"Then—"

"But I've just got to see you today." The voice trembled with agitation.

"What's your number?" asked Meghan. "I'll see if I can rearrange my schedule and call you back."

"I'm not home." The implication was that the caller couldn't go home. "Maybe you could see me after your last appointment," she pleaded.

Meghan looked at her watch. It was almost two. "Okay. Can you be here at five?"

"Any time you say." The voice sounded pathetically grateful.

"Make that four-thirty," Meghan told her. She hung up and buzzed Phyllis to tell her to try to change her last appointment.

"She got to you, eh?" Phyllis asked. "I figured she would. She sounded like a kid, a desperate kid. What's her problem?"

"She didn't say."

But when Meghan saw Stella Cranshaw later that afternoon, she knew immediately. The sight of the young woman's bruised face filled Meghan with remembered agony. Instead of sitting with the desk between them, Meghan led Stella to the leather couch in her office. "Want to tell me about it?" she asked softly.

It was the right note. The situation warranted other than cold formality, but too much pity might cause Stella to break down. Her eyes showed that she had done plenty of crying already.

Stella nodded and swallowed hard, but the words wouldn't come right away. Meghan waited. Stella Cranshaw was young, early twenties at most, but she wore a wedding ring. Satiny dark hair parted in the middle fell to her shoulders; the pallor of her skin was heightened by the bruises beginning to darken on her cheekbone and chin. She was petite, with an appealing frail prettiness that suggested vulnerability. But Meghan had learned that the woman's appearance in such cases wasn't significant. Victims of abuse came in all shapes and sizes. One of her clients had been a female bodybuilder.

"Who did it?" asked Meghan gently.

Stella looked down at her twisting hands. "Brad," she finally managed to say.

"Brad's your husband?"

Stella nodded.

"When did this happen?" From the discoloration of the bruises, Meghan guessed it had been within the past twenty-four hours, but she needed Stella to tell her story.

"Last night." The answer was barely audible.

Meghan reached over and covered Stella's hands with her own. The comforting gesture must have been reassuring. Stella's hands stilled and she looked up at Meghan. "He wouldn't eat any supper. Just kept drinking. He wouldn't talk to me. He wouldn't come to bed. Then he wanted more liquor and accused me of hiding it on him.''

"Did you?"

Stella nodded. ''That's when he hit me. But it was worse this time.''

Meghan felt a sinking thud in her chest, but she tried to keep her voice even as she asked, "Then this wasn't the first time?"

"No."

"Have you called the police?"

Stella shook her head. Meghan wasn't surprised. Like many other battered women, Stella had not pressed charges.

Haltingly, Stella told her story. Brad had beaten her twice before. She had treated the first two assaults as isolated incidents. Brad was having problems at work and was drinking more than usual. "To unwind," he claimed, except that the liquor seemed to have the opposite effect. He would come home troubled and nervous, but after a few drinks, he became agitated and argumentative. He refused to talk to her about what was bothering him, said he needed to forget about the job. If she asked him not to drink, he accused her of nagging. Maybe she did nag, Stella admitted, but she wanted to help him.

"Last night, though, I was really scared," Stella told Meghan. "He didn't just smack me and stop like the other times. Once before, he even cried and said he didn't know what got into him.''

Meghan didn't reveal her disdain for this revelation. She had no sympathy for the tears of a wife-beater.

"This time," Stella continued, "his eyes got all yellowy, and when I screamed, it was like he didn't even hear. I stayed with him after the first times because I didn't think it would keep happening. Brad wasn't himself. He was hurting and I thought I could help. But if he won't let me, there's no point in my staying? Is there?'' After this pathetic question, the tears finally came.

Meghan let her cry. ''What is it you would like me to do?'' Meghan asked when Stella's sobs subsided.

''I can't go back there.''

''No, of course you can't.''

''I can't stay with him when he's like that.''

''Do you want a divorce?''

Stella looked stricken. Meghan wondered why divorce was so hard to accept when it was the only reasonable alternative in a case like this.

''And you want me to represent you?''

Stella nodded again. ''Will you? I'm not sure when I'll be able to pay you but ...''

''That's not what's important now. First, let's find a place for you to stay. Are your parents nearby?''

''My mother's dead. I can't go to my father,'' Stella said fearfully. ''He'd call Brad first thing and tell him to come get me.''

Meghan made a mental note to find out more about Stella's father, but not now. ''Don't worry. Unfortunately, your problem is far from unique. There are several shelters for battered women in the area.''

The term ''battered women'' bothered Stella. ''I'm not that badly hurt,'' she said.

''A shelter's not a hospital, just a safe place to stay for a while.'' Meghan got the secretary on the intercom. ''Phyllis, get me Rose Esposito at the Women's Center. I'll hold.'' She put her hand over the receiver. ''Rose is great in cases like this. I've worked with her before,'' she told Stella.

Phyllis put the call through. ''Okay, what have you got for me this time?'' was Rose's perfunctory greeting.

Meghan smiled. Rose Esposito was short on small talk, but the overburdened social worker was big on problem solving. She had a good heart, but Meghan appreciated her practical intelligence even more. "The usual," Meghan told her. Briefly, and in a matter-of-fact tone so as not to upset Stella, Meghan explained the circumstances. "My client needs a safe place to stay for a while."

Rose sighed heavily. "Easier said than done, my friend. Every shelter is full."

"You've been known to talk them into taking one more."

"I'm talking full to bulging."

"What about The House of Sheila in Arlington?"

"I got turned down there just yesterday on another case. I'll get back to you. I'll make a few calls—maybe find some place that will take her for a day or two."

"I was hoping for more than that."

"Hey, I've got an idea." The new brightness in Rose's voice was encouraging. "I just heard about this new place. I've got the information somewhere here on my desk." Meghan heard the sound of shuffling papers. "Here it is. Midway House. It's privately funded. I heard the director speak at a symposium last week. It's a different kind of program to study and treat domestic violence."

Not another psychology study, Meghan thought. "Rose, my client needs a place to stay, not a shrink."

"Midway House *is* a place to stay, and not just as an emergency shelter for a day or a week. But it can accommodate only a few residents in this start-up phase. Let me call the director and see what's what."

"Call me back."

"Right away."

Rose had an answer within ten minutes. "All set," she announced.

"Great. Are you going to take her over there?"

"Don't I always? I'm on my way."

With a sense of relief, Meghan hung up. "Rose will be here in a few minutes. She's going to take you to a place called Midway House. You'll be okay there."

"But I don't have anything with me." Stella spread her hands helplessly. "Not even a toothbrush."

"Give me your address. I'll go over and pick up some things for you."

"Brad'll probably be there."

"That's fine. He may as well know where we stand."

Rose arrived a short time later and showed just the right combination of sympathy and brisk good humor to reassure the apprehensive young woman.

"I'm going to Stella's house to see if I can get some clothes for her."

"No problem. She'll be fine with me." Rose handed Meghan a card on which she'd written the address of the shelter.

"I'll pick up some of your things and I'll be over later," Meghan told Stella. "Don't worry. You'll be all right."

She knew nothing about Midway House or its director, but Meghan trusted Rose's judgment. She would get to meet the director later and form her own opinion of the woman.

THE CRANSHAW HOUSE in McLean surprised Meghan. It was a miniature colonial mansion on three acres of sweeping lawns.

Brad Cranshaw was also a surprise. The housekeeper had answered Meghan's ring but Brad, hovering in the background, rushed to confront Meghan when he heard her state her mission. He was of medium height, very thin, with a pale complexion and hair so light it looked bleached. He didn't match the picture in her mind. So much for stereotypes. Like victims, abusers came in all sizes and shapes.

"What d'you mean you're here to pick up my wife's things?" he demanded. "Who are you?"

"My name is Meghan O'Brien. I'm your wife's attorney."

"You're what?" His eyes were bloodshot and he blinked rapidly. "What does she need with a lawyer? Where is she? Where's my wife?"

"I'm afraid I can't tell you that, Mr. Cranshaw."

"What do you mean you can't tell me?" His voice rose threateningly. He came closer, seeming to push even though he didn't touch her. "Where's Stella? What've you done with her?"

Meghan smelled the liquor on his breath. With unconcealed disdain and anger, Meghan replied, "The question is what did *you* do to her, Mr. Cranshaw?"

"Nothing."

"I just saw your wife. Her face is all bruised. She's been beaten. You call that nothing?"

"That's none of your business."

"It is now. Your wife retained me to represent her."

"What for? Where is she? I need to talk to her."

"At the moment, it's *her* needs that concern me. And you're in no condition to talk rationally to anyone. If you'll just allow me to get some of her personal things..."

"No way." He almost shouted in his agitation. "Why didn't she come?"

"For God's sake, man," Meghan replied angrily, "you know why. She's afraid of you."

"Afraid?" His face went slack.

"What did you expect?" Meghan turned to go.

"Wait."

Meghan paused.

"Go ahead," he said sullenly. "Take what you want." He called the housekeeper who led Meghan upstairs to the large,

femininely decorated master bedroom. Meghan put some
essential clothing and toiletries into a small suitcase.

Brad came in and watched, red-eyed and sullen. When
Meghan was ready to go, he said, "I fixed this room up
especially for her."

Meghan said nothing. It wasn't the room that Stella
Cranshaw was trying to escape.

IT WAS DARK NOW, and Meghan had difficulty finding Midway House. Finally, she turned into a long lane and up a
circular driveway to a large Victorian house that had seen
better days. There was no bell, just an old-fashioned brass
knocker that needed polishing. A man opened the front
door.

"Hello," said Meghan. "I'm here to see—" She stopped.
The darkness must have been playing tricks with her vision. The dim light of the hallway was behind the man, so
his face was partially shadowed. It couldn't be. Then he
smiled. It was. It was Justin Forbes.

Justin was amused by Meghan's shocked look. But then,
he'd made a habit of surprising people. He had always
questioned rules and stereotypes. Both his brothers, following their father's example, had become engineers. They
all lived in one of the sprawling new communities in Silicon
Valley. Justin had been the maverick, choosing The College of William and Mary instead of Stanford, and then
opting for a major in psychology instead of engineering.

He had been drawn by the sense of history and tradition
that permeated the William and Mary campus, and then
came to love the beauty of the Virginia landscape. For his
doctorate, he went to graduate school in Washington, D. C.,
but chose to live across the river in Alexandria, Virginia.
The beautiful old city seemed more like home than Silicon
Valley ever had. After a stint in the army and four years in

the Peace Corps, it was to this area that he returned. And now, home was this run-down Victorian house.

"What are you doing here?" Meghan asked.

"I live here."

"Do I have the wrong address? I'm looking for the Midway House."

"You've got it. Come on in."

Meghan stood there, as if still disbelieving.

"Look, it's all right, really. This is the right place." He smiled encouragingly and reached out as if to take her arm, at which Meghan bestirred herself and stepped inside.

"I have the advantage," said Justin. "Stella told me her lawyer's name so I expected you. I guess you didn't expect to see me here."

"That's a good guess. What *are* you doing here?" Meghan had her surprise under control now. "I know you said you live here, but . . ." She paused, then asked with a touch of sarcasm, "Surely you're not an abused spouse?"

"No, I'm not any kind of spouse. I'm not married."

"How nice for you."

"Sometimes I wonder," he said with a grin that clearly bothered her.

Justin led her into a sitting room off the foyer. Like the house's exterior, it had a well-used look, but still gave an impression of warmth and comfort. The old Oriental rug had frayed edges but retained its deep toned hues of burgundy and gold. The furniture, oddly assorted pieces which didn't match, somehow worked in this room. Perhaps it was the softening glow from the several tiffany shaded lamps. Meghan's eyes were drawn to a tall, mahogany grandfathers clock against the wall between the two large windows. It read three-thirty.

"It's a beauty, isn't it?" asked Justin. "I picked it up at a yard sale last week."

"It's got the wrong time."

"I know. I'm going to take it apart when I have time. Don't you think it's perfect for this room?"

"Not if it doesn't work."

"It's still beautiful—and I can make it work."

Somehow, Meghan didn't doubt it. His smile was so confident. And disturbing. "Look," she told him, "I didn't come here to talk about interior decorating. Would you mind explaining what you're doing here."

"I told you," he said with an engaging smile. "I live here."

"With the women in the shelter?"

"Don't look so shocked. Actually, my quarters are in that side wing between the house and the garage—so both propriety and privacy are served."

"I still don't understand."

"It's simple. I'm the director of Midway House."

"You?"

"That's what I said."

Meghan frowned. "Are you putting me on?"

"No."

"But you're a man."

His smile broadened. "I'm glad you noticed. I was beginning to wonder."

Meghan ignored the remark. "I don't understand."

"It's very simple. I'm the director here, and I'm a man. There's no conflict."

"Really?" she challenged.

He became serious. "Yes, really. I'm eminently qualified. In fact I'm better trained for this work than most."

"It's not your training I'm questioning."

"My sex?"

He made it sound impertinent and Meghan was irritated. "How can you possibly understand what an abused woman feels, what she needs?"

"Since when," he asked, "do women have a corner on compassion and concern? Maybe it's good for the women who come here to have contact with a man who approaches them with caring."

"At this time? When they're in flight from some man's brutality?"

"Especially at this time," Justin said with quiet conviction.

Meghan met his gaze and was moved by the fiery intensity there.

"Getting Midway House started took a lot of doing," he said. "It's more than a shelter for women to hide in. It's a place to recover, to take stock and learn and grow. We're considered experimental now, but Midway can become the prototype for a different approach to the problem of abuse in the home."

"Very commendable," Meghan said dryly.

"I wish I could believe you meant that."

Meghan softened. "I do. I think all efforts to help are commendable."

"But?"

Meghan hesitated. She felt strongly that there was no therapeutic solution in a case of wife beating. The woman's only recourse was escape. It was Meghan's job to protect her client's interests and effect the best possible divorce settlement she could get. But Justin Forbes was obviously sincere, if misguided, so why assail him with her views? All she said was, "I don't know about a different approach, but I do know we need more shelters. I'm glad you had room for Stella."

"She's the kind of person Midway can help."

"I'd like to see her in a position to help herself."

"So would I," he said with an affirmative shake of his head. "We have the same goal."

"But, I suspect, not the same methods in mind," said Meghan with amiable skepticism.

"You think we're far apart, do you?" Justin cocked his head and smiled. "That can be remedied."

He did have a most engaging smile. Meghan found herself smiling back. Why not? There was no percentage in antagonizing him. "How about letting me see my client now?" she asked.

"Sure."

At the door, he paused and turned to her with a quizzical, teasing look. "Do you believe in karma?"

"What?"

"Karma... destiny."

She gave a short laugh. "I believe in making my own destiny. Don't you?"

"Yeah. But it's nice when fate gives you an extra boost. Know what I mean?"

"I don't think so."

"That's all right." He grinned. "You will." He left the room and returned in a few minutes with Stella Cranshaw.

The young woman seemed more composed, but her face was still etched with anxiety.

"Would you like me to leave?" Justin asked.

Meghan was about to tell him that would be best but Stella answered first. "No, Justin, please stay."

Meghan was surprised.

"Midway's very informal," said Justin. "We go by first names right away."

But Meghan's surprise wasn't due to the informality of address; it was that Justin Forbes had obviously won Stella's trust in the short time she'd been there.

Justin offered Stella a seat on the overstuffed couch. He pulled over a straight-backed chair for himself and looked expectantly at Meghan, who hadn't moved. "Do you object to my being here?" he asked her.

Meghan hesitated. "I guess not." She went over to sit beside Stella.

"Good," said Justin, "because it would help for me to know what's going on."

"There's nothing much going on—yet," said Meghan. She pointed to the overnight bag she had put down near the door. "I brought you a few things, just—"

"Was Brad there?" Stella interrupted.

"Yes."

"How was he?"

"Belligerent."

Stella nodded unhappily. "He would be."

"I think he'd been drinking."

Stella nodded again. "How did he look?"

"Angry and upset. He never expected you to walk out and certainly never expected you'd consult a lawyer. You surprised him."

"What did he say?"

"He ranted at me for a while, then ordered me to leave, then demanded to see you."

"He wants to see me?" There was anguish in the way the words came out. "Maybe Brad needs me. Maybe I shouldn't have left."

Meghan wasn't surprised by Stella's doubts. She had heard such reactions before, the woman feeling guilty at abandoning the man who had abused her. Meghan became aware of Justin's expression as he listened to Stella; sympathy predominated but there was also a questioning look. Meghan hoped he wasn't misinterpreting Stella's words.

"Maybe I shouldn't have left," Stella said again. "Maybe..."

Meghan reached for her hand. "Don't torture yourself with maybes," said Meghan forcefully. "You did what you had to do. You did exactly right." Meghan turned to Justin for corroboration. "Tell her."

Justin leaned forward, elbows on his knees, eyes intent on Stella. "What you did," he said slowly, "was the right thing—for now."

Meghan wasn't pleased that he qualified his statement, but she said nothing. She gave Stella's hand a squeeze and stood up. "You'd better get some rest. We'll talk some more tomorrow."

"Why not wait a few days?" Justin suggested.

Meghan was surprised. "Why?"

"Just to give Stella a breather, a chance to get settled in here, a chance to think?"

Meghan turned to Stella. "Of course, if that's what you want."

Stella smiled feebly and nodded.

As the three of them walked out into the foyer, an olive-skinned young woman with a flashing smile paused on her way upstairs. "Coming up, Stell?" she asked.

Justin introduced the young woman as Carmela Flores, one of the residents and Stella's roommate.

"Glad to meet ya," was Carmela's acknowledgment, accompanied by a hearty handshake. "You're Stella's lawyer?"

"That's right."

"Stell said she got herself a real hotshot."

"I don't know about that."

"You married?"

Meghan was taken aback by the Hispanic woman's bold curiosity.

"No."

"That's smart. You get married and they think they own ya." She turned to Stella. "Come on, Stella," she said and took the suitcase from her. "Let's go up. I can't wait to see what you've got that I can borrow."

"Pretty tough, isn't she?" Meghan commented when the two young women were gone.

"On the surface, maybe. Carmela's a survivor but she's pretty confused right now. She hides behind that toughness." Justin gave Meghan a searching look. "I think you can understand that."

Meghan felt he was making a personal observation. Yet this man knew nothing about her. "Of course I understand. Maybe some of her toughness will rub off on Stella. Is that why you put them together?"

"I put them together because there are twin beds in Carmela's room. There are four women here, Meghan, four very different individuals." He was talking intently, trying to make her understand. "I hope they'll give each other understanding and support, but I don't expect, indeed I don't *want*, any one person to serve as a model for the rest. Each needs time to find her own way."

There was nothing in his words that Meghan could argue with, yet she sensed a basic difference in their thinking. "I believe that Stella's made a good start," she said.

"I'm not sure."

"What do you mean? Did you expect her to stay and be abused?"

"Of course not. But I think she still loves the guy."

"My God, Justin, how can she? She can't even trust him."

"Right now, she can't," he admitted grimly. "What he's done has undermined her trust, but I don't think he's killed her love for him. You saw just now. She's worried about him. She still cares.''

"Habit," Meghan snapped bitterly. "A trained Pavlovian reaction which can be unlearned. A woman *cannot* love a man like that."

Suddenly a gray shadow seemed to cloud the intensity of Justin's eyes. "A man like what?"

"Like Brad Cranshaw. A man who hits a woman."

"You can't categorize such men any more than you can categorize the women. Every one is different."

"Not to me."

"Does everything have to be either black or white? No gray areas?"

"Not when it comes to this kind of abuse."

Meghan left Midway House feeling angry, confused and disappointed. Justin Forbes might have good intentions, but she felt his kind of attitude fudged the main issue. Bradley Cranshaw beat his wife. The guilt was his. Period. Case closed.

AFTER SEEING MEGHAN OUT, Justin went into his office to work, but he couldn't. Guilt was on his mind, also. He stared down at the report on his desk, but his eyes were unseeing. The image in his head dominated. It was over ten years ago, but he'd never forgotten the expression of pain and horror on Samantha's face that awful night—nor the shame and guilt of knowing that he had put it there. He had seen such looks again, but never directed at him.

Meghan had brought it all back to him. Her blanket censure made vivid his remembered self-condemnation.

He had been studying for the Graduate Record Exams, keeping himself awake with cup after cup of black coffee. Without a fellowship, he couldn't afford graduate school, and the fellowship hinged on doing well on those tests.

Samantha had resented the time he spent on his books. They were in love and had been living together for seven months. At first, everything was fine, but their cramped quarters and Justin's concentrated study had put a strain on their relationship. Samantha felt neglected and started partying with a fast crowd that Justin couldn't stand.

One night, he had come home from the library with a splitting headache. He'd intended to set the alarm, catch a few hours sleep, and get up to resume his studying. Furious when he found a rowdy group of Samantha's friends in the apartment, he ordered them out. When he and Samantha were alone, they hurled vicious accusations at each other. She threw a drink in his face. Justin's instant reaction had been to lash back. His hand had caught the side of her head, and she lost her balance, falling against the door.

In horror, Justin watched her slide to the floor. He'd knelt and gathered her into his arms, saying over and over how sorry he was, begging her to forgive him. More stunned than hurt, Samantha clung to him. Shock had sobered her up. They cried together, made up and vowed never to hurt each other again. Samantha blamed herself for not recognizing how much strain Justin had been under, but her understanding hadn't alleviated Justin's guilt.

Justin had sworn that nothing like that would ever happen again. It hadn't. When he and Samantha had eventually split, it wasn't because of any traumatic episode. There was just a mutual recognition that there wasn't enough to keep them together anymore.

During one of their rare meetings last year, Samantha had teased him about owing his professional career to that one time when he'd hit her. It was probably true. Initially, Justin had focused on understanding and controlling his own drives and behavior, but his interest eventually led to a professional study of the causes of domestic cruelty.

Justin was committed to helping people overcome, cope with, or escape from, the violence which could ruin lives. But, unlike Meghan O'Brien, Justin knew that men, as well as women, were its victims.

BY THE TIME MEGHAN had driven the few miles to her high-rise apartment in Old Town, she had recaptured her usual cool-headed logic. Justin Forbes had a knack for disconcerting her, and she had to consciously counteract his effect on her.

He was interpreting Stella Cranshaw's confusion in a typically masculine way. Meghan, on the other hand, knew from bitter experience women's capacity to absorb punishment from men, and then blame themselves. How could he possibly understand?

Meghan entered her apartment and tossed her briefcase onto the white sofa. The cool, modern comfort of her apartment was soothing, all tones of gray and white, nothing to jar. Except her thoughts.

So many times—in the courtroom, among her colleagues and in her social life—Meghan had seen men close ranks in a kind of gender loyalty that always infuriated her. Sure, the women's movement had made inroads in equal employment opportunities and had amassed some political clout, but it was still an uphill battle. As for men's attitudes, was there any real change? She doubted it.

There were exceptions, her friend Stacy insisted over lunch the next day. Meghan had told her about her new client, Stella Cranshaw, and about Midway House and its director. "What do you know?" Stacy exclaimed. "That hunk of a guy in charge of a home for battered women! That has to tell you something."

"It tells me he's chosen an unusual job for a man."

"Come on, you know what I mean. You had him pegged all wrong. I know you're turned off by the macho type, but Justin Forbes is different."

"We'll see."

"Meghan," said Stacy with cheerful authority, "don't fight it. It's fate."

Meghan was startled to hear the same words Justin had used last night. Then she laughed.

CHAPTER THREE

MEGHAN SPOKE TO STELLA the following morning and was glad that the young woman sounded much more self-contained. The person who had initially answered the phone, a brusque-sounding woman, had asked questions before calling Stella. Meghan understood the reason for such screening.

"Who was that who answered the phone?" Meghan asked.

"You mean Dr. Schumann? She's kind of Justin's assistant until the real one comes."

Whatever that meant. Meghan didn't pursue it. Not that it mattered. She just wondered where Justin was. Naturally he would have someone else working with him. Meghan talked to Stella briefly and made an appointment to meet with her the following Monday.

Meghan was late getting to the health club that afternoon. She changed into a sweat suit and started her usual run. The sounds of footsteps coming up behind her made her turn each time, but it was always someone other than Justin Forbes.

Nor was he one of the spectators lounging around the aerobics class. "Looking for someone?" asked Stacy cagily when she caught Meghan scanning the scene. The class had finished and they were on their way to their lockers.

"Not really."

"Who're you kidding?" Stacy teased.

It was just that she had gotten used to seeing him around, Meghan thought, and reminded herself that his constant attention here had annoyed her. Maybe he'd quit the club. Or maybe their meeting yesterday had turned him off.

Concentration was one of Meghan's strengths in tennis, but somehow she couldn't focus on her game and Stacy won two sets.

"Something's happened to one of us," Stacy said happily when they'd finished. "Either I've improved overnight, or you're—"

"Don't say it," Meghan warned ominously. "I'm having an off day. Don't read anything more into it, okay?"

"Okay."

"How about swimming a few laps?"

Stacy shook her head. "Are you kidding? I've had all the exercise I can take for one day. Besides, Tony's coming by. We're eating Mexican tonight. Want to come?"

"No, thanks."

Meghan felt suddenly tired and debated skipping the pool. But maybe a leisurely swim was just what she needed. She slipped into the navy tank suit she kept in her locker, stepped under the shower and went into the vaulted steamy pool area. A gray-haired man with ear plugs was swimming at the far end and two women were standing in the shallow water, more interested in their conversation than any water sports. Meghan made a shallow dive into the deep end and started swimming. The water was pleasantly tepid and felt good. Meghan made no effort at speed and didn't bother counting laps. She was about ready to quit when she heard someone hit the water with a splash. The diver surfaced and swam toward her in her lane.

"Hey," she warned, "you're supposed to..."

With barely three strong strokes, he reached her. It was Justin. Impatiently shaking his head to flick his hair back, he smilingly asked, "What is it I'm supposed to do?"

"Stay in your own lane." But she sounded less than authoritative.

"No fun in that," was his breezy response. "Besides, where would the world be if people always did what they were supposed to do? Columbus would never have left Italy."

She couldn't help laughing. "You've got a point."

"Am I beginning to win you over?"

"My concession is only about Columbus."

"We'll see."

The challenge and invitation in his eyes was disturbing. Meghan swam away from him and hoisted herself out of the pool. Justin followed.

"What's your rush?" he asked, holding on to the edge as he looked up at her. His eyes scanned her body, which the clinging tank suit did little to hide.

"No rush. I had my swim."

"Wait." With a strong, graceful movement, he vaulted out of the pool. "I'll walk you out."

"But you just got here."

"That's all right. I don't like pools much. All that chlorine."

"Then why did you come?"

"To keep you company." He smiled. "I saw you from up there." He pointed to the observation window of the second-floor lobby.

"Thanks for the gesture." Meghan picked up her towel and draped it over her shoulders. "But I really don't mind being alone."

"Togetherness is better."

"To each his own," Meghan said as they walked.

"My sentiments exactly."

Meghan looked at him. His grin was so damn disarming. "I can't figure out if we're arguing or agreeing," said Meghan helplessly.

"A little of both," he said with a laugh. When she turned toward the women's locker room, Justin halted her by grabbing both ends of the towel around her neck. "I'd ask you to have dinner with me but I have to get back to Midway."

"I thought you just got here."

"I did."

"It wasn't worth the effort," said Meghan.

"I wouldn't say that."

Was it her imagination, or was he exerting a slight pull on the towel? She felt her pulse quicken. He was not actually touching her, yet there was an intimacy in the situation, standing close this way, talking low, water dribbling down their scantily covered bodies.

"I do have time for coffee though," he said temptingly.

"Who's in charge when you're not there?" Meghan asked.

"Dr. Clara Schumann." He said the name as if it demanded respect.

"I spoke to her this morning. She sounded very efficient."

"Oh, that she is. I'll tell you all about her . . . while we're having coffee. Okay?"

What was the harm. "Okay."

In the locker room, Meghan toweled her hair, gave it a few blasts from a hair dryer, then quickly dressed. She always hung her clothes as carefully as the cramped locker space allowed so her gray business suit still looked trim. Except for some lipstick, Meghan dispensed with makeup.

Not that she was anxious or anything. Justin apparently didn't have much time.

When she entered the lounge, Justin was talking to two women seated at a table. Hands resting on the table, he was leaning forward, his dark hair, still damp from the water, curling over his forehead. The women were young and pretty, and it was obvious they admired Justin. Seeing Meghan, Justin cut off whatever it was he was saying and excused himself to join her. The eyes of the women followed him and then looked Meghan over. Enviously? Meghan found that she liked the idea. Vanity, she chided herself.

"We'll take those coffees now, Casey," Justin called to the young waiter as they slid into a booth. "You're all damp and shiny," he said to Meghan.

"So are you."

Seconds passed and Meghan became aware that they were sitting there just looking at each other. Suddenly self-conscious, she said, "You were going to tell me about Dr. Schumann."

"I was? Oh, sure."

Clara Schumann was on the board of directors of the private trust which was financing Midway's program, Justin explained. She had agreed to serve as his assistant until the person he had hired finished her employment commitment elsewhere. Justin's description of Dr. Schumann revealed his respect and affection for the now-retired dean of women of a prominent all-female university. It also revealed his impatience.

"She sounds so efficient. Why are you impatient with her?" Meghan asked.

"Because she is with me." He smiled and made a palms up gesture with his hands. "Impatience breeds impatience."

"I think you make up your own proverbs."

"It's my creative mind. Clara doesn't appreciate me, either. You see, Dr. Schumann, by training and forty years' experience, is an administrator. That means she's used to formulating regulations and seeing that people keep to them."

"What's wrong with that?"

"Sometimes nothing, sometimes everything."

The waiter came. Meghan paused until he had put down their coffee cups and then said, "But society needs rules."

"Sure, but not inflexible ones. Society is made of people, and people are complex creatures who act according to all kinds of sometimes unseen motives. Rules are meant to be broken."

"No," Meghan protested with more emotion than she'd intended.

Justin's look was searching, inquisitive and sympathetic. "I think I hit a nerve. Want to tell me about it?"

Meghan backed off. "There's nothing to tell," she said, assuming a casual tone. "I guess we have different ideas."

Meghan got Justin back to talking about Midway and how he'd gotten his experimental project started. "There's still a lot to do," he said after taking his last gulp of coffee. "I'll be glad when Lil gets on board."

"Lil?"

"The assistant I hired. Having her as resident director will be a big help."

"Oh? Then she'll be living at Midway?"

"That's the deal," Justin said happily. "With Lil around, I'll have a lot more flexibility."

"What about Dr. Schumann?"

"Clara will be more than happy to get back to her advisory role. She was just a pinch hitter."

"I guess that's what Stella meant when she said Dr. Schumann was filling in until your real assistant got here."

"Lil's real all right. We worked together before. She's one savvy lady. Has all of Clara's organizational talent but none of the rigidity."

Meghan felt a little irritated by Justin's enthusiasm, but all she said was, "She sounds like quite a lady."

"She is. You'll be meeting her."

I can hardly wait, Meghan thought, but kept the sarcasm to herself.

Outside, Justin walked her to her car. "You're coming to see Stella on Monday?" he asked.

"That's right."

"I guess I'll see you then."

"I guess so." Meghan said goodbye and got in her car. She started the motor and Justin waved and walked off. Meghan drove away feeling strangely dissatisfied. He had made no mention of the weekend between now and Monday. Why should he? There was no obligation—for either of them. But if he had asked to see her, Meghan just might have accepted.

THE DAYTIME ATMOSPHERE of Midway House was bustling. Clara Schumann, whose gray-haired appearance was as starchy as her voice, let Meghan in and then hurried off to answer the phone in the office off the foyer. Meghan stood uncertainly by the office door until the older woman clapped her hand over the receiver and said, "They're all in the kitchen."

"Where's that?"

"Door behind the staircase," said Clara.

Meghan could have found her way by following the luscious aromas coming from the back of the house. She heard women's voices, and then the sound of a man's laughter. She quickened her steps.

It was a large, old-fashioned kitchen, with cupboards and appliances that matched its age, with one exception—Justin was leaning against a bright new, double-door refrigerator. He was watching the four women clustered around the huge oak table in the center of the room. "Hi," he said with a happy smile when he saw Meghan. "Come join us. We're getting a lesson on how to make noodle pudding."

Hardly the kind of activity she had expected. He introduced the portly, red-faced woman in the bib apron as Ida Kremsky. "Ida claims Hungarians are the best cooks in the world," Justin said with a teasing smile at the woman, "so we're letting her prove it." The vibrant, raven-haired Carmela, Meghan had already met.

"Call me Cookie," Carmela asked. "Everybody does."

The stocky woman was Grace Canto, who nodded solemnly when she was introduced but said nothing.

"I have an appointment with Stella," said Meghan, to explain to the group why she had come. "You didn't forget, did you, Stella?"

An anxious look came over the girl's pretty face. Meghan had been happy to see Stella without the strained desperation of last week. She certainly didn't want to upset her.

"No, I didn't forget," Stella said.

Mrs. Kremsky waved her egg beater. "But first we finish the noodle pudding, yes?"

Justin looked at Meghan. "How about it? You're not in a rush are you?"

Meghan glanced at her watch. She had allowed herself time for lunch after meeting with Stella. In two hours she had to be in court, but she could go straight there without stopping at the office first. She had all the papers with her.

Justin pressed his argument. "If you refuse Ida, you risk getting attacked with an egg beater."

"Ach, you," Ida Kremsky chided, but she smiled and turned back to her mixing.

"Then how can I refuse?" Meghan put down her briefcase and leaned against the refrigerator, adjusting her position a little when her shoulder brushed against Justin's. "I didn't know you were interested in learning to cook," she said to him, keeping her voice low so as not to disturb Mrs. Kremsky's discourse.

"I'm interested in all kinds of learning. Aren't you?"

"I haven't given it much thought."

"Why?"

"Why? What kind of question is that? I just haven't. I don't have much free time."

"One should make time for important things."

"There are more important things than noodle pudding, you know," she protested with a smile.

"I'm not so sure."

Meghan shrugged and gave up. He was being whimsical so why argue the point? Still, she was beginning to suspect that there was often a serious basis to Justin Forbes's brand of whimsy.

Preparing noodle pudding was an intricate process. Meghan watched Mrs. Kremsky mix sugar, butter, sour cream, cottage cheese and milk, then add the beaten eggs with vanilla and salt. She told Grace to combine the mixture with the cooked noodles and put the whole thing into the large pan she had prepared. Stella and Cookie were in charge of the topping, and Meghan actually saw a small smile on Stella's face as she sprinkled the topping over the casserole.

Apparently there was something about this whole operation that gave these women pleasure. Meghan couldn't help contrasting this with her own habitual routine of reaching into the freezer for the first package at hand and tossing it into the microwave as per the hastily read instructions on the cardboard container. No rich smells like this in her kitchen. Not since her mother had died. Thoughts of her mother reminded Meghan of why she was here.

"Stella, maybe we can talk now," she said.

Mrs. Kremsky was putting the pan into the oven. "Go, go," she told Stella. "One hour in the oven and it will be ready." She turned to Meghan. "You will be here to taste?"

"Thank you. I'd love it."

Meghan picked up her briefcase and followed Stella out.

"See you later," Justin called.

Clara Schumann was still in the office so Stella suggested they go upstairs. The room she shared with Cookie was minimally furnished—two beds, two pine bureaus, a table and lamp beside each bed, and a couple of ladder-back chairs that needed painting. But the room was large and airy and the colorful braid rug and museum posters taped to the wall added cheerful notes. One print was a Gauguin nude and the other featured sunflowers.

"Cookie says she'd rather have a bullfighter," said Stella with a smile.

"You seem to have settled in okay," Meghan remarked. "You don't mind staying here? I could probably make other arrangements if—"

"No," Stella hastily interrupted. "I'm fine. I really don't want to leave. Cookie says this isn't like the other shelters."

She could well believe that, thought Meghan, with Justin Forbes in charge. "Well, this needn't be for too long. Maybe I can get your husband to agree to some financial arrangement."

"I don't want anything."

"That's ridiculous," said Meghan. "You certainly are entitled to a decent divorce settlement."

"Divorce settlement?" Stella repeated the words tonelessly.

"But before we get to that," Meghan told her, "I'd like you to consider something. I think you should press assault charges against your husband."

The suggestion seemed to shake the young woman. "Against Brad?"

"Yes."

"But why?"

"For one thing, it would help your case when you file for divorce." The way her young client nervously shook her head showed Meghan that this argument wasn't convincing. "More important," Meghan went on, "by not charging him, you're protecting Brad from the consequences of his actions. You're doing all the hurting, mentally and physically—and he's getting off scot-free."

"I can't believe he's happy about all this," Stella said, her words like a plea for Meghan to agree.

"I hope not. But he brought this situation on himself, Stella. Keep that in mind."

"I don't know." Stella now sounded distraught. "Perhaps if I'd..." She stopped, unable to complete the thought. But then she took a deep breath and seemed to summon some strength. Looking at Meghan squarely, she said, "I don't think I want to do *anything* right away."

"I don't understand."

"There's a lot to think about, things I've got to get straight in my own mind."

Stella turned to the window and pulled aside the filmy curtain. Meghan followed her gaze and saw Justin in the back garden. He was wielding a shovel and tossing the large rocks he unearthed into a pile. The women watched him for a minute, then Stella turned to face Meghan again.

"Justin doesn't think any of us should be making decisions at this time," she explained. "He says that's what Midway's all about, to give us time to think things through, in a place where we feel safe and unpressured."

"I'm not sure he's right," said Meghan, "but the last thing I want is to add to your pressure. When you're ready for an attorney..."

"Oh please don't misunderstand," Stella pleaded. "I appreciate your advice and I want you to represent me, but I need to be sure what I decide is the right thing. Justin says you're the best. Don't get angry and walk out on me."

"I'm not walking out on you," Meghan said gently, "and I'm not angry at you. Believe me. I know what you're going through."

What Meghan didn't say was that the annoyance she felt was directed at Justin Forbes, whose advice might prove counterproductive to Stella Cranshaw's case.

They walked downstairs and joined the other women in the kitchen. "Good timing," Cookie told them. "We finished all the cleaning up."

Mrs. Kremsky looked up at the kitchen clock on the wall and sighed. "I wish we had a TV. I'm missing all my shows."

"Ida likes quiz shows and soaps. She's in love with Pat Sajak," Cookie said teasingly. "That's why her husband got jealous and beat up on her."

Meghan felt surprise. She had assumed that Ida Kremsky was the shelter's cook, an employee, not one of the residents.

"Don't talk silly," was the older woman's response.

"There's no television in the house?" Meghan asked.

"It's on Justin's list of things to buy when he can raise some money," Cookie explained.

"I don't miss it," Grace said. These were the first words Meghan had heard from the somber woman.

"That's 'cause you worked all day and never got hooked," Cookie told her. "I liked watching the soaps sometimes, seeing those women who were worse off than me. But Justin says that's an escape. I guess he's right." A look of pain crossed her pert, dark face. "It don't really help none."

A shared quiet descended on the group. Just then, Clara Schumann came in. "Ladies, I need you all in the office, please."

"More forms?" asked Grace.

"Sorry, but the paperwork is necessary."

"You mind the noodle pudding," Mrs. Kremsky told Meghan.

"I'm no cook," Meghan warned.

"You don't have to cook, just watch the time. Check in thirty minutes, and if it's not brown on top, give it five or ten more."

"I guess I can handle that."

The women left and it was quiet. Meghan could hear the sounds from the back garden. Justin was still working. This might be a good opportunity to talk to him, to question him about what he was advising Stella to do—or not to do.

Meghan walked over to the pantry, which had a door leading out to the garden. She opened the door and stepped onto the small open porch. Completely absorbed in his task, Justin didn't notice her. She stood quietly, studying him. How happy and healthy he looked. Dirty, too, in his grimy T-shirt and jeans. But he seemed at peace with himself and his world. Meghan felt a fleeting envy but thrust it away.

After all, she was perfectly content with her life, with her success and her independence. Or was she?

Unobserved, she continued to watch him, becoming aware of the sensual element in her attraction. Nothing wrong with that, she told herself, admiring the play of muscles and the strength of his arms as he turned over the dirt and heaved aside the rocks. Justin Forbes was a fine physical specimen. It was only natural for a woman, any woman, to have such feelings.

He stopped and rested his shovel. Rubbing his brow with the back of his arm, he caught sight of Meghan and smiled, a smile so engaging that Meghan had to remind herself that she was annoyed at him. She stepped off the porch and he walked over. "I'd like to talk to you."

"Talk away," he said. There was a smudge of dirt on his cheek, and she resisted a temptation to brush it off.

"I don't think you should be steering Stella away from taking any action."

A small frown furrowed his forehead. "I wasn't aware of any steering."

"You told her not to act."

"What I said was to do some thinking first to avoid regrets later. That's what I told all of them."

"What regrets? Getting out of a horrible relationship's nothing to regret."

"If it has to stay that way. Meghan, marriages, in fact all relationships, are complicated by many factors, all of which need to be looked at."

"And while the women keep looking, they keep getting beat up," she said vehemently.

"Not here they don't," he protested. "Midway's more than just a shelter from abuse. These women need to figure out where they're going with their lives. That means taking the time to evaluate the past."

"Grandiose ideas."

"Not grandiose. I intend to prove they're realistic." He sounded determined. "That's why I'm working with just a few people at a time and allowing for longer than the usual stays. Most shelters can do little more than get women through a crisis period."

"That's all they're supposed to do."

"Why—if more can be done? Here, they'll get long-term support and counseling."

"It's the men that need the counseling."

His answer surprised her.

"That's also a possibility."

"I take that back. For wife-beaters, it's too late."

"Not always," he insisted. "There's seldom only one culprit in these situations."

"If you're going to dare suggest that women bring this on themselves—"

"You're not hearing me," he interrupted with frustration. "Part of the problem is that a patriarchal society is still the norm for many people in this country."

"A norm that women should not submit to," Meghan insisted.

"I agree—but escape isn't the only other alternative. Meghan, people can change and can also be instruments of change."

"You sound like a textbook."

"Maybe you can learn from this textbook."

"And you expect to accomplish all this with a few women at Midway House?"

"No, but I damn well expect to make a start. I could do more if the foundation funding us was more generous with its support, but we'll make do. Money's not what's important here. Developing a sense of worth and control—that's what's important."

"In my opinion, Stella Cranshaw took control the minute she walked out on Brad and said, 'Enough.'"

"It was a first step. I don't disagree."

"Then why don't you encourage her to see that first step through to its rightful conclusion?"

"Because, dammit, there may be more than one conclusion."

"I don't believe that," Meghan said forcefully.

"You're entitled to your opinion." Then, with lowered voice, he reminded her, "But Stella has the right to make her own decisions."

That hit home. "I know," she said.

There was a long pause. Then Justin touched her shoulder and asked, "Meghan, why are you so down on men?"

Suddenly, Meghan wanted him to understand. "I'm not," she said. "I'm down on men who use women badly." He seemed to wince, but her remark wasn't intended as a personal assault. "I don't mean you."

But how would she react, Justin wondered, if she knew about that episode with Samantha? How would she see him? He told himself that the young man who'd given in to a crazed moment of angry violence no longer existed. Something was happening between himself and Meghan O'Brien, something important. He wanted to offer the tenderness he sensed she needed.

"Meghan, have you been badly used?" he asked softly.

"I will never, never allow that to happen." She looked up and in his eyes found a warmth that seemed to engulf her. Meghan remembered her initial aversion to the macho image he seemed to project. But this man was different, as was the feeling he engendered in her at this moment.

"Being abused is one thing, but there is such a thing as allowing oneself to be used . . . out of love."

His voice had become so gentle, but with a magnetic timbre that stirred her. She felt a surging in her bosom, and a spiral of excitement started deep inside her. He came closer and took hold of her arms. There was an earthy smell to him. His grip signaled strength, but his eyes promised tenderness and warmth. Meghan knew she should be responding to his words, not to the seductiveness of his physical appeal. She opened her lips to disagree with what he had said, but what had he said? His words escaped her. But his mouth was now ready with another message. He kissed her, and any argument she might have offered was smothered in the moist, seeking fire of his lips and in her own surging response.

It was a long kiss and when he drew his mouth away, she realized she was clinging to him, pressing her trembling body against his. Meghan struggled for control. She tried to pull away but he held her. "I've got to go," she whispered. "I've . . . I've got to check the noodle pudding."

"The hell with the noodle pudding," he said and kissed her again.

CHAPTER FOUR

THE MEMORY OF JUSTIN'S KISS stayed with her. Sleep never came easily to Meghan. She often lay awake long after she had put her book away and turned out the bedside lamp. At such times, she tried to keep unhappy memories of the past from rushing in. But this was different. Remembering the feel of Justin's arms and the heady taste of his lips brought back the surging warmth of her own response. A sweet inner tingling made her stretch languorously.

Meghan wondered why she was dwelling on this one kiss. A moment of physical intimacy couldn't erase the differences they had. Still, it was ironic that their argumentative discussion had ended that way.

By design? Was this a technique Justin used on women? The possibility bothered Meghan. If Justin Forbes was betting his physical appeal would win her over to his way of thinking, he was wrong. Sure, she had emotional and physical needs just like other women, but she couldn't let them govern her life.

As for love, the word aroused ambivalent feelings. There was the kind that was supposed to sweep you away into rapture and permanent bliss. But there was a flip side to love, where it became destructive and deteriorated into domination and dependency. She had seen too much of the latter kind. Meghan couldn't help secretly yearning for the ideal, while openly fearing and protecting herself from its unhappy aberration.

On Wednesday, Nate Isaacs called her at the office. "I've been thinking about you," he said, then hesitantly asked, "How about dinner?"

"I'd love to have dinner with you."

He seemed surprised by her enthusiasm. "Good. I'll make a reservation. Le Refuge?"

"Sure." It had been their favorite French restaurant. Meghan hadn't been there since they'd split up.

It was funny, Nate's calling just now after four months of silence. He had been confused and then angry when Meghan had said she couldn't marry him. She didn't blame him. They had been living together for almost a year, and his assumption that their comfortable compatibility would end in marriage was understandable. Meghan had thought she loved Nate and hadn't ruled out making their arrangement permanent. After all, he was an intelligent companion and a considerate and undemanding lover. Why not? But when Nate actually proposed, Meghan had realized that a why-not attitude wasn't enough. What she felt fell short of the love Nate deserved. It wouldn't have been fair for her to marry him. Nate had been hurt but, typically, stoic.

Meghan remembered a perverse disappointment that he hadn't ranted and raved against her decision. Maybe she had hoped a show of passion would persuade her. Was that what Nate now had in mind?

"Everything looks the same," Nate said when he came into the apartment.

"I haven't changed anything," Meghan told him.

He turned his attention to her and his pleased smile deepened. "You're wearing my favorite outfit."

Nate had been with her when she'd bought the beige knit dress with a loose, floral-printed jacket. Meghan was suddenly aware she had chosen to wear it tonight for that very reason. What was she trying to do—move the clock back?

Did she want to reenact Nate's proposal, to try for a different outcome?

If that had been her unconscious intent, Meghan realized as the evening progressed, she would be given her chance. But she also realized something more important—she didn't want it.

Toward the end of dinner, Nate started reminiscing about the past. His look and tone suggested what was coming. "I've missed you," he said. He reached over the table to clasp her hand, and the moment he touched her, Meghan knew it was no good.

"I've missed you, too," she said. But when she saw his face brighten hopefully, she quickly added, "I want us to be friends."

The brightness dimmed. "Friends?"

"Your friendship would mean a lot to me."

It was a sincere statement, but obviously not the one Nate wanted to hear. "That's not what I had in mind."

It wasn't what she'd had in mind either, but it was as far as she could go. "Nate, I'm sorry."

"So am I." He gave her hand a squeeze before releasing it, forced a smile, and said, "I guess that's it."

Meghan was grateful that he didn't press her. Yet earlier, as she'd been getting dressed for this date, she had hoped he would.

It was better this way, she told herself as they walked the few blocks to her building. She wouldn't have known how to deal with an impassioned proposal. But passion wasn't Nate's style. Nor, she had to remind herself, was it hers.

Nate saw her to her door but declined to come in. He kissed her cheek, started away, then turned to ask abruptly, "Is there someone else?"

The question startled her. "No."

He looked at her quizzically.

"It's not that," she said.

His expression was doubtful. Maybe there was something in her tone.

"Goodbye." Nate turned and disappeared down the hallway.

Meghan knew that he wouldn't call again.

"YOU DID RIGHT," Stacy told her at lunch the following day. "If you don't love the guy, that's it."

Stacy's smug summation annoyed Meghan and made her rise to Nate's defense. "There are all kinds of love. Nate's a fine man. We had something good together."

"Not good enough or you'd have married him four months ago."

Meghan couldn't argue that point.

"You've got to follow your instincts," Stacy continued, "and your instincts are telling you the same thing they did before. Don't settle for anything less than the real thing." Stacy took a bite of her sandwich, chewed vigorously, swallowed, and said, "Look at me. I was engaged three times before I met Tony, but each time something told me uh-uh."

Meghan had to laugh. "But with Tony, you got the go-ahead."

"All the way." Stacy grinned. "The first time he kissed me, I just melted. I wanted to crawl into his pocket and never leave. Or," she said with a giggle, "crawl into his bed and never leave."

"I'm afraid I've never felt like crawling into any man's pocket," Meghan said dryly. Maybe she wasn't capable of the kind of love women like Stacy professed to feel, not if it required a submissiveness that Meghan didn't possess.

"How about into some particular man's bed?" Stacy asked.

Meghan knew she meant Justin Forbes. "That's just sex, not love."

"Just sex? Listen to her. Haven't you ever heard that song? 'You can't have one without the other,'" Stacy sang.

"That line referred to love and marriage."

"Whatever. You get the point. Meghan, you're so afraid of getting messed up, you're missing out."

"I don't think so."

"You are," Stacy insisted. "A virile guy comes along and all you see is trouble."

"Virility is okay. Domination isn't."

"Boy, you sure do have an obsession about that. You know, sometimes it's nice to have someone to lean on."

"I don't need to lean."

"Everyone does, at least once in a while. You're too damn independent."

Meghan gave her usual response, "There's no such thing," and then changed the subject. There was no sense arguing with her friend. She and Stacy were different. Stacy was no clinging vine, but she liked the idea of being cared for and protected. Perhaps, Meghan thought, her own fear of domination and dependence was excessive, but she wasn't going to brood about it. That's the way she was, and if she was missing out, so be it. It was her choice. She had her work and her friends, but no special man at the moment. Perhaps another would come along, an attractive lover whose expectations and needs coincided with hers.

Like Justin Forbes? He certainly filled the first part of the definition, an attractive lover. But would his expectations and needs coincide with hers? It was improbable if not impossible. But perhaps for an exciting interlude . . .

Meghan sensed that a liaison with Justin would be more unsettling than comfortable, but it was a disturbingly se-

ductive possibility. If only she could get a handle on the
man, but he was full of surprises.

On Friday, Lester Patterson, the head partner in her firm,
called her into his office. "There's a small case I want you
to handle," he said.

Meghan was free to choose her own clients but, like the
other attorneys, she was also assigned cases the firm had
accepted. "Sure," she said. "What kind of case?"

"Request for a housing variance."

"What?" The cases Lester usually turned over to her had
to do with civil rights or women's issues. "But Harold always takes the zoning and real estate stuff. That's not my
kind of case."

"This client asked specifically for you."

"What client?"

"Name's Justin Forbes. Look, it's no big deal..."

Lester went on talking, something about the case probably being routine and not taking much of her time, but she
was only half listening. Justin Forbes, again. The man had
an uncanny faculty for insinuating himself into her life.

"So he's on your appointment calendar for four o'clock
this afternoon," Lester said. "Okay?"

"Sure." What else could she say?

AT FOUR O'CLOCK, her desk was clear and Meghan waited
expectantly. By four fifteen, she was getting angry. Apparently, Justin Forbes wasn't big on punctuality. At four thirty
she decided he wasn't coming and pulled out the folder of
another case she had to review. But it was hard to concentrate.

He could have called. It was just common courtesy. Unless he'd forgotten about the appointment he had made.
That was even worse. To think she'd actually entertained the
notion of going back to her apartment for lunch and

changing from the business suit she had put on that morning. She was glad she'd decided not to bother. It would have been silly enough to dress up for a client, even sillier for one who didn't have the common courtesy to call and cancel an appointment he'd made. Well, he could just damn well get himself another lawyer, one who didn't mind wasting time sitting around waiting for Mr. Justin Forbes.

At five o'clock, she decided to tell him so herself. She picked up her phone and buzzed the receptionist. "Phyllis, get me Justin Forbes on the phone."

When the phone rang, it was Phyllis again. "He wasn't in."

"Oh great. Is he on his way, at least."

"I don't think so, Miss O'Brien. The woman who answered said he was taken to the hospital."

"What?"

"He was taken to the hospital."

"What for?"

In a how-am-I-supposed-to-know tone, Phyllis answered, "She didn't say."

"What hospital?"

"She didn't say."

"Great." Meghan slammed down the receiver. What could have happened? Was it serious? She had been so angry at his not calling. What if Justin couldn't even hold a phone? Surely someone there could tell her what happened. She looked up Midway's number and was about to dial when the telephone rang.

"Meghan? Sorry about standing you up."

It was Justin. How bad could it be if he could talk and hold a phone? His voice sounded all right.

"Where are you?" Meghan asked.

"At Mount Vernon Hospital."

"What happened?"

"I was trying to repair a gas pipe fitting in the basement. It went boom."

"Boom?"

"Just a little boom."

Did the man make a joke about everything? "Enough, apparently, to send you to the hospital," she said, aware of the relief and exasperation in her voice.

"Nothing critical. A few minor burns. They doctored me up in the emergency room and said I could go home. Problem is, I don't have a car."

"How did you get there?"

"Clara drove me, but I made her go back to the house. I could take a cab, but I thought maybe we'd keep our appointment."

"It's after five."

"Yeah, I know, and I'm sorry. I should have thought to have someone call you."

"That's all right, but I don't really think you're in shape for a business appointment."

"I'm fine now. Except I'm starving. I must have skipped lunch. I've got a great idea. Why don't you pick me up here at the emergency room and we can have our business meeting over dinner somewhere. My treat."

"Are you sure you're up to it?"

"I am if you are."

Meghan wasn't sure about herself, but she said yes anyway.

"I THINK YOU'LL LIKE this place," Justin said as the hostess showed them to a table. "Best seafood in Alexandria."

Meghan was amused to see eyes turn as they walked through the dining room.

"Your waiter tonight will be Donny," the hostess said. She gave them a curious smile and left.

"People are staring at us," Meghan told him.

"Probably because we're such a handsome couple," Justin said with a cheerful smile.

"Odd couple is more like it."

"Why? You look like a perfectly respectable, and quite beautiful, lady attorney to me."

"And you look like a pirate," she countered.

"A perfect combination," he said with a grin.

"I don't know about that." Meghan couldn't help returning his smile. The black patch the doctor was making him wear on his left eye did indeed give him a raffish look. An obliging nurse had snipped off the singed edges of a lock of his hair and it now stood up in a blunt cowlick. "I think you lost part of your left eyebrow," Meghan observed.

"It'll grow back."

"How does your face feel?"

"Sunburned. How does it look."

"Sunburned." The doctor had applied a medicinal salve to Justin's skin and told him he was lucky to have escaped a serious burn.

He shrugged. "I really don't feel bad. It could have been a lot worse."

Meghan shivered at the thought. "How long do you have to wear that patch?"

"Don't know. The ophthalmologist said there was no real damage, but he wants to take another look in a couple of days. I kind of like the patch, though. Don't you think it gives me a debonair look?"

He was wearing a plaid work shirt and stained jeans. "I don't know if debonair's quite the right description," Meghan said dryly. "Do you always find a silver lining in everything?"

"Why not? If there is one. Look what I got out of that little mishap—a sexy eye patch and dinner with you."

"That's hardly recompense."

"Depends on your point of view. I'm not complaining. Why're you shaking your head like that?"

"Because you're weird, Justin Forbes."

"That's one of my charms."

Charm was the right word, Meghan thought, and she was feeling its effect. To counter it, she reverted to her business posture. "Now about your housing variance..."

"Business talk on an empty stomach?" He groaned.

"It's just that I think you'd be better off with another attorney, one who does these cases routinely."

"Well, I don't agree. You're the one I want."

"But why?"

He sighed. "Have a heart. I'm starving. At least let's order first."

Meghan agreed. The waiter brought the menus. "Aren't you going to look?" she asked.

"Don't have to. I always order the same thing. Best dish in the house. Want me to order for you?"

"No, thank you. I like to make my own choices."

Justin smiled at the primness in her tone. He watched her closely as she studied the menu. He knew well enough that any one of a dozen lawyers could handle Midway House's request for a housing variance. His reasons for wanting Meghan O'Brien were personal, not legal. He was attracted by her beauty, by the sharpness of her intellect and by her independence. But he also sensed a softness that she kept subdued, apparently equating it with vulnerability and pain. Justin wanted to know why, and not just to satisfy his professional curiosity. Sure, Meghan was an interesting psychological study, but that was a minor component in his attraction. He liked the many different feelings she excited in him—admiration, respect, frustration, sympathy, desire, impatience, desire... and more desire.

He gazed at her as she studiously read every entry on the menu and a smile came to his lips. Her silky hair draped down, framing her face. So intent. Did she bring that kind of intensity and concentration to everything she did? He remembered her initial surprise when he kissed her, and then the growing warmth of her response. He couldn't help wondering what she would be like in bed, and the thought made his blood stir.

With the women he'd known in his professional and personal life, Justin had enjoyed camaraderie or friendship or sex. He had met women who commanded his respect and others who aroused his compassion. Since Samantha, however, he'd never been tempted to live with a woman. Occasionally, he wondered if fear entered into this. That time with Samantha, his frustrations had mounted and he had struck out at the person closest to him. It had never happened again. He was sure that the memory of that incident, his revulsion at his behavior, precluded a repetition. Underlying his resolve, though, was there a hidden fear?

Like many other youthful lovers, he and Samantha couldn't sustain their relationship after college. Samantha had gotten married, divorced, and then married again. At last report, the second marriage seemed to be working out. Justin was glad for her.

Up until now, Justin hadn't felt deprived. He liked women, enjoyed their company and relished the excitement of sexual attraction. He'd neither sought nor tried to avoid a permanent attachment. If it happened, it happened.

Meghan looked up with a smile, and he was again struck by her appealing combination of sureness and vulnerability. How beautiful she was! Was he falling in love with this woman?

Not yet, he cautioned. There was something missing, something essential. Maybe he would uncover it, or supply it or create it—when he learned just what the hell *it* was.

If Meghan ever let herself love, Justin sensed it would be a consuming emotion. Such a love could reach into his heart and burn away any residue of doubt. But he was getting ahead of himself.

Meghan put down her menu. "What did you decide on?" he asked.

Donny, the waiter, came up at that moment. "I'll have an order of fried zucchini and the blackened redfish," Meghan told him.

Justin burst into laughter.

Frowning, Meghan asked, "Why is that so funny?"

"Because that's *exactly* what I always order. Make that two," he told the waiter, who nodded and went off.

"Are you making that up?" Meghan asked suspiciously.

"Nope."

When the food arrived, they ate ravenously.

"That was good," Meghan said when they finished their entrées.

"You could have let me order for you and saved yourself the trouble."

"But then I wouldn't have enjoyed it as much," Meghan told him.

"Don't you ever take someone's lead?"

Meghan didn't answer right away. "Not often," she finally admitted.

It was the answer he expected, though he knew it would bother him.

The waiter was back. "Care to see the dessert list?" he asked.

Meghan shook her head and Justin requested the check.

"I'm not much for sweet desserts," Meghan said.

"How about fruit?"

"Fruit's okay."

"Or cheese, maybe some brie or havarti and a couple of wheat crackers?"

"That, too. Are you going to tell me that's what you prefer, too?"

Justin nodded happily.

ON THE WAY over to Midway, Justin explained about the variance. The shelter was in a residential zone, but unless there was strong opposition from the residents in the area, there would be no problem.

"Do you expect opposition?" she asked.

"The nearest neighbor's a mile away, so I don't see why. And this is such a worthwhile project."

"I don't know," Meghan said doubtfully. "Some people love worthwhile projects, but only in some other neighborhood."

"Then we'll just have to get them to see things our way, won't we?"

Meghan pulled up and parked in Midway's driveway. "After a day like you've had, how can you be an optimist?"

"I try hard," he said. "Hey, it's easy to be an optimist when things are perfect. Besides, it wasn't such a bad day. Look how it ended."

"Aren't you making too much of a good dinner?"

"I mean the discovery, not the dinner."

"What discovery?"

She was facing him, her hands in her lap. Justin took both her hands and, with a teasing smile, replied, "We like all the same things. You made the exact choices I did. Let's face it. We're made for each other.''

''There's more to life than food,'' Meghan said laughing.

Still, it was a start.

CHAPTER FIVE

THE NEXT MORNING, a sober Brad Cranshaw was waiting for Meghan in her office. He presented a different picture this time. Neatly dressed and subdued, he looked like a proper young businessman—not like a man who drank too much and beat his wife.

"I want to apologize for the way I acted the other night," he told her. Nervousness infiltrated the firmness he struggled to maintain. "I...uh...I know you were just trying to help Stella." He took a deep breath. "But everything's all right now. So if you'll just tell me where my wife is..."

"I can't do that, Mr. Cranshaw."

"Why not?"

"Because everything *isn't* all right. Nothing has changed. Your wife left you because you beat her."

"That...that was just something that happened."

Controlling her outrage, Meghan said coldly, "More than once."

He rose from his chair, started to pace, stopped, and sat down again. "You see, there's all this trouble at work and it was getting to me." He kept talking. Apparently, Brad Cranshaw worked for his father and father-in-law, who were partners in a large mail-order business. There was some problem about a big-ticket order from a prized customer having been lost. "I took all the flak for that one," Brad said bitterly. "So much for the advantages of nepotism."

"So you took your frustration out on your wife."

"That foul-up at work wasn't my fault."

"Was it Stella's?"

The question jarred him. He looked down, his hands tightly clutched together. His answer came in an anguished whisper. "Of course not." He was quiet for a moment, then he looked at Meghan. "Things just started to go sour. I felt all this pressure, see. It seemed everything I did was wrong. Day after day after day...always something." In frustration, he hit a fist into his other hand. "I got put down all day long on the job. At home, I needed to unwind."

His expression begged for sympathy, but Meghan couldn't summon any. "Your way of unwinding was brutal, Mr. Cranshaw," she said bluntly.

"I never meant to take it out on Stella. I never meant to hurt her."

"That's no excuse for what you did. You felt victimized so you made a victim of your wife."

"It won't happen again," he said tightly.

"What's different?"

"I'm different," he cried.

Meghan had little trust in such declarations. She had heard them before.

"I love my wife," Brad continued desperately. "I want to see her. You've got to tell me where she is."

"I'm sorry, Mr. Cranshaw." Meghan stood up to signal an end to their conversation. "I suggest that you have your attorney contact me."

Brad rose, walked slowly to the door, then turned. "At least tell her I'm sorry. I'll make it up to her. Tell her I want to see her. I want her back." Then, with defiance, he added, "You've got no right to keep her away from me. I love her."

"I have every right to protect my client, Mr. Cranshaw, but I'll give her your message."

When he left, Meghan slumped back in her chair. The word *love* was meant to have connotations of tenderness and joy. How had it come to include such frustration and violence?

The ring of the intercom snapped her out of her reverie.

"There's a Barnaby Trask on line five," Phyllis told her.

"Who's Barnaby Trask?"

"I don't know."

Meghan shook her head impatiently. Phyllis conveniently kept forgetting she was supposed to ask the nature of a caller's business. Meghan pressed line five. "This is Meghan O'Brien," she said.

"My name's Barnaby Trask." The caller had a commanding growl of a voice. "I'm Stella Cranshaw's father."

Meghan sat up. She had wanted to talk to her client's father, but had gotten the impression that Stella didn't want him involved. Had she changed her mind? "Did Stella tell you to call me?"

"No. I haven't heard from that girl. You'd think she'd have called her own father before taking off like that."

Now wary, Meghan asked, "How did you get my number?"

"My son-in-law. Now, look here, what's all this nonsense about?"

"It's hardly nonsense, Mr. Trask. I'm representing your daughter in—"

"My daughter doesn't need a lawyer," Trask interrupted angrily. "She needs to stop acting like a prima donna and get back to her husband before the whole neighborhood gets wind of what's going on."

"Prima donna?" Meghan didn't try to disguise her fury. The man was more concerned about a family scandal than his daughter's welfare. "Stella is not acting like a prima donna, but like a battered woman, which is what she has been and what she refuses to continue being."

"We all get hot under the collar occasionally. The boy got a little loose with his hands," Barnaby Trask said brusquely. "It happens sometimes."

"That's your excuse for brutality?"

Trask became angry. "You're making a big thing out of this. If women walked out every time there was an argument—"

This time, Meghan broke in. "We're not talking argument, Mr. Trask. We're talking beating. As Stella's father, you should be interested in protecting her, not sending her back to that situation."

"I don't need you to tell me how to be a father."

"And I don't need you to tell me how to represent my client. I don't think there's anything more to discuss, Mr. Trask."

"You tell Stella I want to talk to her. You tell her to call me."

"I'll relay your message," Meghan said and hung up.

Meghan decided she'd better talk to Stella. With the anger aroused by Barnaby Trask still seething inside, she dialed the number of Midway House. Justin answered.

"How are you feeling?" she asked.

"Pretty good. I played the invalid for a couple of hours this morning just to milk the sympathy factor here, but when the ladies started to boss me around, I recuperated fast."

He sounded so damn cheerful.

"I feel fine," he said.

"I wish I did. I'd like to come over to see Stella. Is that all right?"

"What's got you so fired up?" he asked.

"Male bonding. I've just seen it in action."

"Come again."

"Never mind. You wouldn't understand."

"Try me."

"Not now. Is Stella there?"

"She's upstairs, but come on over. Wear your sneakers."

"What for?"

"You'll need them. We're going running."

"What?"

"Running."

"You've got to be kidding."

"Nope. Come on. It'll do you good."

When she hung up the phone, Meghan wore a slight smile. Justin Forbes's good humor had taken the edge off her anger. Was he serious about her going running with them? It was hard to tell with Justin. She had conferred with clients in all kinds of settings, but this might be a first.

On her way out, Meghan passed the open door to Stacy's office.

"Hey, where you off to?" Stacy called.

"To see a client."

"How about some coffee first?"

"I don't have time. Oh, I forgot something." Meghan returned to her office and picked up the pair of Reeboks she kept in her closet.

Stacy followed her and stood at her door. "What are those for? Are you going to be chasing someone?"

"You never know," said Meghan.

"I'M THE ONLY ONE HERE," Mrs. Kremsky told her. "They all went to run."

So Justin had been serious. But he could have waited for her, Meghan thought. "How come you didn't go?"

"I'm too old and too fat." Mrs. Kremsky patted her portly figure. "But you're not." She looked at the Reeboks dangling from Meghan's hand. "You can catch them."

Meghan hesitated.

"Justin said to tell you where to find them."

"Did he now?"

"They went to the bicycle path by the George Washington Parkway."

"When did they leave?"

"Maybe ten minutes ago. They cut through the woods out back."

Meghan knew where that would bring them. She could probably catch them by driving down the road past Mount Vernon and parking in the picnic area by the bridge.

But did she want to? She could wait here until they returned. Or she could leave and come back later. But she wasn't sure how long they'd be. She wavered as Mrs. Kremsky watched her expectantly. It was a really beautiful Indian summer day, and she had no appointments this afternoon, only desk work. A little hookey playing was tempting. "I'm not exactly dressed for running," Megan said finally.

The older woman pointed to Meghan's brown gabardine pants, "Those slacks are okay, but take off your jacket and that pretty blouse. I'll get you something to wear."

While she was gone, Meghan put on her sneakers. Mrs. Kremsky returned holding an oversize white sweatshirt. "Here. I wear this to work in the garden. It's not glamorous."

Meghan slipped off her jacket and blouse and put on the sweatshirt.

Mrs. Kremsky smiled her approval. "On you, it looks good."

It took Meghan only a few minutes to drive to the parking area. She scanned the few people at the picnic tables and on the path by the river, but no Justin. Disappointed, she wondered if they'd already passed through. Then she saw the group coming from the direction of Mount Vernon, Justin in the lead. His head was turned as he called encouragement to his followers. He looked forward, caught sight of Meghan and headed toward her. He still wore his eye patch, and a delighted smile. Meghan forgot all her qualms about being there.

Justin reached her before the others. "Are you joining us?"

"It looks that way. On the phone, I thought you were kidding."

"You're wearing running clothes," he pointed out.

Meghan pulled at her borrowed sweatshirt. "Mrs. Kremsky's. I happened to have some sneakers in the trunk." Meghan didn't want to admit to any deliberate preparedness.

Meghan waved a greeting as the women came up. They leaned against a picnic table with an exaggerated show of tiredness. Stella, trim in a green jogging suit, asked, "Are you coming with us?"

Meghan nodded.

"Another victim," Grace announced darkly. The stocky, middle-aged woman looked far from athletic in polyester blue pants and a turtle neck.

"You could've stayed behind with Ida," Cookie told her. Cookie's outfit was the gaudiest, black toreador pants and a metallic threaded red sweater.

"I should have stayed behind with Ida," Grace said ruefully.

"Think positive," Justin told them. "You're going to feel great afterward. This kind of exercise is good for you. Good for all of us," he added with a significant nod at Meghan. "We'll take it slow and easy at first."

"Easy for who?" Cookie challenged.

"We're not in shape like you are," Stella told him.

Grace agreed. "You can say that again."

"We been noticin' your shape. You stack up pretty good in those skivvy shorts," Cookie said with a bold grin. "Right, Stella?"

"Right."

Justin shrugged off their teasing. Apparently it wasn't new to him. Meghan was pleased that Stella felt enough at ease to take part, but she surprised Meghan when she turned to her and asked, "Don't you think so?"

Meghan laughed, then made a point of giving Justin a careful scrutiny. He wore gray gym shorts and a navy T-shirt with the logo Save the Whales emblazoned on the front. "No Arnold Schwarzenegger, but not bad," she finally said teasingly.

He wasn't a bit fazed. "Now that you're all through admiring my torso, can we get on with it? Come on. Let's get this show on the road."

Meghan had often driven on the George Washington Parkway, which followed the bicycle path all the way from Mount Vernon to the Fourteenth Street Bridge. On summer weekends, the path was always swarming with joggers and cyclists, but she had never been tempted to join them. It was less crowded now. To Meghan, the tawny colors of autumn, the burnished leaves vivid against a blue sky and the gray-blue of the Potomac, pushed into occasional white caps by errant wind gusts, made a more spectacular setting than summer's hazy lushness.

Beyond the picnic area was a large sign in front of the path. Meghan read out loud, "Welcome to the Parcourse Fitness Circuit." Apparently there were set exercises at stations along the way, each marked with three fitness levels—starting par, sporting par and championship par. A good idea, she thought. "Is this our program?" she asked Justin.

"Our program is what *we* make it, not what some sign tells us," he said. "Maybe we'll stop once in a while to break up the run, but there's no set routine."

"I should have guessed."

"Any objections?"

"No." On her own, she probably would have followed the prescribed circuit. But she wasn't on her own today. She was part of a group and Justin was its leader. "We'll do it your way." For a second, she wondered at her willingness to accept Justin's authority, but then this was only an exercise outing. "Lead on," she said cheerfully.

Meghan jogged regularly at the club, but never enjoyed it much. It was just another routine exercise. This was different. Part of her pleasure came from the others. They grumbled about the pace that Justin set, teased each other, made jokes about themselves and their athletic prowess or lack of it, and seemed to love every minute. So did Meghan.

She and Justin ran together a little ahead of the others, exchanging a few words, laughing at the banter of the women behind them. "Why didn't you wait for me at Midway?" she asked.

"Given your strange priorities, I figured you wouldn't want to come and that you'd make Stella feel she should stay behind with you."

"My priorities aren't strange at all—just different from yours. But you read me pretty well."

He looked at her cagily. "I also figured that if we set out, you just might come after us."

He'd been right again. Meghan gave an uneasy laugh, not sure she was comfortable about this man's ability to predict

what she would do. They ran quietly for a while, and
Meghan's uneasiness faded into the rhythm of her movements. With his long legs, Justin could easily outdistance
her, but he was deliberately matching his stride to hers.

"If we were racing, you'd have me beat," she told him.

"But we're not competing."

"I know. It was just an observation."

He glanced at her. "Maybe I'd let you win."

"Why?"

"Because it's important to you."

Meghan was annoyed. "Don't do me any favors."

"Hey, relax. This is supposed to be fun."

"I thought it was supposed to be exercise."

"Both."

Justin looked back and noticed the others had fallen behind. Grabbing Meghan's hand, he pulled her over to lean
against a tree to wait for them. "Why do you think we're out
here?" he asked.

"We? Meaning you and me, or you and your residents?"

"Meaning all of us."

"We're getting some healthy exercise."

"Sure, but I'm interested in building more than athletic
stamina."

"Like what?"

"Like confidence. Knowing yourself physically is part of
the process. Becoming aware of your body, gauging its limits and then expanding those limits—that's as important as
building muscles."

"Psychologically therapeutic?"

"Do I detect a note of sarcasm?"

"Hey, I'm all for exercise. I wouldn't be paying for an
expensive health spa membership if I didn't believe in it."

"That systematic routine of yours at the club is not the kind of exercise I'm talking about."

"What's wrong with what I do?"

"Nothing, as far as it goes, but it doesn't go far enough. You train your body as something apart from the rest of you."

"Sorry, but I'm not into this self-awareness stuff."

"You should be. You exercise your mind in your work, your body at a health club and your emotions...I'm not sure where, or even *if*, they're getting a workout."

Meghan resented the implied criticism. "Look, I'm not in the mood for a philosophical lecture on the synthesis of body, mind and spirit. Let's just run. Okay?"

By this time, the others had caught up and were eyeing them curiously.

"Whatever you say," Justin told her with a disarming smile.

To break up the run, Justin occasionally stopped at an exercise station. "Time to stretch the back leg muscles," he announced at the fifth station. There were three horizontal bars at varying heights. Justin demonstrated by grasping a bar and bending one leg while stretching out the other, then alternating. "The highest bar's the easiest, so start there," he directed. Cookie and Stella quickly moved to the middle bar, but Grace was content to stay at the high one. "You, too, counselor," Justin told Meghan.

She complied, choosing the lowest bar because she was used to similar stretches in her exercises at the club. Meghan was self-conscious, aware of Justin's watching her.

Justin stopped again at a log hop exercise where six railroad ties were set on the grass like a horizontal ladder, the ties spaced about two feet apart. The object was to hop over them without stopping, which Justin did.

Meghan had to laugh. "You look so funny. Like a jumping jack."

"Oh yeah! Try it," he challenged.

Meghan discovered it wasn't as easy as he made it seem. Awkwardly, the others followed. Cookie stumbled and sat down in the middle. Grace got winded and ended up stepping instead of hopping over. They were all laughing—at themselves, at each other, with each other. Laughter formed a flowing, connecting bond among them.

The women started choosing the stations to stop at. They couldn't always accomplish the called-for skill but they tried. Amid the fun and joking, Meghan detected a purposeful attempt, a serious will to succeed. Even Grace seemed intent on doing at least a couple of push-ups, and she became almost jubilant when she was better at a balancing exercise than the two younger women.

Justin told them to ignore the starting par numbers on the signs and do only what they felt they could. "We'll make our own rules," he declared.

Justin was constantly watchful, Meghan noticed. He hung back to let them test themselves, but was right there if one of them needed a boost. He sometimes suggested that one person help the other. "Don't worry," he would say. "You won't fall. Grace will hold you." Or it might be Stella or Cookie who was helping. The women were wary, however, and preferred to avoid whatever they couldn't do on their own. Justin didn't push.

"They're afraid to trust anyone yet," Justin told Meghan, "even each other."

"Isn't it better that they rely on themselves?"

"Why not both?"

Because it's safer not to depend on others was the answer that flashed through her mind, but she knew that Justin would dispute that. So she shrugged and said nothing.

The ninth station called for a body curl, which Stella and Meghan decided to try. Justin helped them get into position. All that talk about becoming aware of her body... Justin made her keenly aware as the touch of his hands sent a surge of tingling hotness through her. After that, Meghan evaded his touch. She sensed that he knew why.

On their way back, Meghan slowed to the pace of the three other women. To dodge the cyclists using the path, they often had to run single file, with Justin in the lead. "This is just like 'follow the leader,'" Cookie said with a throaty chuckle. "Ever play that when you was a kid?"

"I can't remember that far back," Grace said.

"The way it works is you gotta do whatever the leader does, even if it's nutty. It's a good game."

"Game?" Grace groaned. "This is more like hard labor."

Back at the picnic area, the women sprawled onto a grassy spot near the river's edge. They were tired, but their complaining quips were more humorous than serious. Underlying it all, Meghan detected a feeling of satisfaction.

"Well, we made it," Stella said with a sigh.

"Don't congratulate yourselves yet," Justin told them. "We've still got a fifteen minute jog back to the house."

"Jog? Can't I just crawl?" Grace asked.

"I got a better idea," Cookie said. "How about we all ride home with Meghan here?"

Meghan glanced over at Justin but he shook his head. "Nope. We got here on our own steam and we'll go back the same way."

"I think we ran out of steam."

"That's why we're resting. Okay, now, everybody stretch out like this." He lay down, feet slightly apart, arms extended. "Let yourself go limp."

Meghan watched him for a moment. Against the pale green grass, he looked somehow bigger than before. The expression *larger than life* came to her. His was a form brimming with life, even now in his attempts to quiet it. The three women ranged themselves around him and Meghan stretched out, too.

"Now, tense your shoulders . . . hold them tense . . . relax. Next your arms. Do the same thing . . . tense . . . relax. Make a fist with your hands . . . tight . . . and relax."

This was a yoga technique with which Meghan was familiar. She had even tried using it at night sometimes, when she couldn't fall asleep. It hadn't worked. She was great at the tensing part, but her muscles had refused to obey the command to relax.

Justin's voice took on a cadence, soft and rhythmic, putting them through the motions. "Let your body just sink into the soft grass," he was saying and Meghan felt herself doing just that. His hypnotic power of suggestion was working. In the silence that followed, Meghan became aware of her heartbeat, of the breath entering and leaving her body. She lay quietly content. Her eyes were closed, but through her eyelids, she felt the gold colored heat of the sun. The golden haze dimmed and she opened her eyes to see Justin's head over her, shadowing her from the sun. His mouth curved in a smile that transmitted an almost tactile sensation.

"I thought I had put you to sleep," he said softly.

"You almost did." She stared up at him, then closed her right eye.

"Are you winking at me?" he asked.

"Kind of. It's hard to look into your eyes when you've got one covered with that patch, so I'm making us even." The breath of his soft laughter washed over her face and she laughed with him. He stood and reached down a hand to help her up. Meghan took it, preferring to forget that she was perfectly capable of getting up without assistance.

"Okay, rise and shine," he told the others.

Stella and Cookie complied quickly.

"I'll rise, but I won't shine," Grace told him.

Justin helped her up. "How do you feel?" he asked her.

Grace took a minute. She hunched her shoulders up and down and then seemed to shrug her whole body as if testing its reaction. "I hate to admit it, but darned if I don't feel pretty good," she said finally. Then her plain face creased in a wide smile.

"Way to go, Grace," Cookie said, and Stella smiled and put her arm around the older woman.

Justin looked pleased. "Still want to chicken out and drive back?"

Cookie answered for all of them. "Nah. Lead on, Coach. We're with you."

"You'll have to drive back alone," Justin told Meghan.

"Stop trying to make me feel guilty," she said, but she was smiling. "You know I can't leave my car here."

"Okay. See you in a while." As they started off, Justin called over his shoulder, "We might even beat you back."

"Fat chance," Meghan shouted. She lingered a minute, watching him stride off with his little troop. Cookie had kiddingly called him "Coach," but it wasn't inappropriate. The three women were so different, but they were developing a camaraderie that was like a team spirit. Meghan had briefly felt a part of it.

The rationale behind Justin's fostering such a supportive group spirit made sense. No matter how different they seemed outwardly, these women had a common bond in the painful experience they had endured. Meghan could empathize because of what she'd witnessed as a child. Her father's abuse had never touched her physically, but she had felt the pain.

Meghan got in her car and was about to start the motor when she was struck with a startling thought. What if there had been a Justin Forbes around to help in her mother's case. Would things have turned out differently?

BY THE TIME the others got to the house, Meghan had already changed to her high-heeled pumps and blouse and jacket. Justin looked disappointed. "I see you're back to your lady lawyer role."

"I never left it. That's what I am, a lady lawyer."

"That's part of what you are, not the sum total. You can't fool me. I've seen the evidence of those hidden personalities you try to suppress." He spoke lightly, but she caught the underlying message.

"Well right now, the lawyer has the upper hand. I have to get back to the office."

"Stay for lunch."

"I can't. I came here to talk to Stella."

About to go upstairs, Stella paused when she heard her name. "Do you want to talk now?" she asked.

"Please."

"Won't it wait until after lunch?" Justin asked Meghan, as Stella came toward them.

"I feel guilty enough about killing the last two hours when I should have been working."

Justin frowned. "I believe in using time, not killing it."

"Sorry. An unfortunate choice of words." Here she was on the defensive again. "Can we use your office?"

Justin nodded and opened the door to his office, motioning them inside.

"Justin, will you stay?" Stella asked.

Again Meghan had mixed emotions about his being present when she talked to her client, but she couldn't very well object if Stella wanted him there. Justin looked at Meghan who nodded her approval.

Once they were seated, Meghan described her conversation with Barnaby Trask. She was concerned about how Stella might react, so she chose her words carefully.

"I . . . I could have told you what my father would say," Stella said in a little-girl voice. "I knew he wouldn't understand."

"Any reason why he's taking Brad's side?" Meghan asked.

"I don't think he sees it that way. When my mother died, Dad had to take care of me. Then when I got married, he said he was turning me over to my husband."

"Turning you over?" Meghan's words came out in a sputter. "Like a chattel?"

"Not exactly. He just wanted me to be looked after."

Meghan glanced at Justin. His face was hard. "In the marriage ceremony, a father still *gives* his daughter away," he said grimly.

"How can he expect you to stay with Brad?"

"I never told him how bad it was."

"Why not?"

"I was ashamed."

"Stella, you didn't do anything to be ashamed of. Your father wants you to call him, and when you do, you should tell him why you left."

"Brad must've told him."

"Brad sees things the way he wants to. The fact that he's sorry now doesn't change—"

"Did he say he was sorry?" Stella broke in. "Did you see him again?"

"Yes."

"When?"

"This morning."

"What else did he say?"

"That he wants to see you." Meghan described her interview with Brad Cranshaw. From all the questions Stella asked, it was obvious that she wanted to see him. "I'm not sure that's a good idea," Meghan said. "I told him to have his attorney call me."

Stella looked troubled and confused.

"That may be premature," Justin said quietly. "There's no reason why Stella and Brad can't meet."

"Alone?"

"No," Justin said. "Not alone. Not just yet. They can meet in your office, with you there."

"And you, Justin?" Stella asked.

"If you want."

"But what would such a meeting accomplish?" Meghan asked.

"That's what we'll find out," Justin answered.

Meghan drove back to her office with none of the euphoria she'd had earlier. She had felt very close to Justin that morning, but it was a closeness that apparently required a suspension of her thought processes. The magnetic physical force he exuded would not, however, cloud her professional judgment. She was sure she knew how to help her client.

As for herself, that was another story.

CHAPTER SIX

MEGHAN ANSWERED the intercom.

"Mr. Cranshaw is here," Phyllis announced.

"Tell him I'll be with him in a few minutes."

Stella had stiffened with apprehension.

"I should have told you to get here a little earlier," Meghan told Justin.

"Why? We're not late."

"Just to give us time to prepare."

Justin frowned. "Prepare what?"

"For this conference."

"What's to prepare? This isn't a formal hearing."

"That might have been a better move," Meghan said. She had set up this appointment for Brad and Stella to meet but had her doubts about what it would accomplish.

"I don't think so," Justin said. "Not at this stage. What's wrong with an informal meeting like this on neutral ground?"

"Intimidation is what's wrong."

"Surely you don't think he's going to threaten Stella with us present."

"There are all kinds of intimidation." Meghan turned to Stella. "You're sure you want to see him?"

Stella nodded.

"He's going to ask you to come home."

"I know," Stella said.

"He's going to apologize and swear that it's never going to happen again. If that doesn't work, he'll probably—"

Justin interrupted. "What's the point of all this conjecturing about what Brad will say."

"The point is I want Stella to be ready—so she'll know how to answer him."

"There's no prepared script," Justin said.

"That's arguable. I've heard the same speeches often enough."

"They may use the same words, but each person is different. I don't think Stella has to plan beforehand how she's going to reply to something she hasn't yet heard."

"I'll be all right," Stella told Meghan. She looked pale, but her voice was steady.

"Okay, then," Meghan said. She stepped into the outer office. "Mr. Cranshaw?"

Brad stood up. He looked nervous, but determined.

"Is your attorney joining us?" she asked. Meghan had suggested that he might want to have his attorney accompany him.

"I don't need a lawyer to speak for me."

But when he got inside and saw Stella he could say nothing. She was sitting on the edge of her chair, inclining forward, her dark eyes examining his face, studying him closely. Brad stared at her, his mouth working.

Meghan felt a stab of sympathy. They both looked so young—and so unhappy. She had to remind herself that it was Stella's unhappiness that was her concern, and that Brad was the one who had caused it.

Justin stood. Without waiting for an introduction, he came forward. "Mr. Cranshaw. I'm Justin Forbes."

With a questioning look, Brad took Justin's outstretched hand.

Meghan explained. "Mr. Forbes is the director of a shelter for victims of domestic violence." She deliberately refrained from mentioning the name. "That's where Stella is staying."

"She doesn't need a shelter," Brad said, stumbling over the words. He turned to Stella. "You have a home. I want you to come home with me."

"I can't do that."

"What happened . . . it's never going to happen again, Stella."

She looked away. Brad pulled a chair close and sat, reaching to take her hand, but Stella pulled back. "You said that the last time. I believed you then."

"So believe me one more time. Stella, please."

Meghan felt Justin's eyes on her and realized she had been unconsciously shaking her head. Justin took her elbow and propelled them both a few steps back. Meghan realized he wanted to let the two young people play out their scene without interference.

Brad's apologies continued. "I never meant to hurt you. I don't know what got into me. There was all this hassle at work."

"Why wouldn't you tell me what was bothering you?"

He ran his hand through his hair. "I don't know."

"When I tried to talk to you, you got angry. You said some awful things."

"That was the booze talking."

"Then why did you drink so much?"

"I needed a few drinks to unwind."

"A few drinks! Brad, you got drunk every night."

"I know what you thought—the way you looked at me. I felt like dirt—at the office, and then at home, too. I went nuts. I just went nuts. But it's never going to happen again."

"I wish I could believe you."

Meghan feared that Brad's apologies and promises were softening Stella's resolve.

"You can," Brad was insisting. "Baby, I'd cut off my right arm before I'd hurt you again. Things'll be different. You'll see."

"What's going to make them different?" Stella asked.

"Huh?" The question surprised him.

"Something has to change in order for us to make it. Maybe it's me. Maybe I have to become the kind of person such things can't happen to."

Brad didn't understand. Meghan wasn't sure she did, either, but she recognized Justin's influence in Stella's words.

"You don't have to do anything, Stella, except come home with me," Brad pleaded. "I'm the one who has to change, but I need you with me. Baby, I love you. I'll do whatever you want me to do."

Meghan saw Stella's look of anguish and started to step forward. She had tried to prepare Stella to steel herself against this kind of abject plea, but Brad was getting to her. Justin took Meghan's arm, holding her back. She started to break loose. If Justin was taken in by Brad Cranshaw's contrition, it was just too bad. Meghan had an obligation to protect her client.

Justin held on and Meghan faced him angrily. His eyes, however, were on Stella, and something in their narrowed gaze made Meghan turn around. Stella's face was composed, though her dark eyes reflected emotional turmoil. She stood. Her voice was so soft that Meghan had to lean forward to catch the words.

"Doing what *I* want you to do is no solution unless you want it, too."

Brad rose and started to say something. "No, Brad. Let me finish. I don't think you know what you want right now. I know I don't."

"Baby, I want you."

"Please, don't call me baby. If that's the way you see me, it's wrong. I'm a grown woman. Maybe I didn't act that way before, but I want to." Her voice became stronger. "I intend to."

Meghan felt Justin's hand drop away and caught his satisfied expression. So he'd been right. Stella was handling the situation very well.

But Brad wasn't giving up. "Do whatever you want to, Stell," he said desperately, "but do it at home."

"I don't think I can."

Brad's desperation mounted. "Why the hell not?"

Meghan stepped forward to intercede. "There's nothing to be gained in arguing, Mr. Cranshaw. Stella has told you her decision."

"Her decision, or yours?" Brad almost shouted. He turned back to Stella. "I didn't come here with a lawyer or—" he gestured furiously at Justin, "—whatever the hell that guy is. Why do you need them to tell you what to do?"

His tirade upset Stella, but she held her ground. "I need their support, and I appreciate their advice, but no one's telling me what to do, Brad."

Good for you, Meghan cheered silently.

More subdued, but stubborn, Brad said, "I'm not giving you a divorce."

"Divorce isn't like a gift that's yours to bestow, Mr. Cranshaw," Meghan said. "Stella has a right to sue for divorce if she chooses."

"Do you want a divorce?" Brad asked his wife.

Stella looked at him, then looked away. "I don't know."

Her answer disappointed Meghan. When violence crippled a marriage, there was no other way out. But if Stella wanted to postpone the inevitable, it was her choice.

Brad seemed encouraged. "Can I come to see you at least?"

Stella looked at Justin. Meghan expected him to say no. After all, the purpose of a shelter was to protect women from the men who'd hurt them.

"Perhaps after a while," Justin said.

Meghan was shocked.

"That is if Stella wants to see you," Justin continued. "For now, though, I think you both need time away from each other."

Brad accepted defeat. He'd apparently anticipated the possibility. "I brought some more of your things," he told Stella. "Stuff I figured you'd need. If you'll come out to the car with me... It's right in front."

"Mr. Forbes can help," Meghan quickly offered.

Brad gave her a sharp look. "You don't have to be afraid. I'm not going to beat her up the minute we're alone."

"It's all right, Meghan," Stella said. "I want to go."

A few minutes after they'd gone out, Meghan called the receptionist on the intercom. "Phyllis, can you see the Cranshaws from your window?"

After a pause, Phyllis answered, "Yeah. They're out front. He's opening the door of a red BMW. Real classy car."

"Never mind the car. Just keep your eye on Stella. If she seems to be having a problem with him, call me right away."

Justin was shaking his head when Meghan hung up. "I think you're the one with the problem."

His remark angered her. "Why? Because I'm concerned for Stella's safety? Far more than you are, apparently."

"At the moment, she's in no danger."

"How can you be so sure?"

"I'm pretty good at sizing people up. That's my job. Brad Cranshaw wants his wife back, but he's not going to force her."

"All of a sudden, he's a reformed character?"

"No," Justin said seriously. "He's not a reformed character—not yet. But maybe he could be."

"Are you so gullible?"

"Why is it being gullible to believe that people can change?"

"Because it doesn't happen so easily."

"I don't claim it's easy, but it *can* happen."

"How can you take Brad's side? The man beat his wife."

"It's not a question of taking sides in something like this. Brad Cranshaw may be as much a victim as a villain."

Meghan didn't disguise her scorn. "You can't really believe that. What he did was villainous."

"Exactly... what he *did* was villainous, but the act may not represent the man."

"The only victims I've come across in these cases are the women."

"There are all kinds of victims, Meghan. Until we can get away from stereotypical roles based on gender, men and women will both suffer from it. Brad is immature. He didn't know how to deal with the responsibilities of work and marriage, and he didn't know how to deal with failure."

"So he beat his wife."

"I'd say out of displaced self-hatred, not because he hates her."

"Please spare me your psychological analyses."

"But you've got to understand—"

"No, I don't," Meghan interrupted. "Not when such so-called understanding condones brutality. You claim that people should make their own decisions. Well, Brad chose to act as he did, and I don't think you should interfere with Stella's choosing to free herself from him."

Almost grim in his seriousness, Justin said, "I don't intend to, if that's the decision she comes to after reviewing her options."

"What options? To subject herself to more of the same?"

"And your professional expertise tells you that's the only alternative?" It was his turn to be sarcastic.

"My personal experience is what tells me." The words came out before she could stop them.

Justin looked stunned. "Something…something like that happened to you?"

"To my mother." Meghan suddenly wanted him to understand why she felt so strongly. She had experienced the tragedy of violence in the home, of her father's never-kept promises to change and of her mother's broken hopes.

Meghan told Justin what had happened, emphasizing not her own pain, but her mother's grief. As she talked, he took her hand, and she felt the warmth of his sympathy. "But you know," she said after she described how she and her mother finally left, "Mother was never really happy. She didn't live long enough to learn how to be happy without him. I think she never gave up hoping he would change."

"Did he?" Justin asked.

"No. That's why we left."

"I mean after that."

His question surprised her. "I wouldn't know, but I doubt it."

"You don't hear from him?"

"No. He wrote when he heard that Mother died. I didn't answer."

"That was a long time ago."

"Yes, it was." She knew what he was thinking.

"Time didn't heal this particular wound?"

Meghan forced a smile. "I wouldn't say that. I don't look wounded, do I?" She met his gaze, and its intensity pierced her inner being.

Justin bent and kissed her mouth, a soft, tender kiss. Then he said, "I'm not so sure."

His answer made her pull away. "Well, I am," she said. "I told you all this so you'd understand where I'm coming from. I don't trust Brad Cranshaw's promises."

"Do you trust any man, Meghan?"

Her chin went up defiantly.

"Maybe you don't trust yourself or your own emotions."

"You don't have to worry about my emotions," Meghan told him.

"I wish that was true."

Meghan didn't feel comfortable with the way the conversation was going and was glad that Stella's return brought it to a halt.

"Did you get your suitcase?" Meghan asked.

"Yes. It's outside." A wistful look came over her face. "He packed the woolly robe I always wear. He thought I'd want it now that it's getting so cold."

"That was thoughtful," Justin observed.

Meghan said nothing.

Stella and Justin were about to leave when the call came from Stella's father. Without preamble, Barnaby Trask told Meghan, "I want to talk to my daughter. And don't tell me she's not there. I know she's meeting with Brad in your office this morning."

"Just a minute, Mr. Trask." Meghan pressed the mute button and turned to Stella. "Do you want to talk to your father?"

Stella hesitated, then said, "I guess I should."

"You don't have to."

Stella sighed. "Sooner or later I have to." She took the phone. "Hello, Dad . . . yes, I'm all right. Yes, I spoke to Brad. No, I'm not going home with him. . . . You know why. . . ." She listened for quite a while, then interrupted. "Dad, that's not the way it was. You don't understand. It's going to take more than just your talking to Brad to change things."

Meghan could hear the angry sounds from the other end.

Stella listened, then refused whatever request or demand her father was making. "I'm sorry, Dad. I can't do that. . . . Because it wouldn't solve anything for me to return to your house. I like where I'm staying. It's the best place for me right now. . . . I'm sorry you feel that way but that's the way it has to be. Look, I've got to go. Yes, I'll call you. Good-bye."

Stella put down the phone. Her bravado was fading. "He's mad that I didn't go to him so he could fix things up." She gave a helpless laugh. "Dad prides himself on ordering people's lives for them. He says I'm disgracing him. He wants me home, not in some charity shelter like those losers you read about in the papers."

"I gather that's a direct quote," Justin said dryly.

Stella nodded. "I wish I could make him understand."

Justin put an arm around her. "Maybe you will eventually. But your father's lack of understanding is his problem. Don't let it add to yours. You have enough to deal with right now."

"But everyone's so unhappy with me."

"Are you?"

"I don't know. Sometimes, I feel good, but then . . . I don't know."

"Were you happy with yourself before?"

"No."

"So you made a decision to do something. That was the beginning."

"Beginning of what?" Stella asked with renewed spirit.

"Of something better," Justin declared.

"Of a new life, of independence," Meghan added, then wondered at Justin's slight frown.

They started to walk out and Stella asked to use the lavatory. When she left, Meghan said, "I wasn't disagreeing with what you said, just defining what your 'something better' could be."

"I know that. The problem is I'm not sure our definitions coincide." He cocked his head and his frown creased into an ironic smile. "We don't think alike, Counselor."

"Unfortunately."

"But I don't take offense."

She had to laugh. "Oh, that's big of you."

"I figure the more we get to be together, the closer in thinking we'll become."

"Do you really? And which one of us is going to give in?"

"Neither—or both. We'll see. At least we like the same foods," he said, a teasing reminder of the night he had declared they were made for each other. "If we work at it, I think we might find we have some other appetites in common."

The glint in his eye left no doubt as to his meaning, and Meghan's heightened pulse betrayed her response.

After Justin and Stella had gone, Meghan sat at her desk for a long time. She tried to focus on Stella's situation and review what had happened. The whole encounter that morning had been charged with tension. Stella had handled it very well. Meghan hoped that she would continue to have the strength to resist Brad's pleas for another chance. Those little gestures of his, like packing Stella's favorite robe, could be persuasive, more so than any verbal appeals. Probably

Justin read sincere concern into such gestures. He thought her too suspicious. Maybe so. Perhaps her distrust of motives was extreme when it came to the opposite sex, but Meghan felt it was better not to risk being duped by a show of affection from a man.

Justin's accusation that she didn't trust her own feelings or herself was only half accurate, Meghan thought. She trusted herself to control her emotions, which weren't a very reliable guide in making important decisions. Never would she let herself become a victim.

In a sense, this determination of hers seemed to validate Justin's claim that men weren't solely responsible for the perpetuation of domestic violence. Women contributed to being victimized by their wishful thinking, by a vain belief that words and promises would make things better. Empty words and unkept promises changed nothing, as Meghan well knew.

Justin Forbes was not that kind of man. He would do, she guessed, whatever he said he was going to do. Whether she approved or not.

Meghan didn't know where she stood with him. Sometimes they agreed, sometimes not. Ally or adversary? Or lover? His teasing remarks implied that was on his mind. She couldn't deny the idea was exciting, but threatening as well.

Justin certainly had the power to confuse her, and she didn't like the feeling. But she couldn't help remembering other feelings he aroused, her enjoyment of his humor, her pleasure in his company, and most of all, her sensuous awareness of him as a man—and herself as a woman.

There was no way to avoid seeing him. There was the matter of the variance, and their mutual involvement with Stella. But Meghan was honest enough to admit to herself that she didn't want to avoid seeing Justin Forbes. Perhaps, she reasoned, because there was no other man in her life at the moment. There could have been. She had deliberately shut the door on Nate, this time for good.

And there was that hotshot lobbyist from Capital Hill. When she'd met him at a dinner party last year, he was with his wife. Two nights ago, he had telephoned, anxious to tell Meghan what he apparently assumed would be a welcome bit of news. He was now divorced. Meghan remembered him as being forceful, witty and rather attractive. So why had she put him off? Because she wasn't interested.

At the moment, one man dominated her thoughts. Justin Forbes was like no one she had ever known. As long as she kept the limits of their relationship within her control, why not enjoy whatever it could offer?

With a deliberate and successful effort of will, Meghan turned to the work on her desk. She had a child-custody court hearing that afternoon and an appointment with the personnel director of a manufacturing company about a possible sex discrimination suit. She needed to be sharp, so she put aside all distracting thoughts of Justin . . . for now.

DURING THE NEXT TWO WEEKS, Meghan found herself drawn into the life at Midway House. A strong camaraderie had developed among the four women, and Meghan began to feel herself a part of it. Her visits were work related, at first anyway. She had to pick up a copy of the deed to the Midway House property, or to talk to Stella about a call she'd received from Barnaby Trask's lawyer. When Meghan also agreed to be the attorney for Midway House in all legal matters—she couldn't very well refuse, could she—there were even more reasons to stop by after work, or to make a quick visit at lunchtime.

Soon there was no clear delineation between what was personal and what was professional in her involvement with the residents of Midway—and with its director. But Meghan decided that, as long as neither role suffered, it didn't really matter.

She substituted an hour's run with the Midway crew for one of her weekly health club visits. Meghan enjoyed being with the women and seeing their pleasure as they increased their endurance and skill. She noticed that Justin was gradually retreating from leadership on these outings, letting the others set the pace.

Stacy was curious about Meghan's new interest in outdoor jogging.

"I prefer running in the fresh air," Meghan told her.

"Since when?" Stacy asked. "As if I didn't know."

At the club, her usual singles game with Stacy became a doubles match when Justin and a middle-aged surgeon who played with him, challenged the young women. The doctor turned out to be a tiger on the court, and the women lost the match. The next time they played, Stacy suggested they switch partners so that she and Dr. Clausen were paired. So now, Meghan found herself on the same side of the court with Justin, playing with him, not against him.

This was a different kind of challenge and she floundered at first, uncertain of how they were going to work together. At first she tried to cover too much of the court, as she realized when she and Justin both went for an overhand shot and almost collided. Meghan changed her game. After that, she became as aware of Justin's play as she was of their opponents', and gradually they synchronized their efforts. It was a close score, but they ended up winning the match.

"Partner, we're a natural," Justin declared triumphantly.

"Stop crowing," Meghan told him, but her own pleasure, though unvoiced, was just as great.

Later, as she showered and dressed, she realized that she and Justin had developed their successful level of team play without ever once talking about it. They'd observed, gauged the other's timing, recognized each other's competence and soon learned to anticipate the partner's movements. Sometimes one would try to rescue a point the other couldn't get—and not always successfully. But when it worked, they both exulted.

As if divining her thoughts, Stacy said, "It's nice to have a partner isn't it?"

"On the tennis court, yes."

"You don't fool me. I think you're weakening."

Weakening?

Stacy realized her mistake. "Sorry. Wrong word."

"For me, it is."

Justin was waiting when the two women came out of the locker room. "How about coming over for dinner? You, too, Stacy."

"How can you invite two people over at the last minute like this?" Stacy asked. "Won't your cook get mad?"

"You don't know Mrs. Kremsky. She believes in second and third helpings and lots of leftovers. There's always plenty."

"I thought Dr. Schumann hired a cook," Meghan said. Clara Schumann was afraid that Ida Kremsky's culinary contributions might be construed as unpaid labor by some social services inspector.

"She did, but Ida still commandeers the kitchen when she can. What do you say?"

"Some other time maybe," Stacy answered. "Tony and I are looking at houses tonight."

"How about you?" he asked Meghan.

"I don't think so. I've got some paperwork to do at home."

When Ida Kremsky had found out that Meghan lived alone and subsisted on microwavable frozen dinners, she had issued a blanket invitation for Meghan to eat with them. If Meghan happened to be at Midway around dinner time, it was hard to refuse, but she didn't want to make it a habit. That wouldn't do. Justin's living at Midway also complicated things. Not that her accepting Ida's dinner invitations, even those issued through Justin, could be considered as dates exactly, but the situation certainly limited her and Justin's privacy. It didn't seem to bother him at all.

"You don't have to stay late. She's making goulash tonight," he added coaxingly.

Meghan laughed. "Is that supposed to tempt me? Somehow the name of that dish always had the opposite effect."

"Have you ever tried it?"

"No."

"You don't know what you're missing."

"Well, I'm not going to find out tonight. I've got a case up before the District Court of Appeals tomorrow and I've really got a lot to prepare."

"Okay then." Justin always seemed to understand Meghan's dedication to her work. There was that about him. He accepted and respected women in professional roles—and not with the masculine patronizing she often encountered, and always resented.

She was going to walk out to the parking lot with Justin, but Stacy asked Meghan to keep her company until Tony came. When they were alone, Stacy said, "You were working on that Appeals case all afternoon. I thought you'd finished."

"I want to go over the papers again."

"That's just your excuse for not going with Justin."

"Maybe."

"But why? Meghan, you know you're nuts about the guy."

"I don't like being 'nuts.' It means being irrational. It's not something I do well."

"Come on. You've fallen for him. Admit it."

Meghan shook her head with exasperation. "Just listen to your expressions, 'nuts'... 'falling.' Is that supposed to describe love?"

"Okay, what's your description?"

Stacy's simple question stumped her. Once, Meghan's answer would have included such things as common interests, compatibility and respect, but she was no longer sure. With Justin Forbes, there was a powerful physical attraction. And she felt the influence of his strong personality. But Meghan intended to keep a check on both.

"I'm not sure," she told Stacy, "but one thing I know is that my definition doesn't include yielding yourself up to another."

"You don't know what you're missing."

"I know what I'm trying to miss."

"What happened to your mother isn't going to happen to you."

"You can say that again."

"I give up. If you send that guy away, you'll be sorry."

"Who said I was sending him away?"

"Then you're not going to turn him down?"

"It depends on what he asks."

"Has he tried to make love to you?" Stacy asked curiously.

"Not really."

"Oh."

Stacy sounded disappointed. Meghan felt a reaction that was disturbingly similar.

ABOUT TEN THAT NIGHT Justin called Meghan. "How's the work going? If you're in the middle of something, call me back."

"No, it's okay. I'm done."

"Can you come over tomorrow night?"

"More goulash?"

He laughed. "As a matter of fact, Mrs. Kremsky saved some for you. She couldn't believe you've never tasted it. Tomorrow, your deprivation will end."

"Are we still talking about goulash?"

"What else did you have in mind?"

His provocative question brought only one thing to her mind. His, too, apparently. *Well, you started it,* Meghan told herself. *What do you expect him to think?*

"Nothing special," she said.

"What I'm thinking is *very* special."

Meghan couldn't help wondering if making love with Justin Forbes would be as exciting as her racing heart predicted.

"Are you still there?" Justin asked when she said nothing.

"I'm here."

"Try to make it tomorrow. There's someone I want you to meet."

"Someone new? I thought you weren't going to take in more residents for a while."

"She's new, but not a resident. Lil's here."

"Lil?"

"Lillian Vance. Didn't I tell you about her? I must have. Lil's going to be my assistant. She finished up her other job a little earlier than she'd thought, praise be. Clara and I are driving each other bonkers."

"I gather that you and Lillian are more compatible."

"All the way. We think alike. She's one hell of a gal, sharp as can be, tough and beautiful to boot."

"How nice for you." Meghan felt a twinge of something she refused to acknowledge as jealousy.

"Will you come?" Justin asked.

"Sure. I'd like to meet this paragon of yours."

"Lil's great. You'll love her."

Meghan put down the phone. *Don't be so sure about that,* she thought. Somehow, she was not prepared to love Lillian Vance.

CHAPTER SEVEN

"HI. YOU MUST BE Meghan O'Brien. I'm Lillian Vance."

The woman who greeted Meghan at the door was tall, reed-thin, black and absolutely stunning. Her hair was plaited in corn rows, the severe hairdo perfect for her classic features. When Justin had said she was beautiful, he wasn't exaggerating.

"Justin was afraid you weren't coming," Lillian said. "He just called your office, and they said you'd left an hour ago."

"I had to make a stop." Meghan didn't say that the stop was to her apartment to change into the dramatic black jersey she'd decided was more suitable for the occasion. Seeing this striking woman, she was glad she'd taken the time. Lillian wore her beige ultrasuede dress with the poise of a professional model.

Justin came out of his office. "There you are. You're late. It doesn't matter. You're here now."

He sounded excited and happy. The eye patch was gone, but he still had a singed gap in one eyebrow. It gave him, Meghan thought, an appealingly rakish look. She wondered if Lil thought so, too.

"Mrs. Kremsky's holding dinner. Have you met Lil?" he asked.

"Justin, relax," Lillian told him. "We've already introduced ourselves."

"Good. Then let's eat."

"You have absolutely no manners," Lillian said, giving him a poke. "I'll tell Ida that Meghan's here, and then we'll go into the living room and get acquainted."

"You've hardly been here a day and you're already giving orders."

"You need someone to take you in hand." There was more fondness than criticism in her tone and in her expression.

When she'd gone out, Justin turned to Meghan with a wide smile. "Lil's something else, isn't she?"

"She's very striking."

"I think there's some Masai blood somewhere back in her ancestry. In Kenya we once went to a village where the chief's wife looked so much like Lil, they could have been sisters. Lil was immediately accepted as one of their own. Lucky for me. I had the distinct impression that I would have been in trouble otherwise." He chuckled at the memory. "Because of her, they tolerated me."

"You seem to know each other very well. Did you work together long?"

"Not really. Lil got a bad case of malaria and had to be shipped home before our tour was over. But serving together in the Peace Corps intensifies a friendship. We stayed close. When I got the idea for Midway House, I thought of Lil right away. She's just what we need here."

Such enthusiasm. Meghan wondered if it was based on friendship and professional respect, or something more.

"Wait'll you get to know her. You'll see what I mean."

"I'm sure I will." Meghan hoped her smile was brighter than her thoughts.

Lil returned. "Look what I found," she said gaily. She was carrying a tray with a bottle of wine and some glasses. "We're lucky that Ida believes in using real wine to cook with. She let me steal what was left."

"Is she going to join us?" Justin asked.

"I asked but she said no. I don't think she trusts Clarissa to be alone in the kitchen," she told them with smiling indulgence. Clarissa was the middle-aged midwestern woman Clara Schumann had hired as housekeeper. "The others are upstairs. Stella is combing out the permanent she just gave Cookie, and Grace is watching. So it's just us."

In the living room, Lil poured the white wine. "Excuse the jelly glasses," she said. "Midway's kind of short on fancy stemware."

"Such things aren't important," Justin said.

"Just because *you're* oblivious to aesthetics doesn't mean everyone else is," Lil countered.

"So you can take a couple of dollars out of petty cash and buy some matching glasses."

"Hah! You've got exactly seven dollars and ninety cents left in petty cash. Dr. Schumann showed me. No wonder she was so glad to turn things over to me. You're just as oblivious to details as ever."

"It's the big picture that counts," Justin insisted. With a disarming smile, he added, "And that's where I excel. Right?"

Lil laughed but didn't answer.

"Besides," he continued, "if I could do everything, I wouldn't need you. As a team, though, we'll be unbeatable."

Justin had this faculty, Meghan decided, of being able to draw women close, making them feel a part of his team. If he did this so easily, it meant less than she had been imagining.

"I hope you're right," Lil told him. "I like what you're trying to do here, but it's not going to be easy to make it work."

"That's why I need you two. We'll make it work."

So, I'm included on this team, Meghan thought. *How nice!*

"Justin tells me you're doing all the legal work for us," Lil said.

"Temporarily." Meghan ignored Justin's frowning glance.

Lil noticed and looked curiously from one to the other. "Justin twisted your arm?" Lil asked.

"Not exactly. Stella Cranshaw is my client. I guess that's how it started." But was it? Or had it started when she'd first noticed Justin Forbes, before she'd even heard about Midway House?

"Tell me about your work," Lil asked. "If I'd had enough money after college, I think I would have gone on to law school. It must be fascinating."

Lil's interest was sincere, and Meghan found herself responding. She described her practice and the kinds of cases that were her specialty. The other woman's questions and comments were intelligent and penetrating.

Then Lil talked about her own career, and Meghan sensed the combination of sharpness and sensitivity that Justin had described. No wonder he was so anxious to have Lillian Vance join him in this venture. And in his personal life?

He had used the term "friendship" to describe the bond between them. Was that his euphemism for "love affair?" If so, she admired his taste, Meghan thought, and then complimented herself on her sophisticated coolness. Or was it a sophisticated cover-up?"

"Hi," Cookie called from the doorway.

"The perm looks good, Cookie," Lil said.

"I usually like my hair curlier, but Stell says this gives me class." Cookie's black, shoulder-length hair fell in sophisticated, wavy swirls.

"I like it," Meghan said.

Cookie turned to Justin. "What do you think, Coach?"
"Looks great."

Cookie was satisfied. Meghan realized that, to Cookie, male approval counted the most.

"Thanks," Cookie said. "Oh, I'm supposed to tell you dinner's ready. Ida says come and get it."

At the dinner table, conversation was lively. Ida and Grace were still somewhat reserved with Lil, but the two younger women appeared to have accepted her wholeheartedly. They were about to have dessert when the doorbell rang.

"Keep your seats," Clarissa yelled, coming out of the kitchen. "I'll get it." She was wearing scuffed men's bedroom slippers that made a flapping sound as she padded through. The bell rang again. "Hold your horses, fa' Pete's sake," she shouted. "I'm coming."

"Clarissa used to cook in a logging camp in Oregon. It left an indelible impression," Justin said dryly.

"Your boyfriend's here," Clarissa announced and padded back to the kitchen.

The man following her was so tall he had to stoop to clear the door. He was six four at least, a handsome, lanky black man sporting a fierce-looking mustache. But there was nothing fierce about his good-natured expression as he and Justin greeted each other, or the tender smile he gave Lil as he stooped to plant a kiss on her cheek. There was gruff tenderness in his voice as well. "Hi, Baby. Am I too early?"

"Just in time for dessert," she answered. "Homemade apple strudel."

He pulled a chair from against the wall and wedged himself between Justin and Lil. "I'm in luck," he said happily.

Lil introduced him. "This hungry hulk is Brian Washington. Most people have one sweet tooth. Brian has twenty-eight."

Brian grinned at her. "Which is why I'm going to marry you, sweetheart."

"You're engaged?" Cookie squealed.

Lil nodded. "In a weak moment, I said yes."

"Best decision you ever made," said Brian.

"When're you getting married?"

"Are you getting a ring?"

"Can we come to the wedding?"

The questions came all at once.

It was interesting, Meghan thought, how all four of the other women had such happy and curious reactions to this news of an impending marriage. Despite their unfortunate experiences, they wanted to believe in romantic love.

Analyzing her own pleasure with the announcement, Meghan acknowledged a profound relief. She had been wrong about Justin and Lil. There was no reason for her jealousy. Jealousy? Meghan quickly backed away from the word and its connotations of passion and turmoil.

"We haven't set the date yet—and yes, you all can come," Lil told the group.

"What if we're not here?" Cookie asked.

"Well I certainly expect you won't be," Lil told them, "but I'll see you all get invitations."

"I'll get that ring for you one of these days," Brian promised, "just to make it official."

"I don't need a ring. I feel official enough."

"If that pro ball coaching slot comes through, we'll have it made," Brian told Lil.

"You know you don't want to leave those kids," Lil said. She explained that Brian was a physical education teacher and basketball coach in a local high school, but was being considered for a job on the coaching staff of a professional team. "And I," she said as if reminding him, "don't want to leave Alexandria. Especially now that I'm starting this new job."

"We'll see," Brian said.

"Money's not the only consideration," Lil told him. It was obvious they'd had this discussion before.

"Hey, I haven't been offered the job yet."

"But, if you are . . . ?"

"I said we'll see."

"So who's having strudel?" Mrs. Kremsky broke in with nervous cheerfulness, heading off what she was afraid would be a real argument.

"Count me in," Brian immediately responded.

Everyone did justice to the buttery fruit pastry. Brian had seconds, and then he and Lil left for the school concert they were attending.

Meghan tried to help with the clearing up, but Mrs. Kremsky shooed her out of the kitchen. "We've got a system," the older woman told her. "Take a walk in the garden . . . you and Justin."

"Come on," Justin said, taking Meghan's arm. "We know when we're not wanted." He steered her out of the kitchen door onto the back porch.

The brisk night air had the frosty nip of the approaching winter. "It's cold out here," said Meghan with a shiver. "Not conducive to a walk in the garden."

Justin put his arm around her. "That's okay. Our only garden is that frost-killed vegetable plot out there. Ida's a romantic, bless her heart."

"She was so afraid that Brian and Lil were going to have an argument."

"I saw that. She needn't have worried."

"You mean they don't argue?"

"On the contrary. They've had some humdingers. What I mean is they know how to handle an argument. You know," he said thoughtfully, "it might have been good if the others *had* seen them argue."

"What on earth for?"

"Because Lil and Brian have a loving relationship that's apparently working, a reminder to the others that it can happen."

"So why promote an argument?"

He laughed. "I don't want to promote anything, but if Brian and Lil have a good rip-snorting argument, Stella and Cookie and Grace and Ida will see that differences can be expressed without violence, and that Brian and Lil can make up and still love each other."

"That may be true for some differences and for some people. Brian and Lil aren't typical."

"They're not a rarity, either. Lil is quite a gal, isn't she? Brian's a lucky man."

"Jealous?" Meghan glanced up at him and then away, almost ashamed of having asked.

He gave her an odd look. "So *that's* what you thought."

"Well, I didn't really give it much thought." She stumbled over the lie.

"If you mean jealous in a personal way, the answer is no. I may have harbored a lascivious thought or two when we had to share a hut in the old days." The recollection seemed to amuse him. "But Lil said she had no intention of fooling around with a white dude, so forget it. I did. We've been friends ever since." He took Meghan's chin in his hand and tilted her face up. "Satisfied?" he asked softly.

Meghan had no answer, but a trembling response went through her.

"You're shivering," Justin said. His arms encircled her, drawing her to his warmth. His eyes held hers, but when he kissed her, Meghan closed her eyes to savor the sensuous pleasure of his lips. The kiss seemed to last an eternity.

When it ended, Meghan stepped back. Her knees were trembling and her blood coursed hotly. "We'd better go in," she said.

"You're not still cold?"

"We'd just better go in," she repeated.

Clarissa was alone in the kitchen. "Where's everyone?" Meghan asked.

"I told them to git." Clarissa's speech was as raw-boned as her looks. "All o' them underfoot like that. I need space. You git on out, too."

"Clarissa, you're a dangerous woman," Justin said with mock apprehension.

"You better believe it," Clarissa said, trying not to smile. "Get on with you now."

"We'd better obey," Justin told Meghan. When they were out of earshot, he said, "Clarissa's quite a character."

"Is she under your spell, too?" Meghan teased.

"Too?" At the entrance to the living room, he paused. "I hope that means you're included."

She hedged. "Can't you tell?"

"I get mixed messages."

Considering her own confusion, Meghan thought, that wasn't surprising.

"Justin," Grace called from the living room. "Can you help with this card table, please? One of the legs won't open."

"Sure." He adjusted the hinge and set up the table.

Meghan was surprised to see the four women sit down. Cookie plunked down a deck of cards, cut and slid them over. Grace started to deal.

"What's going on?" Meghan asked.

"Grace is teaching us bridge," Cookie answered. "Stella played before, but me and Ida's just learning."

"You can watch, but you can't kibitz," Grace said with a meaningful look at Justin.

"Just for that, I'm going to let you play without the benefit of my expert advice." Justin took Meghan's arm to lead her to the sofa on the other side of the room.

She held back. "I should be going."

"Must you? It's not late. If you leave me, I'll be forced to go over there and kibitz, and that'll get me in trouble with Grace." His smile was appealingly hard to resist.

Meghan relented. "For a minute then," she said and sat down. "What's with the bridge lessons?" The foursome was too far away for Meghan to eavesdrop, but the players seemed intent and the bidding was spirited.

"It's a kick, isn't it? Cookie's got them doing a half hour of aerobics every morning and Ida's teaching haute cuisine Hungarian style, so Grace decided she should offer something. They're having fun and it sure beats watching TV sitcoms every night."

"You don't even have a television."

"Beside the point. Even if we did, this is better."

"Therapy again?"

"You say that as if it's a dirty word. Any activity is good if you enjoy doing it, and it doesn't hurt anyone else. Work can be therapeutic. So can play..." His voice became softly insinuating. "Especially certain kinds of play."

"You mean like bridge?"

"Not exactly what I had in mind," he said with a laugh, "as I think you very well know."

Meghan did, and what he had in mind was being excitingly duplicated in her imagination. To steer the conversation back to safer content, she asked a question that had occurred to her as he was talking. "Doesn't Stella feel left out?"

Justin knew what she meant. "Because the others have something to offer? I was concerned about that, too, but Lil came up with it."

"What?"

"Did you know that Stella had studied art and design?"

"No."

"I didn't either. That was before she switched to an elementary ed major, which was before she dropped out of college to marry Brad."

"Somehow, I can't see picture drawing as a necessary skill for these women," Meghan said.

"Not drawing—style. Lil thought that Stella's flair for design and creating a certain look could be her contribution."

"A make-over artist?" Meghan glanced over at the foursome. Grace and Cookie and Ida Kremsky were as different as could be. "She'll have her hands full."

"Not make-over. The idea isn't that Stella's going to decide how they should look."

"I don't understand."

"At first, I didn't get what Lil was driving at either, but now I see her point. When a woman wants to change her life, she has to change herself. Creating an outward sign of that change could be a morale booster—sort of a symbol of how she sees herself."

"And an announcement to others." Meghan was beginning to understand.

"Exactly."

"But what's Stella's role?"

"Consultant or advisor...I don't know what you'd call it. When Cookie complained she had no curling iron to frizz up her hair, Stella suggested that new hairdo and even gave her the perm. Looks good, doesn't it?"

"Yes, but not as sexy as before."

"Maybe that's what Cookie wants."

"I wouldn't have thought so. She's a very sexy young woman."

"No arguing that," Justin agreed. "But could be she wants to prove there's more to her than sexiness."

"And the others? Are they going to prove something, too?"

"I hope so. For starters, Grace is going back to work part-time. That's a major step."

Meghan was surprised. "I had the impression she didn't like that job."

"What she didn't like was the way she was treated. Grace was everyone's patsy. Whenever there was something no one else would touch, it was 'Let Grace do it.'"

Meghan frowned. "Is that what she's going back to?"

"Not if she doesn't want it to be. She called her boss yesterday. He wants her back right away and full-time, but Grace held her ground. I think he's going to be in for some surprises when she goes back."

"When's that?"

"She told her boss she'd let him know next week. I'm glad she's not rushing. Grace needs time. They all do."

Meghan frowned. "Just what do you think time is going to accomplish?"

"Nothing. It's what the person accomplishes in a given time that counts."

"I don't know," Meghan said. "I can't see any advantage in Stella's postponing action."

"Doesn't she have to decide first what she wants to do?"

"She doesn't have much choice."

"I don't believe that. People have to realize that they do have choices. Stella has few financial resources now because she chose to drop out of school."

"Come on. Brad probably made her quit. Men like that distrust anything that threatens their masculine domination."

"You have a bad habit of lumping all men into one category," he protested.

"Just the abusive ones."

"Meghan, each situation is different."

Justin's fervency surprised her. "There's a common pattern," she said.

"Don't make a blanket judgment—or a blanket condemnation—because of your father."

"My father has nothing to do with my judgment."

"I think he has everything to do with it. Subconsciously, aren't you branding other men with his guilt?"

Meghan blanched. "No, only with their own. My father was lucky. He got off scot-free."

"How do you know?"

"What?"

"You've lost touch. You don't know what's happened to him. Aren't you curious? Don't you want to see him?"

"No."

"Maybe it's time, Meghan."

"That's not for you to say."

He stiffened. "I'm sorry. You're right, of course."

Meghan stood. "I'd better go."

This time, Justin didn't protest.

JUSTIN SAT AT HIS DESK reading over the budget Clara Schumann had worked out, but the figures didn't register. It was after midnight. He often stayed up to tackle paperwork when the house was quiet like this, but tonight, his mind was elsewhere.

Now that he knew about Meghan's father, Justin could understand why she had such a hard-line approach in cases of spousal abuse. She had described her mother's humiliation and grief, and her own outrage. What she had omitted was the deep hurt she must have felt as a child, and then, as an adolescent, the emotional trauma of the separation for which she probably felt responsible. Was she still trying to justify how she'd felt and what she had done?

In his work at Midway, Justin was trying to encourage examination and evaluation of past actions before the residents decided how to proceed with their lives. He sensed that Meghan had yet to do that. Memory of her father's violence evoked only a renewed and still-raw anger. Her anger had been justifiable, but Meghan's refusal to let it go was destructive.

Justin tilted his chair back and stretched wearily. He stared, unseeing, at the ceiling. He knew only too well how troubling the residual effects of a traumatic episode could be. There was no forgetting what had happened with Samantha. Nor did he want to forget. But he'd been able to put it in perspective, using the insight he'd gained about himself to help others.

"Are you asleep or meditating?"

Lil's voice startled him. He shifted to an upright position. "I didn't hear you come in. How was the concert?"

Lil came in and sat in the visitor's chair. "Loud. This band's big on horns and percussion. But it was fun. What're you doing up?"

"I'm thinking great thoughts."

"Yeah? Well those great thoughts must be awfully weighty, friend. You look burdened."

"An optical illusion."

"You can't fool me, Justin Forbes. I know you too well."

That was true, Justin thought, but she didn't know everything. He had mentioned Samantha to Lil, as the girl he'd loved in college, but that was all he'd told her. In the inevitable closeness that came with their isolated living conditions in Kenya, they'd talked a lot about themselves, but he couldn't bring himself to tell Lil about the argument that had ended so violently. A couple of times, Justin recalled, he'd been tempted to tell her what had happened, but he never did. What would have been the purpose? Was he looking for her sympathy? He had rejected that idea.

Justin was hit by a sudden unwelcome thought. Perhaps what he'd really been afraid of back then, what he'd deliberately avoided, was Lil's judgment. If that were true, if he couldn't talk about what had happened to him, was he really free of the past?

He had turned that terrible experience to professional advantage, but there had been no corresponding compensation in his personal life. He couldn't help Meghan overcome what was blocking her emotionally unless he first resolved his own doubts about himself.

"Are you going to tell me about it?" Lil demanded.

It was an appropriate question, even though Lil couldn't know what he'd been thinking. "There's someone else I have to talk to first."

"Meghan O'Brien?"

"She's the one."

Lil smiled. "She *is* the one, isn't she, Justin?"

He hesitated, not sure how to answer. "I don't know."

"Problems?"

"Quite a few."

"Justin, there are always problems. Don't worry. You'll work them out."

"I'm sure as hell going to try."

CHAPTER EIGHT

IT WAS LIL who answered the phone. "Justin's not here," she told Meghan.

"Oh. Too bad. I wanted to tell him what I found out about the variance."

"Good news or bad?"

"It looks pretty good."

"Great. Come on over and tell me about it."

Meghan hesitated. She and Lil had talked often during the two weeks since their meeting, and Meghan had come to admire the breezy competence of Justin's assistant. A personal warmth had developed between them, and somehow, no matter what their topic was initially, Justin invariably came up in their conversation. Lil had a fund of stories about him, and Meghan was an avid listener.

"Come on," Lil coaxed. "Everyone's out and this quiet is getting to me."

Meghan looked at her watch. She'd had to take over one of Lester's cases when he was suddenly called out of town and had worked late to familiarize herself with the details. It was almost eight o'clock. "Where'd they all go?"

"Gathering information."

"What does that mean?"

"Do we have to talk on the phone? Come over and keep me company."

Meghan gave in. "All right. I'm on my way."

"JUSTIN'S NOT BACK YET?" Meghan asked when Lil answered the door at Midway House.

"Nope. Disappointed?" She had lately begun to tease Meghan this way.

"Don't be cute."

"I can't help it." Lil grinned. "It's my nature."

"I'm just curious about these nocturnal ramblings. Where did they all go?"

"Remember last week when they got into this discussion about setting goals for themselves? All those questions they asked?"

"Which Justin didn't want to answer. Yes, I remember. I thought he was being kind of perverse."

"No, he had a reason. Justin always knows what he's doing."

"I'll take your word for it."

"You don't have to. You'll see."

"You were saying . . . ?" Meghan brought her back to the topic.

"He wants them to find their own answers, so they made a list and tonight he's chauffeuring them around town."

"Like where?"

"Let's see—the library, the 'Y,' George Mason University and the high school. Oh, and that health club you both go to."

"The club?"

"Cookie wants to talk to the aerobics instructor and find out what it takes to be one. She's also decided to get her equivalency diploma."

"Well, what do you know? Has Cookie ever worked?"

"She tried. That's what set her husband off this last time. She'd gotten a job as a barmaid and Manny blew his stack and beat her up. Macho man said he wouldn't have his wife being ogled by a bunch of drunks."

Meghan shook her head sadly. "I wondered what the situation was there. None of them talk much about what their husbands did. Except jokingly."

"That's understandable. The humor alleviates the pain."

"It's a bitter humor."

"I know. I think they're opening up a lot more now," Lil said. "Justin never pushes on that score. He accepts whatever they want to reveal."

"Your being here has made a difference."

"I certainly hope so. But if you mean to compensate for Justin's being a man, that's just not the case. I wondered about that, too, but having a male in charge of Midway is a definite plus. No, I'm saying that wrong. Having *Justin* in charge is what makes it work."

Meghan remembered her initial shock on discovering that Justin was the director of Midway House. Even though they didn't always agree, shock had given way to respect.

There was much to admire in what he was doing, but Meghan still had reservations about Justin's approach. A woman who had been subjected to continued abuse sometimes needed a staunch advocate to help her free herself. That was what Meghan tried to be. Justin saw his role differently. He was probably expecting too much from these women. Meghan feared he would be disappointed. She couldn't help recognizing the incongruity of her feelings. She didn't trust his theories, but she didn't want him to fail.

Clarissa bustled in with some coffee. "Oh, great," Meghan said. "Just what I need."

"I could fix ya something to eat," Clarissa offered. Like Mrs. Kremsky, Clarissa had decided that Meghan was malnourished.

"Thanks, no. This is fine."

"Drink that at your own peril," Lil warned when Clarissa was out of earshot. "Clarissa uses twice as much as the directions call for and then lets it simmer for hours. She says it gives the coffee body.''

"That's okay. I like my coffee strong."

"But not your men?"

Meghan gave her a sharp look. "What does that mean?"

"Justin comes on pretty strong sometimes. I just wondered if you have a problem with that."

Choosing her own interpretation of Lil's question, Meghan said, "We don't always see eye to eye, but I think there's enough common ground for a good working relationship." She added a little milk and a teaspoon of sugar and stirred her coffee.

"I wasn't talking about a work relationship."

"Well," Meghan said lightly, "we found out we like the same foods and we play a good doubles game at tennis."

"That's all? Never mind. You don't have to answer that. But I have a feeling," Lil added, "that if you two delve a little deeper, you'll discover a lot more." She waited, as if expecting a comment, but Meghan was silent. "Sorry if I'm making you nervous," Lil said.

"You're not making me nervous."

"Then why're you stirring the hell out of that coffee?"

Meghan looked down. Her spoon was making a miniature tempest of the dark brew—like the tumultuous feelings Lil had managed to stir up in her.

Instead of answering, she took a swallow of coffee and almost choked on the scorching liquid. Meghan started to cough. Her eyes were tearing. She put down the cup and stood, gasping for breath. Lil started to pound her back. That's when Justin appeared.

"What's the matter?" he asked with immediate concern. "Something stuck in your throat?" Without waiting for an answer, he positioned himself in back of her.

"No, wait—" Meghan tried to protest. But too late. With a deft thrust upward, Justin performed the Heimlich maneuver. "Ooofff..." That awful sound came from her as the air was forcibly expelled. Weakly, she leaned back against Justin. "Ahh," she said as she sucked in her breath.

"Are you all right now?"

"I was all right before," she managed weakly.

"She swallowed some hot coffee," Lil told him.

"Oh." Justin released Meghan, helped her sit down and settled himself beside her. "Sorry. I guess I reacted too quickly," he said a little sheepishly. "I hope my heroic maneuver didn't hurt you."

She gingerly rubbed the region of her solar plexus. "I'll survive, but I owe you one."

"One Heimlich maneuver?"

"One punch in the gut."

He raised both arms. "Have at me. I deserve it."

"I'll take a rain check."

"You're all right?" he asked again.

"I'm fine." She reached for her coffee mug.

"Are you sure you want that?" Lil asked. To Justin, she said, "Clarissa's coffee made her choke."

"It was hot and I swallowed wrong," Meghan said and took a sip. "The coffee's good—strong, but good."

Justin pointed to the other mug. "Whose is that?"

"Clarissa brought it for me," Lil answered, "but I can't drink it."

Justin reached for the coffee.

"There's enough caffeine in that cup to keep you awake all night," Lil warned.

"That's all right. Repenting my rash show of heroics would keep me up anyway." He took a long draught. "Potent stuff. Maybe it'll revive me. I've been driving all over town."

"Was your mission successful?" Meghan asked.

"I think so. Everyone came home with something."

"Did Grace get the civil service test announcements?" Lil inquired.

"Yep. From the library. And Cookie's set to take a practice equivalency test to see what kind of catch-up tutoring she needs in order to pass."

"Did you get to see Fritzi?" Meghan asked.

"Fritzi?"

"The aerobics instructor at the club."

"Is that her name? No, we'll have to do that some other time."

"If you like, I can talk to her...get whatever information Cookie wants."

"Thanks, but that would be defeating the purpose. It's up to her to find out what she wants to know. The others, too. Stella got herself a catalog at the university. The next step is to find out how many of her old credits are transferable."

Meghan nodded approval. She was sure she could get Stella a good divorce settlement, but she firmly believed every woman should be able to support herself.

"What about Ida?" Lil asked.

Justin broke out in a smile that erased away his tiredness. "That's the best yet. I think she came along because she felt she had to do something. All she's known, all her adult life, is housework and cooking. The 'Y' offers all kinds of cooking classes, so Ida thought she might learn cake decorating or something, so that's where I took her...to find out what they offer. We waited in the car. Ida went into the office and there was this big argument going on—a man jabbering away in French at the woman in charge. He went storming out and Mrs. Kellerman—that's the 'Y' lady—said that was her French cooking instructor, and what was she going to do with twelve people signed up and the course due to start next week. Ida tried to console her." He started to laugh. "She told Mrs. Kellerman that it was no great loss because French cuisine is overrated and Hungarians are much better cooks than the French. Can you guess the way it ended?"

Meghan could. "Ida's going to teach Hungarian cooking at the 'Y'?"

"Right. Starting next week. They're going to call it 'European Specialties.' We were waiting in the car and you should have seen Ida saunter when she came out. Was she ever proud!"

"I'll bet," Meghan said.

"You've had a very productive evening," Lil said.

"It worked out fine—up until my unneeded rescue attempt."

"Oh, well, it's the thought that counts," Meghan said lightly. She looked at her watch. "I'd better be off."

"You just got here," Justin protested.

"No. *You* just got here. I've been here awhile."

"Why didn't you let me know you were coming?"

"I phoned, but you'd gone already." Meghan suddenly remembered the reason she had originally called. "I have some good news, too. About the variance—there's no real legal problem. Because this property is owned by a church group and formerly housed a day-care center, there's already a precedent for its not being a single family residence. There should be no objection to its present use."

"Ah, but there is, unfortunately," Justin said. "You see, when the day-care people moved out, the house stayed empty for almost two years. That's how I got to lease it for a token one hundred dollars a year rental. Even though they didn't like seeing it empty, some of the neighbors are protesting our being here."

"But why?"

"Because they don't know what's going on. They think we're some kind of unsavory bunch."

"When did all this happen? Why didn't you tell me?"

"It just started," Lil answered. "We've gotten a couple of calls about it. Seems they're forming a committee."

Meghan frowned. "That could be a problem for you. If you've got public opposition, it won't be a simple matter of filing the necessary papers."

"So what we've got to do," Justin said decisively, "is turn the opposition into support."

"And just how do you propose to do that?"

"By allaying whatever suspicions people have about what's happening here at Midway. People fear what they don't know."

"Do you want me to handle it?" Meghan asked. "I can write a letter—"

"No, a letter won't do it, especially not a letter from a lawyer. That might just make them gear up for a fight. We're going to have an open house."

"A what?"

"An open house."

"Agents hold open houses to sell real estate," Meghan said doubtfully.

"Right. They let people come in to see what's offered. Same principle. We're selling what Midway stands for. We'll invite people in to see what we're all about."

It could work, Meghan thought. If fears were allayed and sympathies aroused, the opposition just might weaken. "That's not a bad idea," she said. "But you'd better get the place spruced up first. Maybe people around here didn't like seeing the old place run down, and if you show what a nifty neighbor you're going to be..."

"Great idea," he responded enthusiastically. "And since you thought of it, you're in charge."

"What?"

"Someone has to be head honcho, and since this was your suggestion, you're it."

His assumption that she'd go along with his outrageous demand made her laugh out loud. The sound of her own laughter was no longer strange to her. She had been laughing a lot more lately, ever since Justin Forbes had come into her life. "Justin, there's a lot of work involved."

"We'll all help. You'll have plenty of willing workers."

"What about time? A twenty-eight-hour day would be nice. Can you manage that?"

He grinned. "I'm good, but not that good."

"I can't neglect my work."

"I wouldn't want you to. But this won't be work. It'll be fun."

"When do you expect this open house to take place?"

"You set the date. You're in charge," he said.

Meghan was caught up by his enthusiasm. It could be a challenging venture and a fun experience. A lot could be done on weekends. It would mean spending more time with Justin. And the others, of course. She capitulated. "This old Victorian has seen better days," she said, "but maybe with some paint and wallpaper and a few pieces of furniture..."

"Right on, Counselor," he cried triumphantly and gave her a beaming smile.

As she drove home, Meghan realized that she had allowed Justin to bulldoze her into agreeing. The funny thing was, she felt good about it.

THE NEXT EVENING, Meghan and Lil and the four women held a conference. Ideas flowed and enthusiasm for the open house ran high.

"I know already what the menu will be," Ida told them.

"First things first," Meghan cautioned. "Midway House needs a face-lift."

"And face-lifts cost money," Lil added, "of which we have little."

"So we'll have to think big, but spend small," Cookie said. "Is that possible?"

"We'll find out," said Meghan.

Certain economies were possible. They could do a lot of the work themselves and might be able to get donations of some materials, but there would still be capital expenditures. They came up with a modest redecorating plan, which they presented to Justin.

"This is great," he said when he read their proposal. They smiled. "Now all we need's the money," he added. Their faces fell.

"Isn't there any money available?" Meghan asked.

"Lil knows what our budget looks like."

"I thought you had something figured out," Lil said helplessly. "Some secret resource or a hidden benefactor. Justin, you gave us the go-ahead."

"The go-ahead to plan. Now I'm giving you the go-ahead to raise the money."

"You are impossible," Lil exclaimed. "How are we going to do that? We're talking a thousand dollars here. Let's forget the whole thing."

Meghan wasn't willing to. "I could pay for the supplies..." she began but Justin immediately cut her off.

"No, you can't. That's not the way to do it."

"What would you suggest?" She threw up her hands. "A cookie sale?"

Ignoring her sarcasm, Justin said, "Ida does make great cookies."

"We'd have to sell over a million," Stella said.

Ida frowned. "A million I can't make. A thousand, maybe."

"What about a garage sale?" Grace suggested. "My sister has one every year."

"Every year? Where's she get all the stuff to sell?" Cookie asked.

"The rest of the year she goes around to other garage sales."

"We don't have time to do that," Stella said.

Lil glanced around the group. "Any other ideas...? I didn't think so."

"Wait a minute," Meghan said thoughtfully. "Maybe the garage sale could work."

"How?" asked Lil. "Midway certainly doesn't have any excess possessions."

"Donations. We could ask people to donate something for a good cause."

"Sure," Grace said. "Everyone's got something tucked away that they're not using. Especially my sister."

"Not just private donations. We could approach businesses. I have some contacts in town."

Justin smiled his approval. "That's a great idea. See. I knew you ladies would come up with something."

"If you finally get around to fixing up that old grandfather clock, that could be your donation," Meghan told him.

"You wouldn't? I love that clock."

"Then you'd better help and see that we get enough other things to sell."

"I'll do my bit."

"We're all going to have to do more than a bit if this is going to work."

"Right, boss," he said, enjoying her enthusiasm.

When Lil's fiancé arrived, he got drafted before he knew what was happening.

"What's with the big powwow?" he asked.

"We're talking about donations."

"Put me down for a buck," Brian said.

"We need your powers of persuasion more than your money," Meghan told him and explained the project. "Got any connections?"

"A whole schoolful," answered Brian. "I'm sure I can get the faculty to contribute."

Lil held out her hand. "But we'll take your dollar, too." She took the bill and handed it to Meghan.

Meghan held it up and waved it. "That's the beginning of our thousand dollar goal. We're on our way." She couldn't remember ever feeling so good.

THE FEELING PERSISTED. It turned out that they had no difficulty getting contributions. Grace's sister stopped by with a station wagon full of serviceable odds and ends of furniture and crockery. The collection from Brian's colleagues included everything from toys and children's clothing to appliances and lawn furniture. There was even a motorbike at which Justin cast a covetous look.

"With a little work, I can make this baby go like a dream," he said.

"You do that," said Meghan sweetly. "If it's working, we can tag it for fifty dollars."

"I thought I might just requisition this."

"No one requisitions anything until we see how much we collect. No arguments. You put me in charge, remember?"

He came over, grabbed her shoulders, planted a kiss on her nose, and said, "Methinks I've created a monster."

Meghan felt her heart do a flip-flop. "Do you usually go around kissing monsters?"

"Only you. I'm a one-monster man."

She laughed and he kissed her again—properly.

SOMEHOW MEGHAN MANAGED to fit it all in. She had told Justin that she couldn't neglect her practice, and she didn't. At the office, with her clients and in court, her attention was completely focused on the job at hand. It was as if her energy level had been heightened. The zest with which she tackled the Midway House project spread into all her endeavors.

Meghan's co-workers, Stacy and Phyllis, volunteered to type up the tags and make posters to place around town, and through her professional contacts, Meghan was successful in getting Alexandria businesses to donate merchandise. A TV repair service gave them three used television sets. "Hey, Ida," Cookie exclaimed when she saw the sets. "Now you can watch your soaps."

Ida gave them scarcely a glance. "I don't have time for that."

Lil and Justin exchanged satisfied looks.

A week before the sale, Meghan took a tally. Even if everything sold as tagged, which wasn't certain, they were short of their goal.

"Tony's brother has that little art gallery on King Street," Stacy said. "I could get Tony to ask him to donate a picture."

"One painting won't do much," Meghan said. She suddenly had an idea. "But twenty or thirty would. Why didn't I think of this before?"

"What?"

"The Torpedo Factory."

"You want a donation of torpedos?" Cookie started to laugh.

"It used to be a munitions plant," Meghan explained. "Now it's been converted to artists' studios."

"Tony's brother probably has some contacts," Stacy offered. "And doesn't Becky Callisher have her sculpture

studio there?'' she asked Meghan. ''I bet she'd help. She'd
do anything for you.''

Becky was a woman Meghan had represented in a child
custody case two years earlier. Meghan called her and Becky
needed no persuasion to cooperate. ''Leave it to me,'' she
said.

''We've only got a week.''

''Don't worry. Creative people are generous souls. They'll
come through.''

Meghan had to fly to Boston the following day to take a
deposition from a witness in a criminal negligence case. The
woman was hospitalized after cancer surgery and couldn't
appear in person. Instead of being able to see her right away
as she'd expected, Meghan had to spend an extra day. On
Wednesday, when she returned, Becky called her at the office. ''Stop by the studio after work. I've got something to
show you.''

''Were you successful?''

''You'll see.''

What Meghan saw left her speechless. From sympathetic
painters, sculptors, potters and weavers, Becky had collected a fantastic assortment of original pieces.

Meghan walked around. ''Becky, this is incredible. They
donated all this?''

''Yup. All us artists have hearts of gold. They tagged each
piece with what they think the price should be.''

Meghan stopped in front of a huge abstract painting.

''You like that one?''

''Oh, yes.'' The left side of the canvas was a black space
interspaced with smoky teal blue. But it also included a lu-
minous streak. In the middle of the painting the black faded
and the blue grew more vibrant. Meghan's eyes followed the
streak which became larger until, on the right side, it ex-

ploded in golden slivers against a startling blue and white background. "Why is it untitled?" Meghan asked.

"The artist wants people to give their own title, according to what each sees in it. What would you call it?"

"I'm not sure. I'd have to give it more thought." She moved away and picked up a colorful woven wall hanging. "All the pieces are beautiful."

"Do you think you'll have enough?"

"With all this? More than enough. We are going to have one hell of a garage sale."

MEGHAN'S PREDICTION wasn't overstated. The cars started coming even before the posted starting time, and they kept coming all day. Everyone helped. Brian directed traffic. Clarissa and Ida presided over a baked goods table. Stella had set up a little play area out back where she supervised the children while their parents browsed. The art objects, set up under a tent with Becky in charge, were attracting many buyers.

Grace's sister, Evelyn, the old hand at garage sales, had Cookie and Grace circulating among the shoppers. At first, those who wanted to haggle were sent to Evelyn, but after a while, Cookie and Grace handled the bargaining themselves.

Justin was the designated floater, appearing wherever he was needed. He'd even had to act as a bouncer once, ushering out some unruly teenagers who were being disruptive. He chose Meghan's station, where she collected money and made change, as his vantage point to keep an eye on what was happening. "Look at Grace getting tough with that old harridan," Justin told Meghan.

Meghan saw Grace standing her ground against a shopper arguing for a markdown on a plant stand. "Are you

sneaking assertiveness training into your group meetings?''
she asked.

"Nope. It comes with the territory."

"What territory?"

"Each person's resources. Grace is just beginning to draw
on her own assertiveness."

"Why not before?"

"Something blocked her. Probably fear of rejection. She
kept submitting to gain approval, but it didn't work. People didn't respect her and she felt demeaned. She doesn't
want to feel that way anymore so she's doing something
about it."

"Good for her."

"What about you?"

"What about me? You think I need to tap my fund of
assertiveness?" Meghan asked.

He grinned. "No. Your assertiveness has adequate out-
lets. But there's something else, I think, that's being
blocked."

Meghan looked up at him. His dark eyes gave off a glow,
as if absorbing the warm October sunlight. The glow spread
through Meghan in a silken, shivery flow. "Like what?" she
asked.

"That's what I intend to find out." His words were a vel-
vety promise.

IT WAS AFTER FIVE when the last customers departed. Practically everything had been sold. After cleaning up, the
weary bunch sat down to dinner. Meghan had finished
counting up the receipts and was the last to come to the table. "Fourteen hundred and thirty-three dollars and eighty-
seven cents," she announced.

"Wow! . . . Way to go . . . Right on," came the cheers.

"That's over our quota," Stella cried, tired but triumphant.

"Way over," someone echoed.

"Where'd that eighty-seven cents come from?" Justin asked curiously. "I thought we'd tagged everything in round figures."

"That was my sale," Clarissa said with a raucous laugh. "Remember that old sun hat I was wearing? Someone wanted to buy it. I asked fer a dollar but he bargained me down to eighty-seven cents. That wuz fun. When we gonna do it again?"

"I hope not for a long time," Meghan said amid the general laughter.

They were all tired, but the prevailing mood was one of exultation. Each person, Meghan knew, felt pride in having contributed. Meghan did, too. It was a different kind of satisfaction from the individual sense of accomplishment she got from her work. This was a shared pride. Meghan liked the feeling.

Ida brought out a platter of chicken paprikash and dumplings.

"A hot dinner after all this," Meghan exclaimed. "How in the world did you manage?"

"I cooked it yesterday and heated it up," Ida said with a happy smile.

"You're a miracle worker," Meghan told her.

"We all are," said Ida.

In truth, they all felt that way.

LATER JUSTIN WALKED Meghan to her car. "What turned the trick were those art donations you managed," he told her. "That was a real coup. I think every one of them was sold."

"Oh, thanks for reminding me," she said and ran back to the house. "I may need your help," she called and Justin followed.

From the hall closet, Meghan dragged a large painting.

"What's that?" Justin asked. "I didn't see that one out there."

"I kept it back," she admitted. She gazed down at the abstract she had first admired in Becky's studio. "It's mine."

"Well, if that isn't devious," Justin accused. "No requisitions allowed. Isn't that what you said about the motorbike I coveted?"

"I paid the tagged price," Meghan said righteously, "so don't be smart. Help me get it to my car."

Justin put the painting into her trunk. "How are you going to carry this up to your apartment?"

"I didn't think of that."

"I'd better come with you. Give me your keys. I'll drive."

"If you come in my car, how will you get back?"

"You'll have to drive me—after we have our nightcap."

Meghan felt she had to point out a logical alternative. "You could follow me in your car."

"That wouldn't be as much fun," he said with a smile that made her give up arguing.

He went back to the house to tell Lil he was going. He returned, got into the driver's seat and started the motor. "I told Lil not to wait up," he said.

It was only eight o'clock. "You're not going to be that late," Meghan told him.

"You never can tell," he said.

Meghan felt an anticipatory warmth that wasn't at all unpleasant.

JUSTIN PROPPED THE PAINTING against Meghan's sofa and stood back to examine it. "I like it. It's unusual. But I didn't peg you as an admirer of abstract painting."

"I'm not. I just happen to like this particular one."

"What do you think the artist had in mind?"

"I don't know. He didn't title it."

"So you're not bound by his vision, just your own," Justin mused. "I like that."

"But it was his vision that created this," Meghan said.

"True, but after a work of art is finished, it exists on its own."

"I'm not sure I understand."

Justin came closer and put an arm around her, a casual gesture as they viewed the painting together, but Meghan's response was far from casual. Maybe all the day's activity and excitement had made her ultrasensitive to any stimulus, and Justin's closeness, his touch, was exerting a magnetic pull.

"What does the painting suggest to you?" Justin asked. "What's your title for it?"

"I haven't decided yet," Meghan answered. Justin started to turn toward her, and she felt suddenly fearful, not of him, but of what she was feeling. "How about some tea?" she asked brightly. "Or a drink? You deserve something for helping me."

"A tip for my services?" His quizzical smile implied that he guessed her emotional state. "How about both? Tea with some brandy added would be nice . . . since that seems to be the only tip you have in mind."

"Would you prefer something else?"

"I would," Justin said with a slow smile that seemed to tug at her heart, "but we can start with the tea...."

CHAPTER NINE

"HOW ABOUT SOME MUSIC?" Justin called from the living room.

"If you like. The tapes are in that cabinet drawer."

"I see them."

"I've got a good collection of classical jazz."

"I'm in the mood for something more soothing. Ah, here we go."

He started a tape, and Meghan heard the soft strains of an Andalusian melody.

"What is that?" she asked when Justin came into the kitchen.

"Manuel de Falla. You don't recognize it?"

Meghan vaguely recalled having received the recording as a gift. "It's not one I play very often."

"It's called 'Love, the Magician.'"

"Romantic title." Busy with her preparations, Meghan didn't meet his eyes. "Is herbal tea all right? This one has an orange cinnamon flavor."

"Whatever you have is fine."

There was a soft resonance to his voice that seemed in harmony with the music. Meghan was very conscious of his eyes on her. Justin's presence in her tiny kitchen was having a strange effect, not so much distracting, as absorbing. A product of the close quarters, Meghan told herself, and the man's sheer physical size.

When the tea was ready, she brought out the brandy. "Does Courvoisier meet with your approval?"

"Perfect. No, not into the pot," Justin said, taking the bottle from her. "The tea bags will absorb it. The brandy goes into the cup. You're in charge of the tea. I'll take care of this."

He followed Meghan into the living room where she set her tray on the coffee table. He sat on the sofa and Meghan was careful to leave a foot of space when she sat beside him. She filled their cups. Justin opened the brandy and slid closer as he leaned over to pour.

"Easy does it," Meghan said. "Remember, I have to drive you home."

"If you get drunk, I promise not to leave here until you sober up."

"How gallant."

"I aim to please."

His teasing was warmly provocative. Meghan was vaguely aware that the warning device she usually relied on was becoming dormant. But that didn't seem important right now.

Meghan took a swallow of the brandy-laced tea, savoring the aromatic steam that touched her face and the hot, honeyed bite of the liquid as it seeped through her.

"Don't gulp it down," Justin cautioned. "I'd hate to have to do another Heimlich."

"Not as much as I would," Meghan said, thinking how she would prefer a more tender touch. She glanced up at him with a teasing smile and felt her eyes caught in his gaze. It was a strange sensation, like a moment of recognition—a recognition Meghan couldn't define, but she felt closer to Justin than ever before. They were quiet for a while, listening to the sensuous Andalusian music, aware of the intimacy between them. When they started to talk, their voices were low, almost hushed, preserving that intimacy.

Meghan asked Justin about his family and his childhood, relishing each detail that added to what she knew. He told her about growing up in California and described his parents and brothers. "They're good people," he said. "You'll like them."

"You're still close?"

He caught her wistful tone and his arm dropped from the back of the couch to her shoulders for a comforting squeeze. "Closer than when I was a kid. My brothers and I fought like animals, and since they were bigger, they kept winning. But at thirteen I shot up to almost six foot and the fights stopped."

"There were times when I wished I were six feet tall."

"When you were a child?"

"Yes." Meghan regretted the intrusion of her childhood memories.

Keeping his arm around her, Justin touched her cheek with his other hand. She looked away but with gentle pressure, he pivoted her to face him. His fingers became softly caressing. "I wish I'd known you when you were a little girl."

"No, you don't." Meghan tried to smile. "I was a sorry thing."

"What you went through—it still hurts, doesn't it?"

"Sometimes as much as it did then." Meghan surprised herself by this admission. She had told Justin about her father's abusive treatment, but it had been a bare facts description, the only way she could verbalize what had happened—until now.

"What hurts the most?" he asked.

Perhaps it was his closeness, perhaps the compassion in his eyes. But more than compassion, she saw there an appeal, as if he needed her response. Released, Meghan's feelings poured out, the emotional memories she'd bottled up, and the hurt she still experienced. This time, she didn't try to cover over the hurt with anger.

Justin said nothing. Most people, Meghan knew, would feel impelled to make some kind of sympathetic comment, well intentioned but meaningless. Justin, however, sensed the inadequacy of such a response. When she finished, he took her into his arms and held her.

For what seemed like a long time, Meghan felt only relief as the remembered pain drained from her. Gradually, her senses reawakened. The music had ended. Her head was nestled against Justin's chest. In the stillness, she became aware of the beating of her heart, or was it Justin's. She didn't stir, but let the impressions come over her, one by one. She inhaled the warm masculine scent of his closeness, felt the strength of his enclosing arms, his cheek against her head and his breath ruffling her hair. To enhance these sensations, she burrowed closer and became conscious of her own body's awakening.

Something was unraveling deep inside, a tight knot loosening into warm filaments that slid through her, sensitizing her skin and heating her blood. She sensed a change in Justin, too. His hands moved caressingly over her back. He rubbed his cheek against her hair, then lowered his head to touch his lips to her forehead. Meghan tilted her chin, bringing her mouth near his. The etched curve of his upper lip tempted her closer. Meghan's hands, resting on his chest, crept up to his shoulders. Justin's grip tightened. Meghan looked into his eyes and was flooded by the depth of passion they revealed.

Meghan welcomed his kiss, her lips eager to taste this passion. At first gently enticing, Justin's kiss gradually caught fire. His tongue teased entry into her parted lips, and Meghan felt her response rise from some closed-off place deep inside. There was more than a surface sensuality in this embrace. Meghan's desire and need arose from her inner being. Surely, she thought, Justin's must, also.

He raised his head, looked deep into her eyes and whispered, "Meghan, I want to make love to you."

His words echoed her own desire, and her smile told him what he wanted to know.

Taking hold of his hand, Meghan led him into her bedroom. By the soft light of the bedside lamp, she started to undress. Justin's eyes never left her. When she was clad only in lacy underwear, she paused. "You're watching me."

"Of course I am. You are beautiful."

"But you're making me self-conscious," she whispered.

"Good." He stepped over and put his hands on her shoulders. "I want you to be conscious of yourself, of your body and what it tells you—and what it tells me." His hands slipped around and undid the clasp of her bra. His touch on her bare skin sent ripples of pleasure through her. Expectantly, she waited for the molding pressure of his hands on her breasts and gasped with pleasure when he obliged. He kissed her mouth, then trailed his lips to her throat and her breasts, and she felt a sweet writhing inside her. Justin lifted her into his arms and laid her gently on the bed.

When he stepped back to shed his clothes, Meghan reached to turn out the lamp. "Don't do that," he said.

"Why not?"

"What are you afraid of seeing?"

"I'm not afraid." In the past, she had always turned out the light. "The darkness just seems appropriate."

"Not to me." He was naked now but with the lamplight behind him, his body was shadowed. Still, he exuded a powerful strength and masculinity that was both fearful and exciting. "I want to see you," he said. "I want you to see me."

Meghan held her breath, anticipating the thrust of his body onto hers, but Justin stretched out on his side next to her and only his fingers reached to touch her. "I want you to see us ... together like this." His caressing hand roamed over her upper body, then slid lower and rubbed against the silky film of the panties she still wore. "And this..." he whispered, moving closer so that she felt the hardness of his erection against her thigh. His voice continued its litany. "To recognize what we both want..."

His hand dipped under the lace to stroke her belly. Meghan's breath caught and when he reached lower, she cried out with the sweet hot pleasure of his touch. When he bent to remove the last lacy impediment, Meghan helped him.

Justin's gaze feasted on her nakedness with a hunger that would not be appeased. His hands caressed her gently and her body lifted toward their touch. His lovemaking was not a demand, but an enticement. He knew exactly where she was most sensitive. His fingers were the seductive initiators and then his lips followed. Each new caress was tentative until he sensed her arousal.

His almost leisurely exploration was tantalizing, and gradually Meghan instigated a quickened pace. Justin's tenderness was melting the cold reserve with which she had always protected herself against total surrender.

Meghan pressed his hands into a closer exploration, drew from his mouth a more fiery kiss and arched her body against his. His passion had evoked hers, and Meghan now wanted to reciprocate. Instead of just allowing herself to be aroused, she wanted to arouse. She started to explore Justin's body, enjoying his initial surprise and subsequent delight.

He had said he wanted to make love to her, but now she was making love to him. All her erotic sensibilities were in play. Meghan had never felt so desired, or so desiring. Justin's pleasure increased her own...more and more...and still she hungered.

Justin finally hoisted himself above her. His eyes flashed their urgent need and Meghan arched to express her own. Even at the height of his passion, Justin didn't assault her body, but eased himself into her. She tensed for but a second, then let herself be drawn into the inexorable movements of the act of love. Deep in her loins, all the sensations coalesced into one and she writhed with the sweetness of it.

She looked at Justin and what she saw melted the last vestige of her reserve. His eyes did not have the self-absorbed glaze of a man intent on his own sexual release, but a tenderness that was centered on her. She drew his head down and in her kiss, told him it was time. Meghan tightened around him, inviting a deeper thrust, and together they reached for the final pleasure.

It came for Meghan with a joyous shattering that she couldn't control and she clung to Justin desperately. She closed her eyes and saw behind her lids a radiance as in the painting she had bought. Then Justin's exultant climax brought her to another shuddering upheaval. It took a long time for her tremors to subside.

They lay together quietly, bathed in a warm mist, their bodies heavy with sated passion. After a while, Meghan became conscious of the weight of him. "You'd better not fall asleep there," she whispered.

"Why not?"

"Because you weigh too much. You're too big."

He raised himself up. His hair fell unevenly onto his forehead. With a wicked arching of his damaged eyebrow, he said, "Funny, I thought I was just big enough."

"Are you being lewd?"

"At the moment, no," he said and rolled away to lie beside her. With a teasing smile, he pulled her close. "But try me later."

Meghan's body softly molded to his and her head found its niche in the hollow below his shoulders. Suddenly the title for her painting came to her—Joy. She had a feeling that the artist would approve.

Meghan closed her eyes and slept.

AT FIRST SHE THOUGHT the light came from the bedside lamp, which was still on, but thin rays of autumn sunlight were filtering through the blinds. It was morning. From Justin's even breathing, she knew he still slept. If she moved, she would wake him. But this was Sunday; there was no hurry to get up so why disturb him, or her own feeling of contentment. They had slept like this all night, barely moving. Remembering her usual restless sleep habits, Meghan smiled to herself.

It was strange, she thought, that she'd awakened with not a trace of confusion or disorientation at finding herself and Justin naked in bed together. The clear memory of their lovemaking was with her the second she opened her eyes. Such a sweet memory! Was this what romantics called the afterglow of love?

But she had never before been susceptible to romantic interpretations of lovemaking. Meghan considered the casual way people went to bed together these days. "Having sex" was a more apt description than "making love." There was a lot of sexual freedom. A lot of bad sex, too, the kind where one person used the other.

Not like last night. What happened between her and Justin had been a mutual seduction, a mutual possession and a mutual fulfillment. Good sex. But it wouldn't do, Meghan told herself, to make too much of one night of love.

She shifted so that she could see Justin's face, its hard contours softened in sleep. Did everyone look vulnerable when they slept? She had never thought of Justin that way. He was so dynamic and strong, could he too be hurt? She felt a rushing tenderness that surprised her.

His lips curved in a slight smile. Was he dreaming? Perhaps of her? *Romantic thoughts again? Better stop this.* She reached over to smooth his scraggly eyebrow. Justin didn't move, but the rhythm of his breathing faltered. "Are you awake?" she asked softly. He made no reply. "Justin, are you awake?" she repeated. His nostrils dilated slightly and one corner of his mouth twitched.

Meghan gave his eyebrow a sharp, playful pull.

"Ow!" he cried. He grabbed for her hand and then flipped her onto her back. He leaned over her. "What'd you do that for?" His voice was a soft growl, but there was a teasing glint in his eyes.

"You were faking it," she accused.

His breath quickened, and she sensed his arousal even before she felt him against her. He let go of her hand to cover the seductive curves of her breasts.

"I'm not faking this."

She had just been cautioning herself not to make too much of their one night together. But why did it have to stop at one night? As long as no one was hurt, why not take advantage of what they had and what they could give each other. There was such a thing as being too cautious, Meghan told herself. Justin quickly demonstrated that he had no such qualms, and Meghan soon forgot all about hers....

IT WAS ALMOST NOON before Justin was ready to leave. Meghan wouldn't go with him. "I'll come later," she promised. She had told Lil she'd be over sometime during the day to plan the next step of their renovation project.

"But I don't have a car."

She'd forgotten. "Use mine."

"What will you use? Maybe I'd better just hang around..." From the look in his eye, he had more than hanging around in mind.

"I can take a cab. Hey wait. It's my car. *You* take a cab."

He laughed. "I'll take your car and when you're ready, call me and I'll come get you. How does that sound?"

"All right. Now go."

The kiss he gave her at the door threatened her resolve. Meghan pulled away.

"Know what I think?" Justin asked.

"What?"

"That you're feeling skittish about what they're going to think at the house."

"Maybe a little."

"I could say I was bushed and fell asleep on your couch."

"Do you think anyone's going to believe that?"

He grinned. "No. But if it'll make you feel better..."

She gave him a shove toward the door. "What will make me feel better is having a little time to myself."

Justin opened the door, then paused. "You really shouldn't worry," he said seriously. "They'll be happy for us. See you later."

She waited until he was out of sight before she closed the door.

Meghan had always lived her private life without concern for the opinions of others. But the people at Midway House were not just "others." They had become friends, and what they thought was important. She sensed, however, that what Justin said was true. From the good-natured teasing directed at her and Justin, Meghan knew the women already suspected a romance. They would be happy to be proven right.

Of course, Meghan told herself, what her friends imagined differed from the real situation. She wouldn't allow herself romantic illusions about Justin. There were no promises. Circumstances had happened to throw them together, and they'd found areas of common ground. Meghan walked into her bedroom, looked at the rumpled bed and started to laugh. Sure, she thought, areas of common ground . . . like the bed.

Meghan had just straightened up her room when the telephone rang. It was Justin.

"How come you're calling? Is something wrong?"

"I just got home."

"And . . . ?"

"And I saw what was in the garage. Lil said you pulled it out of the sale."

"I decided to buy it."

"What are you going to do with a motorbike?"

"The question is what are *you* going to do with it. It's yours."

"You didn't have to do that."

"I know. I wanted to."

"Thank you. That was sweet of you."

Sweet was a word Meghan often used derisively. From Justin, it sounded like a compliment.

"You know," he added, "I'm glad the motorbike present came before last night." She heard the humor in his voice and could picture his smile. "Otherwise, I'd think it was payment for services rendered."

She picked up his teasing tone. "Mmm. The bike was tagged at thirty dollars."

"Are you questioning the value of the exchange?"

"I didn't say that."

"I'll be glad to—"

"Never mind," Meghan interrupted, anticipating what his offer would be.

She heard his soft laughter. "When should I pick you up?" he asked.

"How about three?"

"How about two?"

He hadn't been gone a half hour, so why the rush? But why not? "All right. Two it is."

"OKAY, WHAT'S UP?" Stacy asked Meghan.

"What do you mean?"

The two women were alone in the conference room, waiting for the others to arrive for the weekly staff meeting. A week had gone by since the garage sale, a week in which they'd gotten a good start on Midway House's renovation. Meghan's days were given to her profession, her evenings to the Midway project, and her nights to Justin—and to herself.

"You know what I mean. Something's happened. I've never seen you look so radiant. It started right after the garage sale."

"Well, that's what garage sales will do to you," said Meghan flippantly.

"You're not fooling anybody. How come you're never at the club?"

"I just don't have time right now. Besides, I'm getting plenty of exercise without it."

"What kind?" Stacy asked with raised eyebrows. Meghan chose not to answer but that didn't deter Stacy. "And every time I call at night I get your answering machine."

"Which means I'm out, or asleep."

Stacy grinned. "That's what I figured. I knew Justin would be the one to break you down."

Meghan winced. "That's an unfortunate choice of words."

"Don't take everything so literally. It's just an expression."

An expression that bothered Meghan.

Lester Patterson came in, followed by the others. Sylvester Chaney, the youngest of the law partners, made a big point of greeting Meghan. "Well, Meg! And the first one here, no less. I wasn't sure you'd be able to make the meeting."

Meghan gave him a cold look. Sylvester had come into the firm at about the same time as Meghan. He seemed to resent her success, especially when one of her cases got media attention. In his own mind, he'd created a rivalry between them.

"Really, Syl?" She noted his frown at her abbreviation of his name. She used it whenever he ignored her objection to his calling her Meg. "Why is that? I don't usually miss staff meetings."

"Ah, but that was before you got all embroiled in this little pet project of yours."

Lester and the others sometimes teased her about her involvement, but not with this undertone of nastiness.

"I hope you're getting something out of it." Sylvester continued. "A charity shelter's hardly a lucrative client. There's certainly no profit for the firm."

"What's your complaint, Syl?" Meghan asked tartly.

Her directness took him aback. "Well...no complaint, of course. But you are spending an inordinate amount of time with this one client."

"Are you suggesting that I'm neglecting other clients?"

"I didn't say that."

He couldn't because it wasn't true.

Lester chose to intervene at that point. "No one better say that. Meghan probably contributes more than I do to this firm." To Meghan, he said, "I just marvel at your energy. Where do you get those batteries of yours charged up?"

Meghan just smiled and shrugged. She pretended not to see Stacy suppressing a giggle.

Lester started the meeting. There was the usual discussion of office detail and then the individual reports on pending cases. Meghan had one of the longer lists but, she had to admit, her cases were not likely to enrich the firm's coffers. But then one of the reasons she had chosen to work with Lester was his devotion to the law and his conviction that access to good legal counsel should be available to everybody.

When the meeting was over, Meghan had an appointment with a new client, a woman who had reported her boss for sexual harassment and was subsequently fired. Afterward, Meghan got Stacy working on looking up the legal precedents where judgments favored the plaintiff in cases like this one, and Meghan called for an appointment with the personnel manager of the company. She didn't have to be in court that day, but her appointments were nonstop all afternoon. But that was the way she had always worked, the way she liked to work, challenged and busy so that the day just flew.

The difference was, she acknowledged when she got home at five o'clock, that lately the pace continued after her usual workday. For instance, now she would change into her old jeans and head for Midway House where the gang had started painting the interior. Her involvement with Justin's project had her constantly on the run, but she seemed to be thriving in spite of, or because of, all the activity.

She hadn't expected to get such a kick out of the physical work of fixing up the place. Justin had said it would be more like fun than work, and he was right. He was due to pick her up at five-thirty. At five twenty-five, Meghan was waiting by the lobby entrance. When she saw Justin's car, she ran out before he could park. Meghan opened the door and got in beside him.

"Why didn't you wait upstairs?" he asked. "I was going to come up."

"Like yesterday?"

"Yesterday was nice." His face lit up with a smile.

"We didn't leave the apartment until almost seven."

"That's what made it so nice."

And the niceness, Meghan remembered, had resumed after he'd driven her home at eleven. "I just don't think we should be late again."

"What's late? I'm the boss so I can make my own hours."

"I thought you said I was the boss."

"You're in charge of the whole operation, but there has to be a work-crew foreman."

"Who elected you?"

"It was unanimous."

"I'll bet. Well, if you're the foreman, you should be at the job. Let's go."

He obeyed, casting her a grudging look and saying, "What a hardhearted woman!"

If he thought that, he was certainly misreading the state of her heart, Meghan thought ruefully. "How much got done today?" she asked.

"A lot. All the bedrooms. And Grace and Clarissa stripped layers of wallpaper off the kitchen walls. What a messy job."

"You helped?"

"A little."

Probably more than a little, Meghan guessed. Just as with the jogging, he kept an eye on each member of the group, making sure that no one was overtaxed. Whenever he saw the need, he would be there, grabbing a paintbrush or hammer, suggesting a rest break, or assigning someone to an easier chore, but never making anyone feel inadequate. It was, she decided, a gift he had.

"Did the plumber show up?" she asked.

"Salvatore? Bright and early this morning. He said you talked him into cutting his hourly rate by thirty percent. He also warned me to be wary of lady lawyers. Salvatore says they take advantage."

"What did you say?"

"I told him it was too late."

"You think I take advantage of you?"

He turned to her with a wicked grin. "I try to give you every opportunity."

At Midway, Ida apologized for rushing them into dinner. "I have to go to the 'Y' tonight. There's a meeting for all the teachers." She was flushed with excitement. "Lil's driving me."

The dinner table was where the group talked over their plans and brought up problems. "You know what the outside of this house needs," Brian told them. "Aluminum siding."

"No," Lil objected. "That would spoil its character."

"Besides, we don't have that kind of money," Meghan reminded them.

"Then at least a coat of paint."

"Well, as long as you volunteered," said Justin expansively, "we accept your offer."

Brian groaned and the others laughed. "Justin has his own definition of 'volunteer,'" Meghan said.

"Sounds more like 'commandeering' to me," Brian said. "I think I've been had."

"We'll buy the paint tomorrow," Justin told him.

"I *know* I've been had. Okay, okay, but there aren't that many daylight hours after school anymore, and I have basketball practice every Saturday."

"So we'll do what we can in the afternoons, and there's always Sunday."

"Sunday's a day of rest."

"Not around here," Grace said cheerfully.

"Besides," Lil told Brian, "your idea of a day of rest is playing touch football or three sets of tennis."

"The key word there, my darlin'," Brian said, "is 'playing.' Play is relaxation."

Meghan smiled at the banter. There was no doubt that Brian was going to take on the task. His contrariness was a pose, but his generosity was real.

After Lil had left to drive Ida to the "Y," Brian joined Meghan. She was painting the window trim in Justin's office. "I got snookered again," he said.

"You know you don't mind. I'll do the outside window frames. Windows are my specialty."

"Standing on a ladder for the second floor?"

She hadn't thought of that. "My specialty's only ground-floor windows."

"That's what I thought." He looked over her work. "You're doing a good job. Painting trim is tedious work."

"I really don't mind. In fact, I like it. After what I do all day, physical work's a nice change. Relaxing . . . like a good workout, only better." Meghan had little time for the health club lately, but she didn't miss it. She had become aware of her body, not as something to be exercised like a separate entity, but as integral to her being. She'd begun to feel an immense pleasure in her physicality. And, she had to admit, in her newly awakened sexuality.

"What you're doing would give me muscle cramps," Brian said. "I think I'll go find me a wall to paint."

After a while, Meghan did feel some muscular tension, but she knew how to cure it. She put down her brush and dropped her head forward, then back, then from side to side. She repeated the moves several times. Then she rotated her shoulders to a count of ten and, changing direction, did it again. Finally, she extended one arm over her shoulder and the other around her back and stretched her arms until her fingers clasped.

"That's a funny way to scratch," Justin said coming up behind her. She unclasped her hands as he put his arms around her and pulled her back against him. "I'll help if you tell me where it itches," he said, his lips against her ear.

"I wasn't scratching. I was exercising away a muscle cramp."

"Want me to give you a massage?"

"I think you are," she said, placing her palms on his hands as they traced a circular pattern against her midriff. "That's not where I need it." His hands moved higher. "Nor there," she said, her voice lowering to a whisper.

"You can't isolate one part of the body. Don't you know that the most effective massage is one that covers every inch of you?"

"I'll have to take your word for it."

"No you won't," he said. "I'll be glad to demonstrate."

He kissed her ear, sending a delicious shiver through her. Through her blouse she felt the erotic pressure of his fingers. "Justin, I have to finish this window."

"How long will it take?"

"About a half hour."

"I'll help."

"After that, there's another window to go."

He spun her around to face him. "Go where? That window's not going to move. It'll be here tomorrow and we'll do it then."

It was strange, Meghan thought, how desire was always there, ready for his touch, as if her very skin were underlaid with its potency.

"What's happening to your priorities?" she teased.

"A little reshuffling's going on," he admitted. "Right now, teaching you the joys of overall massage is number one. A purely altruistic motive on my part."

"Then I guess I should take advantage of it."

And later that night, she did. As promised, Justin's massage was thorough, ending with her toes. There was magic in his fingers as he manipulated her muscles, kneading away any accumulated strain. But as her muscles eased, an inner tension started to build. She had been lying face down on her bed. When Justin finished, she rolled onto her back. "That was wonderful." His hands moved over her with a different touch. "Is this part of the treatment?" she asked.

"Only for special subjects." His fingers spanned her waist, traced the curves of her body, then folded over the mounds of her breasts.

Inside her, Meghan felt a strange combination of melting and twisting. "You've got a nice touch," she whispered.

"I aim to please."

The ripples of pleasure spreading through her were proof that he was succeeding. Meghan reached for him, pulling him to her. "You'll have to teach me so I can reciprocate," she said softly.

"Mmm. Just do what comes naturally...yes...like that...." He guided her hands over him. "You're getting the knack of it."

"What about the first part of the massage?"

"We'll start with that next time, darling." He raised himself over her. "I'm afraid I'm beyond that now."

He was, and so was she.

When he made love, Justin's humor and tenderness and fire were a more seductive combination than anything Meghan had ever experienced. There was a duality in the longing he never failed to arouse, a hunger for her own fulfillment and an equally strong need for Justin's pleasure. She had no trouble realizing both.

They couldn't get enough of each other. Meghan had never thought of herself as strongly sexed, but she soon got over her wonderment that her desire kept pace with Justin's. What was happening was good, so why question it?

IT WAS AFTER MIDNIGHT when Meghan urged Justin to get out of bed.

"This mattress is a lot more comfortable than the one I've got at home," he said. "Mine's old and lumpy."

"You're hinting again."

"I sleep better here."

"You'll get more sleep in your own bed. I know I will."

"It's quality, not quantity that counts," Justin told her. "I have sweeter dreams when you're beside me."

Meghan would not admit that she did, too. Her growing reluctance to see Justin leave after making love troubled her. She didn't want his influence to intrude into every aspect of her life. "You know the rule," she said adamantly. She got up and slipped into a satin robe. "On workdays, you go home. Now up."

He gave an aggrieved sigh, but he complied. "You are a tough one, Meghan O'Brien."

"It's the Irish in me." She sat on the bed and watched as he dressed.

"Are you Irish on both sides?"

She nodded. "My mother was from Limerick."

"And your father?"

"He was born here."

"In Virginia?"

"No, New York. There's a section of Queens that probably has more Irish than the city of Dublin, and half of them are O'Briens. An uncle of mine ran a Ford dealership in Woodside. He used to say that if he could sell one car to everybody named O'Brien, he'd be rich."

"Is he rich?"

She shrugged. "I've lost touch."

"Is that where your father is now...in New York?"

"I don't know."

Justin paused in buttoning his shirt to give her a quizzical look. "You could probably trace him if you want to."

"I'm sure I could." She couldn't help her voice going cold. "The point is I don't want to."

Justin's face took on a troubled look. He finished doing up his shirt, then came over and sat next to her, putting his arm around her. She felt his eyes on her but refused to meet his gaze. "Meghan, maybe you should see him."

Her anger flared. "Why? To tell him how much I hate him? There'd be no other reason."

Justin took her in his arms but she held herself stiffly. He waited until he felt her begin to relax against him. Then, his voice deep with compassion, he said, "Hatred is a terrible obsession to live with."

Meghan felt the hotness of unshed tears but, as always, willed herself not to cry. She couldn't expect Justin to understand. It was strange, then, that she found such comfort in his arms.

Justin lifted her face toward him. Just a short while ago, passion had fired her eyes, streaking the emerald color with tints of gold. Now, anguish darkened their hue.

She had been so badly hurt. Meghan had a right to hate what her father had done, but her hatred of the man himself was obsessive. And destructive. Meghan didn't want to acknowledge how much it influenced her thoughts and actions.

That was why he kept postponing his own confession, fearing what her reaction would be. If she would not distinguish between the act and the person, he ran the risk of his becoming, in Meghan's eyes, the representation of what she abhorred. She had come to mean so much to him. He ran his fingers through her tawny hair. How fiery she could be in making love, how rich and deep her sensuality.

What they had together was good, but relationships didn't remain static. Theirs could deepen and grow—or it could end. If he and Meghan couldn't deal with their pasts, they could have no future together.

Justin kissed her slowly and tenderly. "Good night," he said. He left her there, sitting on the edge of the bed. He hoped she would call him back. She didn't.

CHAPTER TEN

MEGHAN WAS LOOKING FORWARD to Stacy and Tony's engagement party. "But you've been engaged for three months," Meghan had said when Stacy first mentioned it.

"So this'll be a postengagement party. Then maybe we'll throw a prewedding shindig. I happen to like parties. Think you and Justin can give up house painting for one night?"

"Sure. It'll be nice to get dressed up for a change."

The night of the party, Meghan made it a point to get home early. After a leisurely bath, she tried a new hairdo, pulling back one side with a pearl clip, while the other side swept to her shoulder in a russet swirl. She took out the dress she had bought that day, a black silk with full puffed sleeves, a wide V-neck and softly draped skirt. She slipped it over her shoulders, enjoying the feel of it slithering over her. Surveying herself in the full-length mirror, Meghan decided her rushed lunch-hour shopping trip had been worth the effort.

"Simple, yet sophisticated," the saleslady had commented. "And black's so dramatic with that kind of red hair."

The pearl necklace and earrings were the perfect adornment—but should she wear both? She took off the earrings, then put them back on and took off the necklace, then decided that the necklace was the better choice. She laughed at herself. She and Justin saw each other all the time, so why the excitement? Because she had never really dressed up for him before. He saw her in business clothes and in work clothes—and out of them, she remembered with a warm flush. But tonight, she meant to look glamorous.

When the telephone rang and it was Justin, she had a sinking fear that he was going to say he couldn't make it.

"I'm running late," he said.

"Is something wrong?"

"No. I just didn't count on this first meeting taking so long. I don't want to break it up just yet."

"But you're still coming?"

"Of course."

She sighed with relief. "Why don't I pick you up? It'll save us time."

He seemed to hesitate, then said. "Sure, if you want to."

When she hung up, Meghan wondered why Justin had said this "first meeting" was running late. He'd been having regular meetings with the women residents from the beginning.

Clarissa let her in. "Well, ain't you the spiffy one," she said.

"Spiffy? I was hoping for glamorous," Meghan told her.

"Same thing."

Meghan followed Clarissa past the closed door to Justin's office. She heard voices. Then the door opened and a tall man in his forties came out, closing the door behind him. His mouth was set in angry lines. He gave them a cold look and left. Meghan wondered what was going on.

In the kitchen, Cookie and Stella were having coffee. Their nervous expressions turned into smiles of admiration at Meghan's appearance. "You look beautiful," Stella said.

"Sensational," Cookie agreed.

"Thank you."

"Justin's gonna flip when he sees you," Cookie added.

"Which he's apparently not in a hurry to do. What's with the late meeting tonight?"

Their apprehension returned.

"Were you two excused?" Meghan asked curiously.

"It wasn't our meeting," Stella said.

Lil came in. "Ida's with Grace. They'll be down later." She gave Meghan an admiring once-over. "That's one wicked dress. You look fabulous."

"Will someone please tell me what's going on?" Meghan asked. "What kind of meeting is Justin having without all of you?" She paused. "I just saw a man leave his office."

"What did he look like?" Cookie asked anxiously.

"Tall, sandy hair, fortyish and very angry."

"That wasn't Manny," Cookie said.

"Sounds like Grace's husband," said Lil. "Especially the angry part. He gave me a lot of flak when I called him to set this up."

Meghan finally understood. "You mean Justin's been meeting with..." Shaking her head, she left the sentence incomplete.

Lil filled in the ending. "He's meeting with the four husbands."

"But why?"

Lil raised her eyebrows, surprised at Meghan's vehement tone. "That was always on the agenda."

"Whose agenda? Justin's?"

"We talked about it," Stella answered. "We all agreed."

Meghan said nothing. It would serve no purpose to voice her disapproval here. Perhaps they had all agreed, but Justin should never have asked.

After his male visitors had gone, Justin came into the kitchen. In response to all the questioning looks, he said only, "I think we made a good start." But his smile must have reassured Stella and Cookie. They visibly relaxed.

The smile turned admiring when he saw Meghan. "Give me a few minutes to change," he said. "I'll try to make myself as gorgeous as you are."

When he left, Stella said, "I wonder what they talked about."

"Us—and them," Cookie answered. "What else?"

"He said it was a good start," Lil offered.

"Not exactly an informative summation," Meghan couldn't help saying.

"Oh, he can't tell us everything they talk about," Stella explained seriously, "just like they've no right to know what we say unless we decide that's what we want."

Meghan knew enough about therapy groups to understand Justin's adherence to confidentiality, but why was he meeting with these men at all?

Justin was ready in no time, in a handsomely tailored blue blazer and gray pants. "Now I'm worthy of you," he told Meghan.

"You look terrific," Cookie said. "Right, Meghan?"

She had to agree.

They walked out to her car. "Want me to drive?" he offered.

"If you like." Meghan handed him the keys. When they were settled and on their way, she asked the question that had been preying on her mind. "Justin, how can you allow those men into Midway?"

He sighed. "I knew that question was coming. I figured you wouldn't approve."

"That's putting it mildly. Having them there just doesn't make sense. It's a violation of the sanctuary your residents have a right to expect," she declared forcefully.

"There was no danger. The ground rules were carefully spelled out."

"But what's the purpose?"

"Working with the husbands is part of Midway's program."

"It shouldn't be."

Justin obviously disagreed. "I think it can help."

"Wife-beaters aren't the ones who need help. They know exactly how to help themselves."

"That's just the point. They don't."

"I can't feel sorry for them."

"I can. Meghan, they're not all sadists. There are some who take pleasure in inflicting hurt, and maybe they'll never change. But that's not always the case. If these men can come to grips with their real motives, they may be able to find a healthy way to satisfy them."

"And if not?" she asked with angry sarcasm.

"Then," he said with grim fatalism, "they'll probably repeat the pattern." He had stopped at a red light and turned to face her. "I'm not such an idealist that I believe every marriage can be saved—or *should* be saved. I don't think Grace and Herb Canto can salvage their marriage. There's a man who thinks brutality and authority are synonymous, to be freely exercised by men only. He sees Grace as a servant, not a person. And that's what she would be if she returned to him. Some people never change. But there are those who can alter their lives, with some help." His brow furrowed with the conviction of what he was trying to say. "That's the whole idea behind Midway House."

"I thought the idea was to help the victims, not the perpetrators."

"It is, but what you won't accept is that women aren't the only victims. In fact, they have to take some responsibility for what's happened." He noticed her frown. "You don't buy that, do you?"

"Only if you mean that it's up to them to extricate themselves from the situation."

"Or to change it. They have to redefine their roles in the relationship, just as the men do. Both parties have to want to make the marriage work. If they do, they've got a chance."

"You must believe in miracles."

"No, but I believe in people."

"I'm afraid you're going to be disappointed," Meghan said sadly.

The light changed and he drove on. Meghan was silent for a long time. This inability to accept each other's point of view on this basic issue created a chasm between them. They could bridge it when they made love, but they couldn't ignore its existence.

Justin did not break the silence. He had long since decided not to engage in lengthy arguments with Meghan. Like the lawyer she was, she rose to a debate, feeling challenged to defend her position and refute her opponent's claims. If she didn't recognize that her personal biases were influencing her judgment in cases like Stella's, arguing would be counterproductive. She would not be bullied, or overridden or persuaded by theoretical argument. She had to see things for herself.

Her participation in the life at Midway House had been spurred by him, but proceeded only at Meghan's will. She had already changed, though she might not be willing to admit it. The woman who turned to him with such passion at night was not the unapproachable beauty who had first spurned him. But sexual closeness would never be enough, for either of them.

Seeing what evolved from his program at Midway might prove a vicarious experience for Meghan, more compelling than any argument. Justin didn't expect that he would be universally successful in his program. But he was confident, from signs he had already, that some of the people now involved could change their lives. They had to deal with fear and hatred and loss of confidence and need for love—the men as well as the women. They had to balance what they would lose and what they would gain by changing, and make a choice.

Everybody was faced with such choices, though not under such desperate circumstances. Meghan, too. She had to deal with her feelings, open them up to examination and decide if she would continue to let the old fear and hatred inhibit her life. Justin could provide a stimulus, but it had to be Meghan's decision whether or not to act.

THE PARTY WAS GOING STRONG when they got there. "Sorry we're late," Meghan told Stacy.

"Doing a little preparty partying?" Stacy asked archly. She didn't wait for an answer. "Meghan, that's a smashing dress. I'm going to lose ten pounds just so I can borrow it. My diet starts tomorrow. Are you hungry? Better get to the food before it's all gone. Tony's mother did most of the cooking so everything is Italian and luscious—and fattening." She chattered away until someone claimed her attention elsewhere.

It was a good party, Justin thought, an eclectic mixture of legal types, accountants, old-world Italian relatives, people in the arts and, for added spice, a few politicians from both parties. Meghan knew many of the guests. How quickly, he noted admiringly, she seemed to become the center of every group she joined.

Inevitably, they got separated, but Justin's eyes kept seeking her out. With that vibrant hair and emerald eyes, she was easily the most striking woman there. She would stand out in any gathering. He'd never particularly noticed women's clothes, but Meghan seemed to have a way of carrying herself that made anything she wore, be it work jeans or a business suit, look good.

Tonight, she had a special aura, more sophisticated and more alluring. Whenever she sensed his eyes on her, she would disengage herself briefly from whatever she was doing, to meet his gaze and smile. He was glad their earlier conversation hadn't made her brood. Between them were differences that could be divisive, but there was also this strong feeling of connectedness, and it was the latter that Justin wanted to nurture.

He wandered over to the bar where Tony Nicoletti was officiating. "Want me to spell you for a while?" Justin offered. "Give you a chance to circulate with your guests."

"No thanks. I'm fine. Most people find their way over here sooner or later. The thirsty ones, anyway. How about you? Ready for a refill?"

"No thanks. I'm still working on this one."

"Let me freshen it up for you. Gin 'n tonic, right?"

Justin pulled his glass out of reach. "Not when I'm driving."

"Let Meghan drive," Tony said. "Hell, she likes being in the driver's seat... even when there's no car." He laughed, apparently thinking he'd said something funny, but Justin didn't respond. "You know what I mean," Tony said.

"I can't say that I do."

"A cuddly kitten she's not. Meghan O'Brien's a tiger, or is it tigress? Always protecting her territory from men," Tony proclaimed. "When it comes to the battle of the sexes, that little lady just doesn't know how to give in."

"Why should she have to?"

The question startled Tony. He'd apparently expected some kind of man-to-man agreement. Justin's tone indicated he didn't appreciate Tony's attempt at witticism.

"Hey, no offense, man," Tony said apologetically. "All I meant was..." He groped for words to finish his sentence. "Well" he said lamely, "she's not Stacy."

"No, she's not," Justin agreed. With a slight smile, he added, "I'm very happy for you."

And for me, Justin thought to himself. Tony was a mild-mannered man, practical-minded and amiable. Meghan had mentioned that she had gone out with him briefly a long time ago. It was easy to see where he'd have been intimidated by her strong personality.

Someone asking for a refill diverted Tony's attention, and Justin walked away. He did not see Meghan as Tony did. He liked her strength and independence. Sure, she argued for what she believed, but she was capable of friendship and loyalty. And love, Justin told himself. Fearing submission, she had kept herself from loving.

In the give-and-take of their lovemaking, Meghan's fear of abandonment had abated, enabling her to respond joyfully. If she could transfer that same freedom, that trust in herself and in him, to other aspects of their relationship... but, he was getting ahead of himself.

MEGHAN HAD ENJOYED THE PARTY. It was funny how, even when they were separated, she felt she was with Justin. Someone told a funny political story and she made a mental note to repeat it to Justin later. Her eyes kept seeking him like a magnet and she'd felt a warm pleasure whenever she met his gaze. A young man started to play old show tunes on the piano and she and Justin, as if on cue, joined the group that gathered round.

"You're a Gershwin lover. I should have known," Justin said.

Meghan didn't bother to correct him. The show tunes were familiar, but she had never thought of herself as a fan.

Someone started singing along, others followed suit, and Justin's deep baritone joined in. He put his arm around her shoulders and his encouraging smile was an invitation. Meghan realized that she knew the words, probably from watching all the old-time musicals on television when she couldn't sleep. Tentatively at first, then with gusto, she started to sing. It was fun. The party didn't break up until almost two in the morning.

As they walked to her car, Meghan said, "I knew it was time to leave when our singing started to sound really good to me."

"What do you mean?" Justin demanded. "We *were* good."

"We were enthusiastic. There's a difference."

"How about we were good and enthusiastic?" His laughter sounded crisply in the cool November darkness.

"Have it your way," Meghan said, joining in.

The uncharacteristic words hovered in her mind as they drove back to Alexandria. *Have it your way.* It was a trivial concession and, in the context of their light banter, meant nothing. Or did it? Was she, unconsciously, absorbing Justin's way of seeing things? Was he steering her into a new role, as he was attempting with the other women?

They got to her apartment and, without any discussion, Justin came up with her. He refused a nightcap. "Tea, instead?" she offered.

"No. I'm thirsty, but not for liquor or tea." He opened the refrigerator. "Got anything cold? Ah . . . just the thing. How about a cranberry spritzer?"

"A what?"

He took out a container of cranberry juice and a bottle of seltzer water and poured a half-and-half combination into two tall glasses. "Taste this. Great, isn't it?"

"It's nice."

"You don't go overboard with your compliments, do you?" he teased.

"It's not my style."

But lately, she was doing many things that weren't her style. "You know, I've been thinking of what you said before," she told Justin.

"That's a good sign. At least you're listening. Now, which of my pithy sayings are you talking about?"

"The pithiest," she said lightly, not sure just how serious she wanted this discussion to get. "That bit about women redefining their roles . . . ?"

"Yes?"

"I'm not sure I understand."

His eyes narrowed speculatively, but he seemed gratified by her interest. "What I meant was that change has to start someplace. If two people get into a destructive routine where one plays the tyrant and the other the slave, the routine can't continue if one of them moves out of his or her role."

"I don't disagree with that."

"Don't misread what I mean by moving out. Extracting yourself from the situation isn't enough."

"Why not?"

"Because you never learn to deal with whatever in you contributed to what happened."

"Do you really believe that two people can completely reverse themselves?"

"It doesn't have to be a complete reversal. Meghan, it's a fascinating phenomenon." He warmed to his subject. "If one changes, the other can't continue as before. The relationship is altered. He, or she, has to accommodate the change, or leave. So eventually, both learn to behave differently. Look what's happening with Grace."

"What's happening?"

"She's saying no when her boss asks her to do things that aren't part of her job. She refuses to continue being a patsy, so if he wants to keep a good secretary, he has to behave differently."

"Or he could fire her."

"That's one of his options," Justin admitted. "Grace is even prepared for the possibility. That's why she's looking into civil service work. Hey, there's no guarantee. All I'm saying is that there's an alternative to submitting to the status quo or escaping from it. Show how you want to be treated and see if the other person will come around. It if works, both people benefit. Incidentally, this applies in all kinds of relationships."

Justin put down his glass and came around the counter to where she was standing. His look told her that he'd veered into a very personal interpretation of his theory. "For example?" she asked.

"For example, have you noticed that I'm the one who always initiates making love?"

"I can't say that I have."

Justin took her glass and set it on the counter. "What if I didn't?" he asked, giving her a wicked grin. He put his hands on her shoulders. "What then?" His thumbs stroked her bare neck.

"I don't know." Meghan felt the now familiar surge deep inside. It was as if Justin tapped into an ever-present reservoir of desire that needed only his touch to overflow.

"If I didn't make the first move, you would have to act differently." His fingers traced the outline of her wide neckline, then barely grazed over her breasts, just a tantalizing suggestion of the passion he could offer.

"Meaning?" she asked.

"That if you wanted to make love, you would have to come on to me."

"And if I didn't?"

"Then it wouldn't happen, and you would lose out."

"Is that so?" she said with a teasing laugh. Yet Meghan knew he hadn't overstated the case. She was still surprised and elated by the intensity of her continued sexual response to Justin. Each time they made love was more stirring than the last, as if their growing familiarity added depth to their passion. It couldn't keep on, she kept telling herself, hoping she was wrong. But so far, it had.

Justin put his arms around her and pulled her to him. "You're an enchantress tonight," he whispered, as he bent to kiss her throat and the enticing cleft at the bottom of her neckline.

"I thought you were going to wait for me to make the first move," Meghan said.

"I was," he said softly.

He ran his hands down her hips and pressed her close. She felt him against her and thrilled at the knowledge that his desire was as quickly aroused as hers.

"But I figured I'd put the role reversal off awhile," he said, his lips so close that his words were like feathery kisses, "... just to be sure."

She brushed his lips with hers. "Sure of what?"

"That our making love becomes a habit you won't be able to break."

As Meghan parted her lips to receive his fiery kiss, she suspected that she may have already reached that point.

He kissed her long and hard and passionately, then lifted her into his arms. "Which means," he said, his eyes golden with promise, "that I'll have to make sure to gratify your every desire."

He carried her into the bedroom and proceeded to make good his promise.

"Yes. Serviceable enough if you like that kind of stuff. I thought I'd do everything modern, black-and-white lacquer pieces with a few touches of wicker for a beachy look."

"I'm sure that'll be lovely," Meghan said untruthfully. "But about the furniture that's in there. Perhaps you'd be willing to donate some of it to a worthy cause." Meghan explained about Midway House. They had almost finished with the repairs and painting, but some of the old furniture now looked even seedier by contrast.

"Why not?" Imogene agreed. Her husband's unexpected, albeit forced, generosity had made her feel generous, too. "You take what you want and I'll have The Salvation Army or Goodwill pick up what's left. You have the address?"

Meghan nodded, pointing to the file still on her desk. "It's in here."

"You'll need a key. I can drop it off tomorrow morning when I come to town to get my hair done. When do you think you'll be going out there?"

Midway's open house was scheduled for right after Thanksgiving which gave them only about ten days to get everything ready. "Would this weekend be all right?" Meghan asked.

"Whenever you want, my dear. Of course, it'll be awfully dreary. There's nothing more depressing than a beach resort in the off-season."

"That's all right. We're not going out there for fun."

Justin had a different opinion when Meghan told him. He was enthusiastic from the beginning. "If you're busy, Lil and Brian could drive out there with me," Meghan had offered.

"Are you kidding? I wouldn't miss this opportunity. I love the beach at this time of year."

CHAPTER ELEVEN

THE LUCRATIVE SETTLEMENT she had gotten for her client in the Tedford divorce didn't particularly thrill Meghan. She couldn't sympathize with either party. Ralph Tedford was pompous, overbearing and a philanderer, but his wife Imogene was a heartless shrew. Imogene had found out he was having an affair with his secretary and sued for divorce. To Meghan, she confided that she'd had her own private liaisons, but she'd had the sense to be discreet about them. Imogene was out for blood. Meghan was surprised when Ralph acceded to most of her demands, but then realized he was anxious to get the marriage over with.

When Ralph Tedford and his lawyer left Meghan's office after agreeing to the settlement, Imogene was jubilant. "I never expected he'd give up the beach house, too. I thought he loved that place."

"How come you wanted it?" Meghan was puzzled. "He said you never wanted to go there."

"Because he wouldn't fix it up. All that tacky early-American furniture. It was in the house when we bought it, and just because it was almost new, Ralph wouldn't hear of redecorating. I'm going to junk it all and start fresh. You'll have to come out for a weekend next summer."

The prospect had not one whit of charm for Meghan. But she did have an idea. "You said the furniture in the house is in good condition?"

"It's a three-hour trip, and if the Bay Bridge gets backed up, even longer. You're not going to have much time for frolicking on the beach."

"So we'll get an early start. If we leave at seven—"

"Oh, no!"

"All right, eight. We'll get there by eleven. We can do whatever we have to do in a couple of hours and still have time for a little . . . what did you call it . . . frolicking?"

He made it sound feasible—and tempting. "How are we going to get the furniture back here?"

"I think I can borrow a small truck. If not, I'll rent one."

"Maybe Brian should come with us."

"I don't think he's into frolicking, not without Lil, anyway."

"I mean, to help you load any heavy stuff."

"I have a helper—you." His grin softened as he added, "The two of us will manage just fine."

Meghan didn't feel like arguing.

Their early start never materialized, however. First there was a brake problem with the small truck Justin had rented, so they had to return it and pick up a replacement before they could start. Then near Annapolis, they had a flat tire and had to pull over onto the shoulder. Meghan didn't like the looks of the rusty jack Justin used to prop up the truck. She was about to caution him to be careful, voice her apprehension that he might get hurt. Just like a wife, she thought, and stopped herself in time. But she was relieved when he finished. He showed her the nail that had caused the damage.

"Luckily, the tire's repairable. We'll have it fixed when we get to Rehoboth," he told her.

"Should we be driving without a spare?"

"For a couple of hours, we can take a chance." He looked out at the highway. "Traffic's getting heavier. We don't want to lose more time on this side of the bridge."

But they got stuck anyway as the cars slowed to a crawl just before the bridge entrance.

"Who ever expected so many potential frolickers," Meghan said. "Do you suppose they're all going to Rehoboth?"

Justin laughed. "I hope not. That's not the romantic idyll I've been picturing for us."

"What have you been picturing?"

"Just like in the movies. You know how the lovers always walk on a deserted beach with their arms around each other, the wind blowing their hair, and nothing around them but ocean waves, sand dunes and sea gulls?"

"No people?"

"Of course not. Except maybe a kid with a kite, or a crusty-old-salt-type in an oilskin slicker..."

"Smoking a pipe?"

"You know the scene," he said happily. "Yeah, smoking a pipe and breaking his weathered face into a benign smile as he passes the young lovers."

"Schmaltzy."

"I like a little schmaltz now and then. Don't you?"

"I never thought about it."

Justin took her hand and brought it over to rest on his thigh. "Think about it now."

There was certainly no harm in that.

The trip took much longer than planned. If she had been alone, Meghan would have been exasperated and upset with all the delays, but Justin kept her calm. "Relax and enjoy the scenery," he told her.

The Chesapeake Bay itself was beautiful, dotted with sailboats leaning with the wind, but on the other side, Meghan felt there wasn't much to look at.

Justin didn't agree. He pointed out a dry cornfield that hadn't yet been cut down and plowed under, then a pretty white farmhouse circled with evergreens in the middle of now barren fields, and when they saw goats grazing on a hilly enclosure, he actually slowed down. "Look at those goats."

"It doesn't take much to make you happy," Meghan teased.

"Not true. It takes a lot, but it's all out there, if you let yourself see it."

There was charm, Meghan decided, in what she had always thought an uninteresting landscape. It was nice seeing things from Justin's perspective—for a little while.

It was after one when they arrived. The house was in the northern section and only a hundred yards from the beach. When Meghan opened the door, a musty smell greeted her. In spite of the brisk November weather, they opened windows to let in some air and sunshine. In the living room, Justin looked around with a pleased smile. "Why does your friend want to change any of this?"

Meghan understood his puzzlement. It was a lovely room. There was a chintz-covered love seat, two easy chairs and an antique rocker. The tables were rustic pine, and a braid rug was in front of the brick fireplace. The decor was invitingly warm and cozy.

"Imogene calls this tacky."

"But it's perfectly good furniture."

"She prefers a shiny lacquered look." Remembering her client's brittle attractiveness, Meghan said, "She's got a point. This doesn't suit her."

"I'm glad you don't share her taste," Justin said.

At one time, Meghan might have claimed that she did. Her own small apartment was attractively efficient and modern, but she had come to appreciate the old-fashioned charm of Midway House. Apparently, her tastes weren't as rigid as they'd once been.

"We should have brought a bigger truck," Meghan said as they went through the rooms.

"Don't get greedy," Justin told her. "We can't take everything. Remember our list of what we really need."

For the next three hours, the two of them worked. Luckily, the rooms were all on one floor, so the only stairs to be navigated lead from the deck down to the driveway. A neighbor came over to investigate their activity. The man returned to his house where he called Imogene Tedford to verify their story, but once his suspicions were allayed, he offered to help. Justin and Meghan accepted gratefully. The larger pieces like the love seat and a bedroom dresser would have been a problem without his assistance.

When all was loaded except some smaller pieces, the neighbor took his leave. They thanked him, but declined his invitation to come over for coffee. While Justin went up into the attic to look around, Meghan plopped down on the rocking chair in the living room. She heard a racket when he came back down. "Are you all right?" she called.

"Fine." He came into the room holding a wicker bassinet.

"What have you got there?" Meghan asked.

"A baby's crib. There's also a playpen and some other children's furniture."

"It must have come with the house when they bought it. The Tedfords don't have children. You're not thinking of taking it, are you?"

He nodded. "Any reason why we shouldn't?"

"You don't need it at Midway."

"In the future we might. Lil and I are talking about gearing up to accommodate women who have small children. Sometimes the kids are the ones who require the most help."

And Justin, Meghan was somehow certain, would be just the kind of person who could give it to them. "If you keep on this way, you're going to need a second Midway House," she told him.

"What's wrong with that?"

She shook her head and gave a little laugh. "I don't know if I can handle it. I've never before had a client where I ran garage sales, painted houses and moved furniture."

Justin took her hands and pulled her up from the rocker. "See how I've enlarged your horizons."

"That's one way of looking at it."

He gazed deep into her eyes. "Meghan, you're not sorry, are you?"

"About getting involved with Midway? No, I'm not."

"How about getting involved with me?"

"Are we involved?"

"You'd better believe it."

"Depends on how you define involvement."

He gave a raucous laugh. "Is it a legal definition you're after, Counselor? Never mind...don't answer." He bent and gave her a light kiss "Right now, I prefer to forget that you're my lawyer. You must be starved. I know I am. Let's get something to eat."

Meghan drew back and checked her watch. "It's after four. Maybe we should get started and eat on the road."

"Damn!" said Justin.

"You don't like my suggestion?"

"It's not that. The tire..." he reminded her.

They had forgotten to drop it off at a gas station. "Is it too late to get it fixed?"

"We'll find out."

At the first station, the proprietor said he would have it for them in the morning and Justin agreed.

"We could have tried another station," Meghan told him as they drove off.

"Meghan O'Brien, you have to learn to stop fighting what's meant to be."

"Karma again?"

"Without a doubt. We were late arriving, we haven't quite finished loading the truck, and, most important, we haven't had our walk on the beach. Fate has decreed that we spend the night and go home tomorrow."

"Lil expects you back."

"I'll call her."

"Where will we sleep?"

"In the house."

"But the heat's turned off."

"I'll build us a fire."

"The beds are all on the truck."

"We'll put a mattress in front of the fireplace. Darling, I guarantee you'll not be cold."

From the smoldering look in his eyes, Meghan knew exactly what he had in mind.

"Any other objections?" he asked.

Meghan couldn't think of a single one.

WHEN SHE AWOKE in the morning, there was a chill in the room. The fire had gone out. Her body, nestled against Justin's under the blanket, was warm, but her face felt cold. Meghan pulled the blanket higher and buried her face against his shoulder.

Justin woke up. "Your nose is cold, like a puppy's."

"Is that supposed to be a compliment?" she asked, her voice muffled against his skin.

"It is if you happen to be mad about puppies' noses like I am." He reached out to lift her face and kiss the tip of her nose. The movement dislodged their blanket and Meghan shivered.

"Justin, it's cold in here. Maybe you'd better start the fire again."

"That means getting up."

"There's no other way."

"I can think of one." His voice was a throaty purr. Justin rolled onto his back, and in a deft motion, lifted Megan atop him.

Momentarily startled, Meghan supported herself on her hands and arched her upper body. His murmur of pleasure at the involuntary grinding pressure of her against his loins made her repeat the movement and intensify the rotation. The blanket fell away, but Meghan no longer noticed the chill in the air. Justin's body below hers exuded a steamy heat, and she lowered herself against him to absorb it, her mouth on his, her breasts against his chest, her lower body pressed and undulating on his.

They had made love the night before, but Meghan was rocked by the ferocious intensity of her need. When Justin caught her arms and held her away from him to taste the sweetness of her breasts, she felt a convulsive shudder, which echoed in him. Then Justin eased her body lower and, without thinking, Meghan moved her thighs to straddle him, lifting her body so he could enter her. It was a different sensation for Meghan with a new freedom of motion that seemed to generate an even fiercer passion.

Meghan looked into Justin's eyes for confirmation that this time they need not postpone their final pleasure. She found what she sought. Meghan felt the mounting tension and rode it, uttering little cries she did not even hear herself make, until the final convulsive release that shook them both.

She lay against him for a long time, her body spent. After a while, Justin pulled the blanket up over them. He rolled onto his side and held her close.

Later, when they tried to dress under the warmth of the blanket, the confusing tussle had them pummeling each other and laughing.

Once they were up and dressed, it didn't take long to finish loading the truck.

"What about the rocker?" Meghan asked as Justin made some final adjustments to the load.

"There's no more room."

"We can move things around."

"I don't think so."

"Justin, it's a great chair. You can use it in your office."

"I have a chair in my office."

"Not like this. A rocking chair is relaxing."

"So's a mattress." He smiled wickedly. "I don't know when I've ever felt more relaxed."

"You're depraved," she accused with a laugh.

"That's better than being deprived."

Meghan scurried away from his reaching hands and went inside. She returned carrying the rocker.

Justin shook his head. "You are one stubborn woman. I told you that there's no room."

"I'm sure we can make room. If not, we can put something else back."

"Meghan, that's foolish. I've gone to a lot of trouble getting things set up so nothing rattles or breaks."

"Look, give me a boost up there and I'll do it."

"Nope."

She was surprised. "What do you mean, *nope*?"

"Why mess things up?"

"I'm not going to mess up anything. See where those two chairs are back there. I can turn one upside down on the other and that'll do it."

He shook his head.

"Justin, don't try to intimidate me," Meghan said with a teasing smile. "It won't work. You don't have what it takes."

"What does it take?"

"Someone much more threatening than you. You're just not the type." Justin gave her a look that she couldn't decipher.

Meghan's offhand remarks troubled Justin. In her view, men capable of violence were permanently branded by their action. She had said that he wasn't threatening, that he wasn't the type who could intimidate her. Would she feel that way if she knew he had once acted out of unreasoning anger and struck a woman he cared for? Or would she shrink from him? He had postponed telling her, waiting for Meghan to reconcile herself to her own past. Or was that just his excuse? Perhaps he was afraid that if Meghan refused to trust him, it would shake his trust in himself.

THEY FOUND a little coffee shop open for breakfast. The morning special of eggs, bacon, home fries and coffee was huge, but Meghan managed to finish it all. "I think I ate more than you did," she told Justin. "You didn't finish your home fries. Aren't you hungry?"

"Not anymore. Want these?"

"Okay. Just a few."

He smiled when she speared some potatoes with her fork and popped them into her mouth. He had seemed strangely pensive during breakfast. Meghan had caught him looking at her questioningly at times. But whatever the question was, he didn't voice it. She was glad he was smiling again.

"Must be the sea air that's making me so ravenous," she said.

"Don't tell me I'm going to have to feed you again after our walk on the beach."

"I don't know. We'll see."

When they pulled into the parking area by the beach, the wind was blustery, but the sun was almost harshly bright. It was one of those November days that straddled the seasons, a combination of Indian summer and the wintry weather to come.

There was a long boardwalk, but Justin headed for the stairs down to the beach. "Mind getting sand in your shoes?" he asked.

"I'm not going to." Meghan sat on the bottom step and removed her sneakers.

"Good thinking." Justin followed suit. "Here's what you do with them." He fastened the laces together and looped them over the belt on his denims. "This way, you don't have to carry them."

Meghan did the same and also rolled her jeans up to her knees.

"Now you look like a true beach bum," Justin said with a grin. At her offended look, he quickly added, "That's a compliment. Beach bums are high on my list of aesthetic marvels."

"All right then."

They walked down to the water's edge. The tide was just starting to come in.

"Look at the sandpipers," he said. "It's amazing how they manage to skitter around just ahead of the wave and not get swamped."

A wave broke, then another immediately behind it. The double force impelled the flow farther up the beach. "Watch it," Meghan cried. Too late. Justin didn't move fast enough to keep the water from splashing over his feet and wetting the bottoms of his pants. "The sandpipers are doing better than you are." Meghan laughed. "Why don't you roll up your pants?"

"Your advice is a little late."

"No need to get even wetter."

"You've got a point." He bent and rolled his pants above his ankles. "Now we can slosh along," he said, taking her hand.

"Funny how the water's warmer than the air," Meghan said.

"Are you cold?"

"No." She was wearing a white turtleneck with her denim jacket and jeans.

"I can give you my sweater. These Irish knits are warmer than fur."

"I'm fine."

They stood facing each other. The wind was whipping Meghan's hair around. Justin reached up and pulled a clinging tendril from her face.

"You look fine," Justin said softly. "You know your eyes have changed color? They're almost turquoise...as if they've picked up the blue of the sky."

There was such tenderness in his voice. It made Meghan feel treasured. She smiled up at him. He put his arm around her shoulders and they resumed their walk.

The beach was deserted. The wind folded the sea into high crested waves that broke near shore in a crescendo of foam. As the waves ebbed, they left a frothy scalloped edge on the sand. Justin smiled as he watched Meghan carefully avoid trampling the lacy pattern.

"Is this idyllic enough for you?" she asked after a while.

"Almost perfect."

"Only almost?"

He didn't answer but a slight shadow seemed to cross his face. Meghan didn't like seeing it there. She let go of his hand. "Come on," she said running ahead of him. "I'll race you to that jetty."

He took off after her and caught her just before they got to the jetty. "It's a tie," she said breathlessly.

"What tie? You sneaked in a head start."

"Well, don't you think I'm entitled to a handicap? Your legs are longer than mine."

"Okay," he conceded, "it's a tie."

"Oh, look!" Meghan shielded her eyes and pointed down the beach. "A kite. There's a boy flying a kite."

"What did I tell you?" Justin cried. "Just as I predicted."

Meghan laughed. "So you did. Except he's not exactly flying that kite. He can't seem to get it in the air."

As they approached, they could see the boy's frustration. He was a sandy-haired youngster of about eight or nine. He would get it up about six feet, the kite would float for a few seconds and then plummet into the sand.

"Maybe if you ran with it," Justin suggested.

"I tried, but I got tired. My father can do it. He's big like you." There was an unmistakable appeal in the way he said it.

Justin found that appeal irresistible. "Want me to try?"

The boy nodded. "Okay."

Justin took the spool of string. "You hold up the kite, and when I say okay, let go and I'll run with it." They got into position. Justin moved ahead a little, yelled, "Okay," and when the boy let go, he took off, letting out string as he ran. A gust of wind took the kite, sending it spiraling upward.

"All right!" the boy shouted and raced over to Justin, beaming as he took back the spool.

"See," Justin said with satisfaction when he came back to Meghan, "it's all just as I pictured." He gestured expansively. "Beach, sand, ocean . . . and a boy with a kite."

"The only thing missing is the crusty-old-salt you said would be walking the beach."

They continued on, talking little. Meghan felt keenly alive—enjoying the taste of the spray-laden air, the warmth of the sun on her back and the contrasting colors of sand and ocean and sky. She knew, however, that without Justin beside her, there would be a dimming of these sensations.

On their way back, they spotted an elderly woman searching through the sand with a metal detector. "There we go," Justin announced, "the crusty-old-salt to complete the picture."

"Now you're reaching," Meghan told him. "She's just an old woman with a metal detector."

"She's got a salty weathered look, and she's searching for treasure."

"Where's her yellow slicker?"

"That old sweater's just as good. And she's smiling benignly at the young lovers—that's us."

Indeed, the woman was giving them a cheery smile.

"What more can you ask for?"

"Nothing. You're right. It's perfect. Too bad it has to end," Meghan said as they reached the stairs where they had started.

"It doesn't have to."

"You don't expect us to be beach bums forever, do you?"

"No," he said reluctantly after a long pause. "I guess not."

Meghan bounded ahead of him to the boardwalk and started toward the parking area.

"Where are you going without shoes?" he called.

"The truck's not far."

"You can't walk barefoot. Come back here and put on your shoes."

"What if I don't?" she teased, but she returned and sat on the bench next to him. "You sure are bossy today. But as I told you before, Justin Forbes, you don't scare me one little bit. I'm putting my shoes on because my feet are cold."

"Okay," he said, but his smile was strained.

Meghan finished tying her shoes. She started to get up but Justin caught her arm. "Sit a minute...please. There's something I want to tell you."

Meghan looked up at him. The sun glints were gone from his eyes, leaving them shadowed darkly. "Sounds ominous," Meghan said lightly, unwilling to lose the blithe magic of the past hour. "If it is, I don't want to hear it."

Very slowly, almost painfully, Justin said, "I don't ever want to seem ominous to you. I don't ever want to scare you, Meghan."

Her smile was uncertain. "You couldn't. It's not in you."

"The potential for violence isn't always obvious."

The word jarred her. "Violence...Justin, what are you talking about?"

"Something happened once...something I did. It was a long time ago." With grim seriousness, Justin described what had happened with Samantha years earlier. He didn't spare himself, characterizing what he'd done as hurtful and unforgivable.

Meghan found it impossible to reconcile the action he described with the man she had come to know, a man who chose to work with victims of physical abuse. "You're exaggerating," she said when he had finished.

"Why would I want to?"

She shook her head with confusion. "I don't know...perhaps to support what you're doing at Midway...your theory about change."

"You're right in one way," he said. "Maybe I am using myself as an example, both of what can happen when anger isn't controlled, and of what can happen when a man judges his actions and decides never to repeat them. I wasn't exaggerating, Meghan. What I did was inexcusable."

"I can't see you hitting a woman or hurting anyone. You care about people. What you're telling me doesn't fit."

He reached for her hand. "That one act doesn't embody my whole being. What I *did* was reprehensible, but I don't think I am." His grip was almost painfully tight. "What are you thinking? That I'm an ogre?"

His eyes compelled her to look at him and she saw his desperate need for understanding. She tried to find in his face a trace of the person who had unleashed his anger in physical violence, but what she saw was a man who cared about others. Meghan might fault some of his theories, but not the compassion, intelligence and humor he brought to his work. And not only his work. This was also the man with whom she shared a tenderness and passion in love-making unlike anything she had ever experienced. "No," she said with a sigh, "I don't think you're an ogre."

On the drive home, Meghan made conversation, remarking on the landscape or a billboard advertisement or a town they were going through. Trivialities, but she kept chattering. On Kent Island, they pulled off the highway for gas. There was a diner next to the station. "How about some lunch?" Justin suggested.

"I'm not hungry."

"Well, I am," he said, so they went over.

Justin ordered a hamburger for himself and coffee for both of them. He took a couple of bites of his burger and pushed the plate away.

"I thought you were hungry," Meghan said.

"So did I. Whatever it was I wanted, this isn't it."

"Order something else."

"No. I'll just finish my coffee."

She was uneasy with the intensity of his gaze and started talking again, about the furniture and where they would put it and the open house.

Justin interrupted. "Meghan, don't you want to ask me something?"

"About the open house?"

"No . . . about what I told you at the beach."

"There's nothing to ask."

"I get the feeling that something's dangling . . . unfinished."

"Justin, it happened long ago. Let's just forget it."

"I don't think we can—or should."

"It's past. Bury it."

Justin shook his head. "Isn't that what you've tried to do? But it doesn't work, does it?"

Meghan refused to answer. She was silent for the rest of the drive home.

Pulling up in front of Midway House, Justin turned off the engine. Meghan reached for her door handle but he grabbed her arm, holding her back, forcing her to turn to face him. "Meghan, you have to acknowledge the past . . . what it did to you, how you felt then and how you feel about it now."

She couldn't pretend that she didn't know what he meant. "I feel exactly the same. I wish I could block out the memory of my father, but I can't."

"Don't block it out. Deal with it."

"It's too painful."

"But don't you see? You're stuck in that time warp. You'll never get beyond those feelings."

"What do you expect me to do? Pretend nothing happened, that my father was a saint?"

"Of course not. But maybe you should find out what he's become."

"What for?"

"So you can put the past to rest and get on with your life."

"What do you want from me?" she cried.

"Everything you can give."

As he said the words, the impact of how true they were hit Justin. He was in love with Meghan, completely and irrevocably, and he would not settle for anything less from her.

CHAPTER TWELVE

JUSTIN LEFT THE NEXT DAY for a speaking engagement in New York. He had been invited to talk about his program at a symposium for social service professionals. He was also going to check into sources for additional funding. When he'd first mentioned the trip a couple of weeks ago, Justin had teased Meghan about getting along without him. She had breezily countered that she'd managed just fine all these years and would have no trouble filling her time. It turned out not to be true.

Her workday was no problem. Clients and meetings and court appearances demanded her concentration, and the hours flew...until it was time to go home. The first night, she brought files home to read, but found she couldn't concentrate. Yet, for the past couple of months, she had been a dynamo, making productive use of every minute so that she would be free to spend time with Justin. Now here he was gone for a few days and she felt at loose ends.

On Tuesday, she asked Stacy if she wanted to go to the club, but Stacy was in a whirlwind of wedding preparations so Meghan went alone.

The aerobics instructor greeted her like a returned prodigal. "Haven't seen you lately," Fritzi said.

"I've been busy."

"So I hear. Your little friend's been telling me about what's going on at that place. Midwood, is it?"

"Midway House."

"That's it."

"What little friend?"

"Carmela Flores. As a matter of fact, she's coming tonight. She wants to see how we do the classes."

Meghan remembered Cookie's ambition to be an aerobics instructor. "Could she teach in a place like this, Fritzi?"

"Not without experience. But she's a good dancer and she's got spunk. What she's talking about is starting a class for Hispanic women up in Adams Morgan at a community center. She wouldn't get paid, but it's a start."

Meghan was surprised. With everyone involved in work projects at Midway, she hadn't kept up with individual developments. So much seemed to be happening. The women had all come a long way in the past two months. Meghan had little confidence that Justin's efforts with their husbands would pay off, but he certainly could be proud of what he had accomplished with the residents. Justin functioned as a catalyst for change—for all of them.

"Meghan, hi!" Cookie raced up, a streak of vitality in a bright orange leotard. "I didn't know you'd be here. Your guy's out of town, eh? Got nothin' to do?"

This kind of kidding was something Meghan had gotten used to. "All the heavy work's finished at Midway," she pointed out. "I've got to get my exercise some way."

"You can go running with us."

"Not when you go so early." Now that the days were short, the women no longer took their run in the afternoon. "I've got to go to work."

"Speaking of which," Fritzi interrupted, "let's get to it. Come on, ladies," she called to the women waiting around and started the music. The hard rock tempo roared out of the speakers. Fritzi led them through a warm-up and then into one of her routines. Cookie followed easily and was thrilled when the instructor called her up front to demonstrate.

"D'you think I can come again?" she asked after the class.

"Sure," Fritzi said.

"The guy at the desk told me my pass was only for one visit. I don't have the bread to join a fancy club like this."

"Can Cookie use my membership?" Meghan asked.

Fritzi shook her head. "Against the rules. But I'll talk to the manager. Maybe he'll let you in as my unofficial assistant. You can be up front demonstrating while I circulate and give some individual attention. You know, that wouldn't be a bad idea."

Cookie gave a whoop. "A great idea."

"I'll see what I can do," Fritzi promised. "Give me a call tomorrow."

Meghan and Cookie showered and changed into street clothes. "How are you getting back?" Meghan asked.

"There's a bus goes down Route One that drops me at a shopping center. Then I'm supposed to call Lil to come get me. Of course, if someone wanted to give me a lift . . ." she hinted.

"Why not?" There was nothing drawing Meghan home. When Justin was there, he filled the apartment with his presence. Without him, it seemed cold and empty.

"Wait'll Manny hears about the club," Cookie said when they were on their way.

It seemed to Meghan that her husband's name was cropping up frequently in Cookie's conversation lately. "Are you going to see him?" she asked.

"Not for a while. Not after last time."

"What last time?"

"Thursday night. After his meeting, he asked if me and him could talk privately. Justin said it was up to me so I said okay. Then in my room, all he wanted was to lock the door and get laid.''

"Oh, no." Meghan knew that it was Cookie's rebellion against her husband's sex-on-demand pattern that had started his violent behavior. She'd finally had the sense to walk out.

"Yeah." But Cookie didn't seem much perturbed. "No way, José. That's what I told him. He doesn't own me, or my body. I don't have to let him if I don't want to and I'm not gonna stand for his forcing me no more." She looked determined.

"I hope you got out of there fast."

"Funny thing is, I wasn't afraid. Then you know what? He said he loved me, so I told him he better change how he shows it. Macho man didn't say yes, but he didn't say no, neither."

It was obvious to Meghan that Cookie was pleased with the outcome. "Are you thinking of going back to him?"

There must have been something in her tone. "You don't think I should, do you?" Cookie asked.

At one time, Meghan's immediate response would have been a definite no, but she wavered. Justin's influence again, and he wasn't even here. "That's not for me to say," was the answer she gave.

At Midway, Cookie ran upstairs to tell the others what had happened. Meghan found Lil alone in the office.

"Hi. What brings you here?" Lil asked.

"What a question. I'm always here."

"Not without the main attraction. I know, there's a window frame you forgot to paint."

Meghan laughed. "No. Thank goodness, all the painting's done with. How's the open house shaping up?"

"No sweat. Ida's got her menu planned. Stella's sent out personal invitations to everyone in the neighborhood and to a whole slew of town VIPs. That friend of yours in social services, Rose Esposito, said she thought she could get the mayor to come. Next week, we're going to follow through with a phone call to everyone."

"Sounds good," said Meghan. "So why aren't you smiling?"

Lil forced a grin. "How's this?"

"It doesn't make it. What's up."

Lil dropped the pretense. "Brian got that pro ball offer. Assistant coach . . . at twice what he's getting as a teacher."

"Is he going to take it?"

"He hasn't decided."

"I know you don't think he should, but what if he does? Will you go with him?"

Lil gave a heavy sigh. "I don't know. Probably . . . because I think he'll regret it, and I can't stand the thought of his being unhappy without me there. Does that sound weird?"

"Strangely enough, I understand."

"I figured you would. How does it feel . . . two days without seeing Justin?"

"I haven't thought about it."

"Liar," Lil accused, but her smile was sympathetic.

"Well, I'm surviving."

"Think you can survive until Friday?"

Meghan was taken aback. "I thought Justin was due back tomorrow."

"Didn't he call you?"

"I haven't been home."

"He called here late this afternoon. He met someone who offered to help him write up proposals for a couple of grants he thinks we might qualify for. That's why he's staying on. He'll probably call you tonight."

"He doesn't have to report to me," Meghan said, aware that her voice sounded testy. "He's a free agent."

"When you love someone," Lil said with a rueful smile, "being a free agent has a different connotation. Believe me—I know."

"No one said anything about love," Meghan told her.

"Why are you afraid of the word?"

"I'm not." The word was harmless. The problem was it covered a range of emotions and was subject to individual interpretation. Love could be used destructively. That was what she feared.

JUSTIN DID CALL HER later that night. "I've been trying to reach you since five o'clock."

"I went to the club." She explained about meeting Cookie and then visiting with Lil.

"Then you know I'm staying until Friday."

"Lil told me."

"Samuels, the guy I'm working with, he's going to be a great help."

"I'm glad for you."

"Meghan, I miss you."

"I miss you, too." Meghan suddenly realized she had never before used that expression and meant it. Ever since her mother's death, she had made it her business never to need anyone. Companionship was nice, romance even better, but she had prided herself on being able to manage on her own.

"Then why don't you join me?" Justin suggested.

"What?"

"You can take a shuttle flight out of National in the morning and be here in an hour."

"I can't leave just like that. I've got work... appointments."

"Can't you postpone them?"

"In an emergency, yes, but not just to have a fling in New York. Besides, you'll be busy with Samuels. What am I supposed to do while you're working?"

"I won't be working around the clock. What about all your O'Brien relatives here?" There seemed a studied casualness in his tone. "You could visit with them."

"I don't think so. We lost touch years ago."

"They'd probably be glad to hear from you."

"What would be the point?"

"Connecting the present to the past. You could find out what happened to your father."

A cold hardness crowded out her pleasure at his call. "I'm not interested."

"You should be," Justin said, dropping his attempt at nonchalance.

"As far as I'm concerned, my father might as well be dead."

"He's not."

"You don't know that."

"As a matter of fact I do. Your father is in a VA Hospital in Brooklyn."

Meghan's head whirled and she drew her breath raggedly. "You have no right to interfere."

"I have no intention of interfering. This is as far as I go. Meghan, listen to me." His voice took on emotional intensity. "You've tried to lock a door on something painful in your past, but you're locking part of yourself behind that door, too."

"You can't make me see my father."

"Of course not. I've no intention of trying. All I've done is find out where he is—so the information is available if you want to use it. Anything more is up to you."

"I hope you didn't go to a lot of trouble because I have no use for your information."

"One phone call is all it took."

She caught his inference. "It was a phone call I never cared to make."

"All right." If he was disappointed, he hid it. "I'll be home Friday afternoon. How about dinner?"

"I don't know. I may have to work late."

"I'll call you when I get in."

"If you like." They said goodbye. Meghan heard the click when Justin hung up. She stared at the receiver and finally replaced it in its cradle. It had been an unsettling conversation.

When she got to the office the following morning, Stacy was solicitous. "Are you sick or something?"

"No. Why?"

"You don't look right. Your eyes are all red. You been crying?"

"Of course not." She hadn't cried in years. Suddenly, Meghan had a vivid recollection of herself at twelve, stifling her sobs in a pillow so no one would hear. She shook off the memory. "I didn't sleep much last night. That's all."

"Justin keeping you up?" Stacy asked archly.

"Don't be cute. He happens to be away. I probably drank too much coffee."

"I should've guessed it wasn't Justin. You're different when he's around."

"Oh?"

"Mellow—and excited at the same time."

"Transitory feelings at best. They never last."

"You *are* in a down mood," Stacy said. "When is Justin coming back?"

"Friday."

"Good. Then you'll get back to normal."

Normal? Perhaps, Meghan thought, she had veered too much from what had been her normal behavior lately. Justin had challenged her intellectual ideas, broken down her sexual restraints and put her in touch with her physical self. She had tuned in to his moods, his humor and passion and concern for people, and this had made her more sensitive to others. But was she losing something in the process? Was she debilitating the qualities that comprised her strength?

Justin had probably called her father's brother to get the information he wanted. But why? He was entitled to differ with her professional opinions, but he had no right to challenge her personal attitudes.

Yet, didn't his very being challenge those attitudes? He had told her about a time in his life when he had succumbed to violence. Meghan needed to unlink that person from the compassionate man she cared for, else how could she allow herself to care? Justin, however, didn't deny the connection. He had refused to be defined by that one violent act and had made his subsequent life reflect the values he considered important.

He was implying that Meghan had mired herself in the past, unable to change the way she viewed herself, her father and her mother, except through the eyes of the child she had been. Was that true? But if so, what of it? Justin talked about opening a door, but what good would that do? Reviewing the past couldn't change what had happened.

ON FRIDAY Meghan stayed late at the office. When Justin called, she would tell him she was too tired to go out, and it wouldn't be a lie. But he surprised her.

"How about skipping dinner out?" he said. "I'm beat."

"That was my line. I was going to beg off."

"Good. I'll bring over a pizza and we'll just relax at home. Anchovies or pepperoni?"

"Neither."

"You want it plain?"

"No..."

"Pepperoni, then."

"Justin, hold it. What I'm trying to say is I'm tired, you're tired, maybe we should forget about dinner and just go to bed..."

His laughter revealed how he read her words.

"If you've got a leer on your face, forget it," she told him. "That's not what I meant."

"Consider the leer erased. Now, about that pepperoni pizza... If I consume the whole thing myself, I'll get sick. Look, I promise I'll eat and go, if that's what you want. You're the boss. I just want to see you for a little while. You've been on my mind all day."

Meghan could have truthfully used the same words. "Okay then," she conceded.

"Great! One pepperoni pizza coming up. I'll be there in a half hour."

He made it in twenty-five minutes, just time enough for Meghan to shower and change into a green, cotton twill jumpsuit.

He charged into the kitchen, put the large flat box on the counter and bent to kiss her. "Hmm, you smell so fresh," he said, rubbing his face against hers. He drew back to look at her. "That fresh scrubbed look becomes you. I'm grimy. I had to check out of my hotel this morning and I've been on the go all day. Why don't you take out a couple of pieces of pizza, keep the rest warm in a low oven and get out the beer while I wash up."

"I don't have any beer."

"Oh. How about wine?"

"There's some red wine."

"Chianti?"

"You're in no position to be fussy."

He laughed. "You're right. Whatever you have will do fine. You can pour us some." He headed for the bathroom.

"I thought you said I was the boss."

He paused at the door. "You are."

"Then how come you're issuing orders?"

"Suggestions, not orders," he said with a grin and disappeared.

But Meghan knew the persuasive power of Justin's suggestions. When he returned, he had taken off his jacket and tie and rolled up the sleeves of his shirt. His face was drawn. Had he, too, been losing sleep these last few days? If he had, it couldn't be for the same reason.

He sat wearily at the kitchen table. Meghan brought two slices of pizza and joined him. She reached for the decanter to pour the wine, but Justin grabbed her hand. She glanced at him and was puzzled by the intensity of his gaze. "I thought you wanted wine," she said.

"Meghan, when you look at me, what do you see?"

"What?"

"Tell me what you see."

"That's a crazy question."

"Indulge me, please."

"Well, I see a tall, attractive man who's had a long, tiring day and who is foolishly letting his pizza get cold."

Justin would not buy her lightness. His hand tightened around hers. "Meghan, are you afraid of me?"

He was referring to what he'd told her on the beach that day. She knew that she had to respond seriously. "No. You would never hurt me." She knew this with a rare certainty.

"But I did hurt someone once."

"That was a long time ago. Justin, why are you bringing this up again?"

"Because, now that you've had time to think, I need to know how you feel about what I told you. We can't just leave this hanging. If you have questions, ask. If you have doubts about me, let's deal with them."

Meghan could see how important this was to him. "I have no doubts—not about that issue. The Justin Forbes I know would never physically abuse a woman. That other person is dead."

"Not dead...changed. Whatever I've done is part of what I am. A deplorable act can't be erased, but it can lead to change. I need to know that you can accept me as I am, knowing that it includes what made me this way."

Meghan was caught by his gaze and, for the first time, realized the depth of anguish he still carried from that youthful experience. "I do," she said with feeling. "It's hard for me to believe that you could lash out at someone as you say you did, but what's important is what you've done since then. I know you as a compassionate man, dedicated to helping people who have been hurt. I may not always agree with your methods, but that's another story."

"I'm not asking for a professional judgment, Meghan. It's your personal reaction I'm after...your gut feeling about me as a man." He paused and then released her hand, but his eyes held hers. "Do you trust me?"

"More than anyone I know," she replied so quickly that she surprised herself. She had tried to disconnect Justin from his past, but he wouldn't let her. He was acknowledging what he'd done and linking that experience to the present. He wanted her acceptance and trust, and he had it. But Justin's case, Meghan thought, was unique. If he expected her to generalize that other men were equally capable of such change, he would be disappointed. She knew too well that it didn't happen.

Reassured, Justin smiled at her.

"There's one thing, though..." she began.

"What?"

"If you were so concerned about my reaction, why did you tell me what you'd done? I'd never have known."

"I wanted you to know. I owed it to both of us. Skeletons get to rattling their bones if hidden away in closets for too long."

He gave her a searching look, and Meghan stiffened apprehensively, expecting him to make some reference to the skeletons in her closet. But he didn't, and she was relieved.

"Enough about skeletons," Meghan said. "The pizza's getting cold."

"Then let's get to it," he said with a smile. The tension lines in his face had eased. His mood changed. "Man, this is good," he said, proving it by finishing half a pizza and two glasses of wine in short order.

Meghan asked about his trip and Justin described the symposium and some of the people he'd met. He told her about the pompous trustee of the Jacoby Foundation and about Alan Samuels's advice on where else to apply for aid. He talked about everything—except what he'd mentioned when he had called her from New York, that he had learned the whereabouts of her father. Meghan was thankful. When Justin said that anything more had to come from her, he'd meant it.

"You're not eating your share," Justin said. "And you're leaving the best part. Stop filling up on crusts."

"I like the crusts. Here—" she pushed her dish toward him "—you can take the gloppy part."

Without the hard crust edge, the triangle of pizza that Justin picked up folded and sagged. When he raised it to take a bite, some sauce oozed onto his shirt. He wiped it with his napkin.

"You're making it worse," Meghan told him. "I'll get some cold water."

When she got back with a clean cloth soaked in water, Justin was standing. She dabbed the stain, which was on the left side of his chest. The water soaked through and ran down. "Hey, that's cold," he protested.

"It's supposed to be. Hot water will set the stain. Look, it's coming out."

She folded her cloth over to a clean section and resumed rubbing. Then Justin covered her hand with his as if to assist, and the circular motion gradually became more sensuous than practical. Through her fingertips, she felt his heartbeat and the rise and fall of his breathing, which was quickening under her touch.

"That's the best I can do," Meghan said, stepping back.

Justin started unbuttoning his shirt.

"What are you doing?"

"Taking this off so it can dry." He draped the shirt over the back of a chair. He touched his damp skin and showed her a sticky finger. "Tomato sauce . . . it soaked through."

Meghan rubbed it off with her wet cloth. Again, some of the cold water dripped.

"Hey, I don't need that." Justin pried the cloth away.

"I was just being helpful."

He took her hands and held them against his bare skin. "If you want to be helpful, I've a better idea."

As he drew her hands up to his shoulders, her fingers savored the smooth tautness of his skin. He put his arms around her and Meghan waited to be pulled against him, but he held her loosely.

"Such as?" she asked softly.

"Do you need to ask?"

The liquid desire in his eyes compelled her forward and she closed the space between them. Only then did he tighten his hold, pressing her against him. Her fingers molded to the hard curve of his shoulders and then slid around his neck.

"I never knew I could want anyone so much," he whispered. "God, how I've missed you."

His mouth on hers was hot and demanding, but Meghan knew she was transmitting an equal imperative. She welcomed the flood of desire that was drowning out the emotional turmoil of the last few days. Sexual need was understandable and appeasable. On this plane, she and Justin had no problems communicating.

He led her to the bedroom, and they resumed their sensual explorations. When she felt Justin's fingers fumble with the buttons of her jumpsuit, Meghan helped him undo them. He stripped her of panties and bra and her body tingled, anticipating his caressing, delving exploration. She loosened his belt and Justin quickly shed his clothes. He reached for her again and Meghan molded her body to his, savoring the feel of him, the rough texture of his chest, the muscular strength of his thighs, his hard, concave abdomen and the thrusting heat of his erection.

There was a frenzied hunger in their lovemaking, which brought a quick and tumultuous consummation. Then, sated and exhausted, they slept....

"MEGHAN...MEGHAN, I'm leaving."

She opened her eyes. Justin, fully dressed, was standing over her. "What time is it?"

"Almost eleven."

"Is that all?" She must have slept deeply. Meghan sat up, pushing her tangled hair back from her forehead.

"Go back to sleep," he said. "I'll let myself out." He leaned over, brushed a kiss on her lips and was gone.

Meghan felt confused. He hadn't even given her a chance to ask why he was rushing off. She had expected he would

stay the night. Not that he had to, of course, but he usually
wanted to. Meghan had an unwelcome thought. Had their
positions somehow become reversed so that *she* was now the
one reaching for him, trying to keep him close to her?

It had been a strange evening. When Justin had asked her
to look at him, and tell him what she saw, Meghan realized
he was asking her to accept the reality of what he'd done.
Not to condone his violent act—he himself never could. But
it had happened, and what Justin had done with the experience was the important thing. He'd been reassured by her
affirmation of trust. But was that trust reciprocated?

She had an uneasy sense that one matter between them
had been resolved, but there was still a barrier. Profession-
ally, despite different views on some issues, they respected
each other and worked together. When they made love, they
seemed perfectly synchronized. Why couldn't that be
enough?

Meghan lay back down on her bed. The pillow Justin had
used was crumpled against the headboard. She took and
squeezed it against her bosom, seeking vestiges of his scent
and his warmth. Annoyed with herself, Meghan thrust the
pillow away. She tossed restlessly for a while and then got
up. There was no sense staying in bed when she knew she
wouldn't sleep. The room seemed stuffy. She opened a window and looked out over the lights of Old Town. But a cold
November wind made her shiver and she closed the window again. Some warm milk might help.

She put on a robe and went into the kitchen. The unfinished pizza was still in its box on the table, along with the
dirty dishes and wineglasses. She busied herself with cleaning up. She hated leaving things messy...always had. Except with Justin, sometimes she forgot. Her priorities
became confused. Not that neatness was a top priority in

itself, but it connoted orderliness and control, qualities that *were* very important to Meghan.

When she finished, she took out a container of milk and measured out a cup, which she poured into a small saucepan and put on the burner. She remembered reading it was the calcium in the milk that helped you sleep. Her mother hadn't needed any such scientific validation. When she heard Meghan cry at night, she used to heat up some milk, stir in a spoonful of honey and bring it to her. Then she would hold Meghan until she fell asleep. Meghan got older, stopped crying and became the one to soothe her mother's tears.

Tonight, though, she felt the need of solace, and she didn't know why. Something was happening between her and Justin, something she couldn't explain. Their physical need for each other was as strong as ever, but there was an emotional adjunct to it that was interfering. Why couldn't things just stay as they were? Working together, talking and laughing, making love . . . Wasn't it enough?

He expected something of her that she wasn't sure she could give. It had to do with her father. Why else had Justin made it his business to find out about him? But it wasn't his business. The way she felt about Justin had nothing to do with her father, with the hatred and pain that the memory of him evoked. It was a personal matter, not subject to Justin's approval. Yet tonight, he had sought hers.

Justin hadn't brought up the subject of her father, but it hovered between them. She sensed that the way Justin felt about her was linked to this whole business. Was he putting the brakes on their relationship? Was that why he'd left her tonight?

Justin had never told her he loved her. Meghan wasn't sure she wanted to hear those words from him because with them would come a demand for a total commitment. She wasn't ready for that. But then Justin might not be ready, either. His leaving her tonight showed that he was holding back until— She broke off the thought. Until when? Until she disposed of her closeted skeletons?

Justin would be true to his word—he wouldn't pressure her to see her father. The next move had to be hers, and Meghan could simply continue as before, pretending that her father didn't exist.

But could she?

Ever since that phone conversation, she kept hearing Justin's words, "You father is in a VA hospital in Brooklyn." Present tense...*is* in a hospital in Brooklyn. Timothy O'Brien had existed, for Meghan, only in the past. His being alive in the present seemed to obscure that reality.

Justin had told Meghan that she had to open the door to her past because part of herself was hidden there. Perhaps it was better left that way.

The milk boiled, frothed up and spilled over. "Damn." Meghan whisked the pot off the burner and poured the contents into a cup. As it cooled, the milk formed a skin that stuck to her lip unpleasantly. She wiped it away and took another swallow. It had a scorched taste, not like she remembered. Something was missing. Perhaps it was the honey. It just wasn't the same. Meghan poured the milk down the drain.

CHAPTER THIRTEEN

THE OPEN HOUSE was scheduled for the Friday after Thanksgiving, and this was the last weekend to get things ready. Meghan had delayed going over to Midway. She wasn't sure why. She had gotten up in the morning feeling edgy. The kitchen still smelled like burned milk, so she didn't even bother with breakfast. Instead, she'd put on a sweat suit and taken a long run by herself, from Old Town past the marina and the airport and then back. She ordered breakfast in a fast food place but the egg was runny and the muffin soggy so she left most of it. It was almost two by the time she had showered and changed and driven over to Midway.

She pulled into the driveway behind a large black Lincoln. A heavyset man was in the driver's seat, drumming on the wheel.

Meghan was about to ring the doorbell when Stella opened the door. She was holding a small overnight bag. "Hi," she said.

"Where are you off to?" Meghan asked.

"That's my dad in the car." Stella's father had switched from demanding that she go back to her husband to pleading for her to visit him.

"I told him he could visit me here, but you know how he is. He wouldn't even come inside." Stella gave her a nervous smile.

"You don't have to go with him," Meghan told her.

"I know that. But he is my father. I can't cut him out."

Meghan started to say something, but changed her mind.

Barnaby Trask opened the window on the passenger side and called, "Stella, come on already."

Stella leaned over to give Meghan a kiss on the cheek. "Don't worry. I'll be all right."

"When are you coming back?" Meghan asked.

"Sometime tomorrow."

"Call me if there's a problem."

"There won't be."

Meghan hoped Stella was right.

She found Justin out back putting a coat of redwood stain on some lawn furniture. He greeted her with a big smile. "Hi. I wondered when you'd get here."

"I took a long run this morning."

"Why didn't you tell me? I'd have gone with you." He gave her a quizzical look. "Or did you want to be alone?"

"Something like that. I just saw Stella with her father. Justin, do you think that's wise?"

"What?"

"Letting her go with him."

"I'm not a warden. Stella's free to come and go as she pleases. It was her decision."

"Under her father's pressure."

"A pressure she can resist if she wants to. That's something we all have to learn."

"Barnaby Trask is trying to run Stella's life. He has no right."

"Nor do we," was Justin's sharp response. "Look, I'm not saying you're wrong, but maybe he's kept on treating his daughter like a child because she encouraged it. Stella may want to get on to a new footing with him."

"Can she?"

"I think so. You know my theory. If one person changes, the other can't continue as before."

"Is there a hidden message for me in all this?"

"It's not hidden."

"You think my father has changed?"

"I have no idea. Maybe he hasn't."

"So why should I see him?"

"To test those feelings you've been hanging on to."

"Ha!" Her laugh was harsh. "I don't have to test them. They're very much with me. Maybe you're right," she said defiantly. "Maybe I *should* see him—tell him all the things I had to store up as a child, and how much I hate him for what he did to us."

Meghan was half expecting Justin to try to argue against her venom, but there was only sympathy in his look.

"Give me that address," she said with sudden determination. "I will go. For my own reasons—not yours, whatever they may be."

"All right." His quiet tone was a contrast to her vehemence. "In fact, you can come with me when I go to New York this week. I was thinking of driving up this time. After work on Monday. Does that suit you?"

The mention of an exact date shook her for a moment, especially one so soon. But why not go now? "All right," she agreed. "I may as well get it over with."

"Good. It's settled then."

"How come you're returning to New York so soon?"

"To have Samuels look over a grant proposal I'm getting ready."

"You didn't say anything before."

"I wasn't sure I'd have it done this week, but I can work on the proposal tomorrow and Lil can type up the forms Monday morning."

Meghan suspected that Justin's New York trip was a sudden decision, but she had no desire to question it. It was somehow reassuring to know that he would be with her. She had no desire to question this feeling of hers, either.

ON SUNDAY MORNING, Justin called Meghan to ask if he could use her apartment to work. "But I won't be home," she told him. "I'm meeting with the others over at Midway to discuss the open house."

"I know. Do you think I could concentrate with you around? It's quiet I'm looking for."

"Come on over then. I'll wait for you."

"You don't have to."

"You don't have a key."

"I'll borrow yours when you get here."

"If that's what you want to do." Meghan hung up. She was puzzled. Was Justin avoiding being alone with her? Perhaps he sensed her confusion and meant to be considerate by not making any personal demands.

When she got to the house, he was waiting. He took the key and gave her a peck on the cheek. "Thanks. When do you think you'll be going home?"

"No special time. I can wait until you get back."

"I'm not sure how long I'll be. Three hours, maybe. Do you mind hanging around?"

"No problem."

When Justin left, Meghan went in search of Lil. She found her in the living room.

"Am I glad you're here," Lil said. "The troops are deserting. Brian's got a game this morning, Justin's off to work on that proposal, Stella's at her father's and Cookie and Clarissa are both in bed with the flu."

"Where's Grace?"

"Spraying her room with disinfectant. I told her she didn't dare get sick. She'll be down in a minute."

"How about Ida?"

"In the kitchen baking. She's decided that the way to get support is to appeal to people's taste buds."

"She may be right." Meghan sat down. "What's left to be done? I'm sure we can handle it."

Lil went over her check list item by item. "We're in good shape," Meghan declared. "There's not that much."

"Following up every written invitation with a phone call is going to be time consuming," said Lil. "There are more than fifty on this list. Justin was supposed to take half, but now he's got this proposal to do, and you'll both be gone next week."

"Only for a day. Maybe we can postpone—"

"No," Lil interrupted. "Justin said you've got some personal business in New York, something you've waited a long time to do. If it's important, you shouldn't postpone it."

"It's not that important."

"That's not the impression I got from Justin."

"I think I'm the better judge."

Lil gave her a doubtful glance. "Maybe."

Grace came in and greeted them. "I think Cookie's a little better," Grace said, "but Clarissa's moaning that she aches all over."

"I hope you didn't get too close," Lil told her. "Some of us have to stay healthy."

"I feel okay."

She looked more than okay, Meghan thought. Grace had lost weight and had bought herself a few new outfits now that she was working part-time, separates that could be worn in various combinations. Instead of the drab tans and grays she had favored, she now wore jewel-toned colors that added warmth and interest to her appearance. Her hair was cut shorter and a rinse brought out its chestnut highlights. Grace had followed Stella's suggestions skeptically at first, but now took pride in the changes she'd effected.

"You look great," Meghan said. "That suit is very becoming."

"Thank you." Grace was still shy about compliments. "It's all Stella's doing."

"Not all," Meghan said with a smile. "She couldn't have done it without you."

"Let's get down to business," Lil told them. "If we get the major shopping done today and make a dent in those phone calls, we'll be okay. How about if you do the phone bit, Meghan?"

"I think I'd rather do the shopping."

"But you know the people on that list."

"Not all of them."

"Still, it makes a difference. A call from you would mean more," Grace said. Though she was still the most reserved, Grace was no longer afraid to give her opinion.

Meghan gave in. "Okay. I'll stay here and man the phone."

"Great," Lil said. "We'll get back as soon as we can."

When they had gone, Meghan stopped in the kitchen to say hello to Ida, who easily persuaded her to have a still-warm apple pastry and visit for a while. Then she looked in on Clarissa who was in no mood for conversation, and Cookie, who was asleep. Having run out of excuses to postpone her chore, she finally went into Justin's office. Meghan hated asking for favors and, even though this was for a good cause, she was reluctant to get started.

It turned out not to be such an ordeal. Apparently the people in the neighborhood, the ones Justin most wanted to reach, were planning to come out of curiosity. Rose Esposito had connections in City Hall and had persuaded the mayor and a few other dignitaries to put in an appearance. Meghan was able to use this as a wedge when she met with resistance.

"You're not sure you can make it? Oh, that's too bad. Everyone's so busy at this time of year. We're all so pleased that Mayor Holscomb was able to arrange his schedule... Yes, the mayor is coming... You might... Well, I certainly hope so. Midway House needs the support of people like you. That's what this open house is all about."

Meghan was sincere, but by the fifteenth call, her words sounded hollow, so she took a break. She leaned back in the chair, stretched, and looked around. Despite the accumulation of furniture from various sources, the room reflected Justin. He had made it his. There was the grandfather clock he hadn't gotten around to fixing yet, the bookcases of unfinished wood, which he'd stained himself, the deep red Oriental rug with the threadbare center medallion that he'd rescued from the attic—and the rocking chair from Rehoboth that Meghan had insisted he take.

Meghan remembered the night they had spent in the beach house, cuddled together in front of the fireplace, the time they had discovered they shared the same taste in food, and all the hours working together on the house—and their lovemaking...oh yes, that most of all. Such a short time and yet so many memories. She had let him become too important in her life. Was it too late to extricate herself? Did she want to? She would have to come to some decision... but not yet. First there was this New York trip to get through, then the upcoming holiday weekend and the open house—which reminded her to get back to her chore.

Meghan looked over the list again. She had already called most of the people she knew. The name Barnaby Trask caught her eye. Stella had asked that her father be put on the list, hoping that he would change his opinion about Midway House. Meghan doubted he would even come. Remembering that Stella was with her father this weekend renewed Meghan's uneasiness about that visit. The open house invitation was a good excuse to call and check on what was going on.

A woman answered the telephone, probably the housekeeper. Meghan gave her name and asked to talk to Mr. Trask. A second later, Stella was on the line. "Meghan, is that you?" She sounded upset.

"Yes. Stella, what's the matter?"

Stella gave a nervous laugh. "You must have some kind of radar."

"What do you mean? Is something wrong?"

"Brad's here . . . he's drunk."

Meghan felt her anger rise. "Has he hurt you?"

"No . . . no. He's fighting with my father. I can't stand to hear them."

Meghan reacted instinctively. "I'll come get you. What's the address?"

Stella hesitated. "Are you sure . . ."

"Of course I'm sure. Never mind. I have the address here. I'll be there as soon as I can." Leaving a message for Lil with Ida, Meghan took off.

Meghan expected trouble when she arrived at the Trask house, and she wasn't disappointed. Barnaby Trask was bull-like in his rage. Brad had been drinking, but he was not drunk. Trask tried to order Meghan out of his house, telling her not to interfere in his family's affairs. White-faced, Stella appeared and told her father she intended to leave with Meghan. Then a strange thing happened. Brad stood up to his father-in-law.

"You can't keep running our lives," he cried. "If Stella doesn't want to stay, stop trying to make her."

"You idiot," Trask bellowed. "I arranged this whole thing for you."

"I know—and I never should have let you." Brad turned and faced his wife. "Stell, I'm sorry. Your father thought if he got us here together, everything would be all right. But nothing's all right is it?" He flung up his arms in frustration. "I knew it couldn't work, even though I wanted it to. I should never have gone along with this." He turned back to Trask. "I want Stella back, but not because you're making it happen. Not that way. Do you understand?"

"You're a fool," Trask told him. "I'm trying to help you."

"Then leave us alone," Brad cried. "I should have told you that from the beginning. Stella," he said without turning around again, "go on—leave. If that's what you want, get out of here. Your father's not going to stop you."

Stella's face contorted as she looked from her father to her husband indecisively.

"Come on," Meghan said and took her arm. "Let's go."

Justin's reaction was a complete surprise. He was at Midway when they got there. The message Meghan had left was that she'd gone to the Trask house to pick up Stella, so he had to know that something had gone wrong. Meghan would have expected him to sympathize.

He took them into his office and closed the door. "Are you all right?" he asked Stella. She nodded. "Want to tell me what happened?"

Stella threw up her hands in a helpless gesture. "My father had this big scenario all planned. I was his little girl, back in his house, and Brad was supposed to come courting, and then there'd be this reconciliation. It was like he was giving me away all over again." She shook her head sadly. "You know, he even had cruise tickets for us as a present...a second honeymoon. He still doesn't understand.''

"What did you tell him?''

"That he can't plan my life. So he got angry at me—and then Brad blew up at him.''

"Brad must have been part of this whole scheme,'' Meghan said.

Stella shook her head with confusion. "I guess he was...but he didn't seem too happy about it. He drank a lot at dinner and then he started fighting with my father.''

"Physically?'' Justin asked.

"Oh, no. Not like that. It wasn't that kind of anger.''

"But you were frightened enough to call Meghan to come rescue you.''

"No. I wasn't really frightened for me.''

Meghan explained about the phone call. Justin was frowning. "Surely you don't think Stella should have stayed there?'' she asked him.

"I think you should have let her decide what to do.''

"I did,'' said Meghan hotly, "and she decided she wanted to leave. You can't be sticking up for those two men.'' She didn't want to believe that Justin was acting out of the kind of misguided male loyalty she despised. "How can you have confidence in anything they say?''

"What I have confidence in is Stella's ability to handle the situation.''

"Why should she have to?''

Stella intervened. "Look, you're both right,'' she said. "I knew I wasn't in any danger, but there was no point in my being there just to listen to them argue...as if they're deciding what's going to happen to me.'' She turned to Meghan. "I guess I shouldn't keep putting off the divorce.''

"Do you want me to start the proceedings?''

Stella took a deep breath. "Yes," she said. "Then maybe they'll both realize that they can't run my life."

Stella left. Meghan could see that Justin was troubled. "You don't think that was a good decision, do you?" she asked.

"I think it's a premature decision. Don't move on it too quickly, Meghan."

"Delay just postpones the inevitable. Why can't you see that?"

"Brad stuck up for her today. I think he may be trying to shake off his father-in-law's influence."

"He was part of this whole scheme. Maybe it was his idea from the first."

"I doubt it."

"Then it means he's easily led. That's another mark against him."

"What about your influence on Stella?"

"That's not the same thing," Meghan declared. "I'm her attorney, and her friend."

"I know, but you're also an authority figure whose opinion she respects and whose strength she may be trying to emulate. Meghan, I think those two just might have a chance if they're encouraged—and allowed—to rely on themselves."

"Stella has decided she wants a divorce."

"I'm not so sure. Maybe what she wants is a symbol of her independence. There are other ways to prove she's her own person."

"Not by going back to Brad!"

"Depends on her reason... should she decide to. If they love each other, they can make it work."

"You're such an idealist."

He finally smiled. "Don't say that so sadly. It's not a bad way to be."

She shook her head. "I wouldn't know." She started for the door, then remembered. "Can I have my key?"

"You don't have to go now."

"Yes, I do. I'm tired."

He handed her the key. "Meghan . . . ?"

At the door, she turned. "Yes?"

"About tomorrow, I'll pick you up at five. Is that all right?"

"Our pilgrimage to New York . . . I almost forgot," she said with faint sarcasm. For a second, she considered calling it off.

"You're not reneging, are you?"

Was he challenging her? "No, I'm not reneging. I'll be ready." She closed the door behind her.

CHAPTER FOURTEEN

MEGHAN WASN'T IN A conversational mood during the long drive to New York. Justin had talked at first, describing the proposal he was bringing to Samuels and what the additional money, should he get the grant, would mean for his program. Finally he'd asked, "You want me to shut up?"

"No, why do you say that?"

"I've been rattling on, but you haven't heard a word."

"That's not true."

"Then what have I been saying?"

"Something about your proposal."

"That's a vague answer."

She gave an exasperated laugh. "I didn't realize I was going to be tested."

"That's all right. I know you've got a lot on your mind. Are you apprehensive about tomorrow?"

"A little."

"When was the last time you saw your father?"

It was funny—she had just been thinking about that parting scene.

Her mother had finally agreed to leave, probably more for her daughter's sake than her own, but Meghan didn't care. She knew it was the right decision. Her father hadn't been home in two days and Meghan had hoped she and her mother would be gone before he returned from his latest binge. But he staggered in just as they were about to go.

It was the morning after St. Patrick's Day and Tim O'Brien wore a drunken grin and a green derby hat. He had tried to give Meghan a Kewpie doll dressed in green, one of those cheap plastic dolls on a stick that they give away in arcades. Meghan had refused to take it. Couldn't he see that she was almost an adult? Her mother had taken the doll and made some kind of comment about how cute it was. Still trying to mollify her husband, to stem his temper. Meghan had seen her do this hundreds of times. It didn't always work. This time, it did. Tim O'Brien lay down on the couch and promptly fell asleep.

Meghan remembered how she'd gone into the bedroom to fetch their packed suitcases and returned to find her mother removing her husband's shoes. "You can't change your mind, not this time," she had whispered vehemently. Her mother's face was etched with pain. "We have to go," Meghan had urged.

"Yes, we have to go," her mother had listlessly agreed, her eyes filled with sadness. The sadness had remained until she died.

Meghan sensed that Justin was looking at her and realized she hadn't answered his question. "It was over ten years ago."

"Do you think you'll recognize him?"

"Of course." Timothy O'Brien had the brash redheaded handsomeness and commanding voice that made him the center of attention—whether he was carousing or brawling, merry or somber. How could she not recognize him?

"Do you think he'll recognize you?"

She hadn't considered that. "Probably not," she said thoughtfully. "I'm not what he remembers . . . if he remembers me at all. I've changed."

They were silent for a while, and when Justin glanced at her, Meghan had put her head back and closed her eyes. Not to sleep, but to indicate that she didn't want to talk anymore. He wouldn't prod. He understood her apprehension. Justin could picture the frightened but determined young girl who had been forced to grow up too soon. She had watched her mother endure, without resisting, until escape seemed the only solution for them both.

It was no wonder that Meghan had steeled herself against a similar fate. She had willed herself to become strong and independent—but at great cost. She feared the consequences of love, but Justin knew that loving did not mean subjugation.

When they made love, Meghan seemed to forget her fear. She was able to acknowledge her needs and passion and to rejoice in their mutual pleasure. But he wanted more—he wanted the love he knew she had to give, once she freed herself from the past.

It was something she had to want to do, not for him, but for herself. Justin knew how hard it was to turn a traumatic experience into something positive. Justin had done that, but it wasn't until he'd been able to tell Meghan about what had happened with Samantha that he felt he'd placed that episode completely behind him.

Meghan had just said that her father might not know her because she had changed. Yet she was certain she would recognize him—because she still saw him through the agonized eyes of a child. Justin desperately hoped that something more than the renewal of pain would result from tomorrow's meeting.

It was almost eleven when they got to the hotel. Meghan refused his offer of a nightcap. Justin had reserved adjoining rooms to allow her the choice of privacy or being with him. She chose to be alone.

ALAN SAMUELS had a continental breakfast with them in the hotel dining room and took his leave. He patted the folder Justin had given him and said, "I'll give this a thorough read this morning. Give me a call about one and I'll tell you what I think. It was a pleasure meeting you, Miss O'Brien. I hope you have a pleasant visit here."

Meghan hoped he didn't notice her strained smile. She nodded and said goodbye. When he left, she turned to Justin. "I thought you were going to meet him at his office."

"I was, but since his office is just a couple of blocks away on Fifty-Seventh Street, I called and told him to hop over and have breakfast with us. I hope you didn't mind."

"No, he's very nice. It's just I assumed you two had work to do together."

"That may come next. It depends on what he thinks of the proposal. But for now, I'm free. Alan doesn't need me around while he goes over it. I figured I'd drive you to the hospital whenever you're ready."

"You don't have to come with me."

"I know I don't, but since I have the time, why not? You might get lost taking the subway." He smiled. "People have been known to disappear forever in those labyrinthian depths."

"I could take a cab."

"You'd have the devil of a time getting a taxi to take you all the way out to Brooklyn. What's the matter? Don't you like my driving."

"I love your driving." *And I love you,* she almost added, knowing that his light tone was deliberate and didn't mask his concern. She wondered why she didn't resent his hovering as intrusive. But she didn't.

"It's settled then. What time do you want to go?"

She took a deep breath. "What about right now? Why put it off? That's what I came for."

On the long drive out to Brooklyn, Meghan felt the tension build inside of her. It was a combination of fear and anger and guilt. She knew the guilt part was illogical. Children often blamed themselves, undeservedly, when their parents fought or separated. Another dimension of her guilt stemmed from having ever allowed herself to love her father during those years when she hadn't known about, hadn't wanted to know about, his abuse. Love had turned to resentment and resentment into hatred. Her mother had kept her from telling her father how she felt. There was no one to stop her now.

Justin let her off at the front door. "Do you want me to come up with you?"

"You don't have to."

"I wish you'd stop saying that. You should know I want to be with you. Look, why don't I park and give you some time alone, and then I'll come up. Okay?"

"All right. What I have to say shouldn't take very long."

"You father may have something to say to you."

That hadn't occurred to her. Was Justin suggesting that her father had become a reformed character who wanted to atone for the past? If Justin expected her to forgive and forget, he would be disappointed. It was too late for that. There would be no sentimental reconciliation scene. She was here for one reason only, to confront Timothy O'Brien, to let him know exactly what she thought of him as a husband, as a father, as a man.

"I'll see you in a while, then," she told Justin, and got out of the car.

In the hospital lobby, Meghan went through the preliminaries mechanically, inquiring at the desk, getting the visitor's pass and listening to directions on where Timothy O'Brien's room was.

In the elevator was a nurse managing the IV for her patient in a wheelchair. The young man looked hardly old enough to be a veteran. He gave her a cheery smile. "What's it like out?" he asked.

"You know, I didn't even notice." Meghan forced a smile. "But since I'm not wet, I guess it's not raining."

"That's okay. You probably got other things on your mind. You visiting someone here?"

"Yes."

The elevator stopped and an older man in pajamas and a robe got on. His sad expression was a sharp contrast to the young man's. This was a large hospital. She wondered how many patients it held, men of all ages, men with all kinds of illnesses—her father among them. The elevator stopped at the fifth floor and Meghan got out.

"Hope your friend's all right," the young man called as the doors closed.

Meghan started down the corridor. A nurse at the desk asked, "Can I help you?"

"Room 511?"

"You're going the wrong way." The nurse pointed. "It's on the other side of the elevators, third door on the left."

"Thank you."

Meghan's steps slowed as she approached 511. The two men in the elevator had stirred her sympathy and she hadn't wanted to feel any softness of emotion this day. Justin's information was that her father was in the hospital to dry out. Meghan was gratified that he wasn't seriously ill. She couldn't say what she had to say to a sick man. Outside his door, she stopped. She hadn't felt the need to plan what she would tell him. Words of silent accusation were implanted in her mind, stored up for years. She took a deep breath and was about to enter when an old man came out and almost collided with her. "For Pete's sake," he complained, and shuffled past.

Meghan went inside. The large room held four beds. Three were occupied. A young man about thirty looked up from his magazine and smiled. "Hi," he said.

"Hello." Meghan looked around. An elderly black man was asleep, and the only other occupant was a burly middle-aged man with a scar on his face.

"I must be in the wrong room," Meghan said.

"Who ya looking for?" the young man asked.

"Timothy O'Brien."

"He just went out this second. Didn't ya see him?"

Meghan shook her head. Not that short old man. It couldn't be.

"He's probably lookin' to bum a cigarette from someone," the burly man offered. "Then he goes to the lounge for a smoke."

"He won't be long," the other offered. "Have a seat. You a relative or something?"

"Kind of."

"Only person comes to see old Timmy is his brother. He says none of his other relatives can stand him." The burly man laughed. "I can see why. He's a real pain in the ass sometimes."

"You shouldn't be saying things like that, Frank," the younger man told him.

"Sorry."

Meghan felt uncomfortable. "I think I'll walk over to the lounge...see if he's there." She backed out. "I'll see you later."

"Sure."

As predicted, the man she had bumped into was in the small lounge at the end of the corridor. He was sitting on a plastic chair in front of the television watching a quiz show.

A couple was at the far end by the window talking in low tones. They looked up and stared. Did she seem as out of place as she felt in this dreary hospital lounge? She was wearing a simple black suit, but nothing could subdue the fiery brilliance of her hair. When she was little, her father used to boast that she was a chip off the old block, and it was only later that Meghan began to hate his claim. The couple lost interest and turned back to their conversation. The man who was supposed to be Timothy O'Brien hadn't even looked around. He was intent on his half-smoked cigarette and on the television screen.

Meghan stood just inside the door. No wonder she hadn't recognized him. He had lost most of his hair and what was left was a faded russet and gray. Had he shrunk, or was it because his shabby plaid bathrobe was too big for him? The man Meghan remembered had been wiry and robust ... taller than she. But of course she had continued to grow after she and her mother had gone away.

This man was in his late fifties, but he looked twenty years older. Had it been the drinking that withered him so? What had he done with his life these last ten years? But why was she thinking this way? It had nothing to do with her—nor with her mission here. Yet, what would she do if he apologized and turned to her with love? How would she handle that? For a moment, she considered walking away. He wouldn't even know she had been here.

But she realized that she couldn't. Sooner or later, this moment had to come.

As Meghan approached, she heard him muttering. "Damn stupid fool ... any idiot knows that." He was cursing the ignorance of some contestant on the program. He looked up at Meghan. "Where the hell do they find these jerked-up people to put on these shows?" he asked. It was obvious he didn't expect an answer. He had spoken to her, but without really seeing her. Meghan drew up another chair and sat down.

"Hello," she said.

He looked around. There was little left of his cigarette, and he was holding it between thumb and forefinger to get the last few puffs out of it. Suddenly she remembered that this was a habit of his, and something tightened in her chest. He brought the cigarette to his lips and took a deep drag.

"You want something?" he asked. The tone was suspicious, but he was looking her over carefully, and she could see the beginnings of recognition in the faded green of his eyes.

"I..." Meghan stopped. How could she answer? What did she want here? Where were the words she wanted to say, words for all her pent-up rage? "Don't you know who I am?"

His eyes narrowed as he peered at her through the spiraling smoke. "Meggie...?"

"Yes," she said through a constricted throat. "I'm Meghan."

"Well, how about that? What do you know about that?" He paused and shook his head. "You're looking good, girl." The cigarette burned his finger. "Damn," he cried and dropped the butt, which he ground out under his slipper. "Been a long time, hasn't it?"

"A long time."

"You know I figured you'd come around sooner or later."

"I'm not sure what you mean."

"Running out with your mother like you did. You never should've done it. That wasn't right."

The words should have been inflammatory, but his whining tone and pathetic appearance kept her from anger.

"I hear you're a big shot lawyer. My brother Paddy read your name in the paper last year...said you won some kind of big case. You live in Washington now?"

"In Virginia."

"Doing well, are you?"

"Well enough."

"Say, do you have any cigarettes on you?" he asked.

"No. I don't smoke."

"There's a machine in the lobby. Can you get me some?"

"Are you supposed to smoke?"

"What the hell do these doctors know? I can do what I want. I signed myself in here and I can sign myself out when I'm ready. A pack of cigarettes for your old dad won't break you."

Meghan got up. She would take this excuse to get away and collect her thoughts. She had been prepared emotionally—but for a different kind of meeting.

When she reached the door, her father called, "Meggie, make that a couple of packs, will you? You can afford it."

Outside, she headed for the elevator. A jumble of thoughts assailed her mind. She saw Justin outside her father's hospital room and rushed over. His presence didn't change anything, but she was so glad he was here. There was another man with him.

"Meghan, this is Dr. Zelinsky. He's been looking after your father."

"I didn't know Tim had a daughter," the doctor said.

"We haven't seen each other for years." Meghan guessed that her voice betrayed her emotional turmoil. Justin, who had been studying her intently, came close and took her hand. "He asked me to buy him some cigarettes, Doctor. Is he supposed to smoke?"

Dr. Zelinsky shrugged. "He should have stopped years ago. At this stage, I don't suppose it makes much difference."

"If he's here just to dry out, then he's not really sick, is he?"

"I'm afraid that's not true."

"But he said he'd signed himself in and could sign himself out when he wanted to."

"Your father, Miss O'Brien, is a sick man. He's an alcoholic." The doctor spoke with the impersonal gentleness of his profession. "This isn't the first time we've had him here. After a really bad bender, he'll come in to dry out, especially if he has no place else to go. When he feels better, he says goodbye—until the next time. The man's liver is shot. There may not be a next time."

"But he could stop drinking...?"

The doctor shook his head. "Tim won't stop, and at this point, it wouldn't help. But I'm glad you're here. He must have been happy to see you."

"I couldn't tell."

The doctor gave her a curious look, said goodbye and left.

"Meghan, what happened?" Justin asked.

"Nothing much. I said hello, told him who I was, and then he asked me to get him some cigarettes. Justin, I didn't even recognize him. He's not the man I remember."

"A lot of years have gone by," he said gently. "Time doesn't stand still."

But for Meghan, it had. She realized that, in her mind, her father had been fixed in those painful memories. And she, too, had been imprisoned in them, unable to let go of the child's vision and feelings, refusing to acknowledge that they warped her view of the present.

"Come on," he said. "I'll buy you some coffee."

"No. Let's get the cigarettes."

"You don't have to go back."

"Of course I do. I'll be all right."

"Are you sure?"

"I'm sure."

They got the cigarettes and went back to the lounge. Her father snatched them eagerly. "I wondered what took you so long," he said. "I thought you were after pulling another one of your vanishing acts on me." He ripped open a pack and immediately lit a cigarette.

"This is Justin Forbes. He's a friend."

Tim O'Brien barely acknowledged the introduction with a nod. "You know, you and your mother never should have left like that. A man goes to sleep and wakes up to find himself deserted."

Apparently, while she was gone, he had been rehearsing what to tell her. It came out in a torrent of words, a jumbled mixture of accusations against Meghan's mother, excuses for himself, and finally cajoling requests for money from his newly discovered daughter. There was no repentance or apology, no admission that he'd done anything wrong. He was unpleasant and pathetic, but Meghan let him talk. Her rage was gone, leaving an emptiness. Meghan was grateful when Justin said they had to leave.

She seemed almost numb as they drove back to Manhattan. Justin's heart went out to her, but he respected her silence. He dropped her off at the front door of the hotel. "I have to see Samuels, but I won't be long," he said. "Will you be all right?"

She nodded and then mustered an ironic smile. "We were both wrong, Justin."

"How do you mean?"

"I expected a confrontation and you wanted a reconciliation. Neither worked out, did it?" She didn't wait for an answer. "I'll see you later. Don't rush because of me."

It wasn't true that he'd wanted anything specific, Justin thought as he walked over to Samuels's office from the parking garage. He'd had no preconceived notion of what would happen. From what Meghan had told him about her father, a sentimental reunion scene hadn't seemed likely. If the man had reformed, he would probably have wanted to contact his daughter before this. Any responsibility or guilt that Tim O'Brien might have felt was drowned in booze.

No, what he had hoped for was a different kind of confrontation than Meghan had in mind—where she could confront the past and her feelings, but from the perspective of a compassionate and mature woman. If she didn't, then this whole venture had been futile.

WHILE JUSTIN WAS GONE, Meghan kept thinking about her father, but she could no longer summon up the red-headed rogue whom her mother had loved, nor the bully who had expressed his rage with his fists. Instead, she kept seeing the shrunken man in the shabby bathrobe. What was that man to her? She had not been able to unload onto him the burden she'd carried around with her for so long. Yet where had it gone? The emptiness it left was no relief.

Justin returned and she was grateful that his business with Samuels hadn't taken long. "Samuels recommended a few changes," Justin told her, "but he'd already made all the necessary notations. All I have to do is incorporate his suggestions and have the proposal retyped. There's nothing more to do here. We can leave whenever you want."

"Let's go now," she said. Meghan had no desire to remain in New York.

The trip home seemed endless, punctuated by toll booths and road signs. Meghan offered to take the wheel for a while, but Justin said he wasn't tired. He looked tired, however, or was she just projecting her own weariness onto him? About an hour from home, it started to rain and shafts of lightning split the sky. Thunder rumbled in the distance. A fitting way to end their venture, Meghan thought.

They drove over the Woodrow Wilson Bridge. ''We're almost there,'' Justin said.

Meghan stared out at the dark waters of the river. An idea had been forming in her mind. ''Justin, I'd like to make some kind of financial arrangement to help him,'' she said.

He knew she had been thinking about what had happened at the hospital. Justin had made several casual overtures, hoping to get her to express her feelings, but she hadn't responded. Her focus was inward, and he had to accept that. This was her first statement, and it surprised him.

''What kind of arrangement?''

''To pay for private medical treatment if he wants it. And whatever expenses he needs to live comfortably when he's out of the hospital.''

''Dr. Zelinsky said he lives with his brother off and on. You may want to talk to your uncle about this.''

''All right.''

''It didn't turn out the way you thought it would.''

''No, it didn't.''

''Are you sorry?''

''Of course, I'm sorry. I knew what to say to the man I remembered. I had no words for the man I saw today.''

''Why do you want to help him?''

''Because he needs help. Because he asked for money. I don't think he wants anything else from me.''

''Maybe forgiveness.''

''Compassion is the best I can do right now. Forgiveness is too much to expect.''

''You still hate him?''

''No. In the man I saw today, there was nothing to admire...but nothing to hate, either.''

When they arrived at her apartment building, Justin carried her overnight bag upstairs. At her door, he said, "I don't think I'll come in. You're tired."

"No, please come in." Suddenly Meghan dreaded the thought of being alone. "I'll make us some tea, with a hefty shot of brandy. I think we both need something."

"All right."

Inside, Justin excused himself to wash up. Meghan used the microwave to get hot water quickly and had the tea bags steeping in the cups when he returned. "The brandy goes in after the tea bags come out," she said. "See, I remembered."

It seemed so long ago that they had first performed this little tea ritual—so much had happened since. Meghan removed the tea bags and poured the brandy without measuring.

"Whoa," Justin cautioned. "You don't want to get us drunk."

"I don't know about that. Maybe I do." She put the cups on a tray and went into the living room. Justin followed and sat beside her on the sofa.

"That wouldn't solve anything," he said gently.

"What's to solve? A solution implies a problem. What we have here is not a problem, but a situation." She took a large swallow of tea, welcoming its comforting warmth. "The situation being that of one elderly unrepentant alcoholic who is drinking himself to death, and one daughter who should feel there's some poetic justice in his ending like that. Why don't I feel that way?"

"Because you're not vindictive."

"I was . . . I was," she cried.

He took her cup from her and set it down, then folded her hands between his own. "That was in the abstract, before you met him face-to-face. You don't feel that way now."

"I don't know how I feel anymore." Meghan shook her head, trying to clear it. "None of the things I'd thought of telling him seemed to fit. I'd even steeled myself in case he tried to apologize."

"Is that what you wanted—for him to apologize?"

"After all this time? No. He could have gotten in touch with me long ago if he'd wanted to make amends. He didn't."

"Maybe it's just not in him," Justin said. "But there could be something else that kept him from contacting you, an undercurrent of shame that he's never acknowledged. He probably never will. Timothy O'Brien isn't given to introspection. He's also not a very nice man."

She gave him a bitter smile. "But he got to me anyway, didn't he?"

"Which reflects on you, not on him." Justin reached and put his arm around her. Feeling her compliance, he pulled her close. Meghan rested her head against his chest. When he spoke again, she felt the soothing reverberations of his voice.

"There's nothing wrong with what you're feeling," he said. "You just need time to put it all into perspective." His solidity felt so warm and satisfying. Remembering how engulfing his passion could be, Meghan lifted her face and pressed her mouth to his.

Justin returned her kiss and his arms tightened around her. But then he pulled away and, holding her at arm's length, looked at her searchingly. He leaned forward again for a light kiss, but when her lips sought to cling, he let her go and stood up. "I'd better go."

Meghan got up. "Why?"

"It's been a tough day. We're both tired."

"Not that tired." She meant to sound flirtatious, but her words didn't have the right ring. Meghan reached out a cajoling hand and was gratified when Justin took it. "Justin, stay with me tonight." She moved closer. "I don't want you to leave. I want you to make love to me." When she couldn't find acquiescence in his dark gaze, she asked, "Don't you want me?"

"Yes, but not like this."

"What?"

"I don't want to make love to you as a solace, or as an escape from what you're feeling."

Meghan didn't understand. "Why not? Don't people seek to lose themselves in making love? Isn't that what it's all about?"

"Not in my book. I think it should be the opposite, that people can find themselves in loving."

That was not the reaction she wanted. She wanted him to sweep her into his arms and smother all conscious thought in an onslaught of passion. Feeling affronted, Meghan pulled her hand away. "Your book?" she repeated sarcastically. "What book is that? One of your therapy manuals? You sound so damn patronizing," she accused.

He seemed startled by her sudden flare-up. "I don't mean to."

"I don't think you know what you mean," Meghan cried. "I thought you wanted me to take the initiative."

"Not like this."

"Why not?"

"You want to use sex like a drug. That's not for me."

"Such scruples all of a sudden."

His mouth tightened as he tried to control his anger. "Not all of a sudden. I haven't changed."

"Really? I remember when you couldn't get enough of making love."

"Making love is not what you're offering."

"You're so insufferably righteous." She shot the words at him and started to turn away, but Justin grabbed her by the shoulders and held her.

He looked ready to shake her. She faced him defiantly, almost hoping that he would. He gazed intently at her and then his anger seemed to drain away. "Meghan..." He paused, then said, "I'll stay if you want..."

She wouldn't let him finish. She brought her arms up and broke his hold. "Don't do me any favors," she said sharply, hoping her words reflected her anger and not her hurt. She had let her guard down and made herself vulnerable. Whether he was right about her motivation didn't matter. It was her own fault, Meghan thought bitterly, for exposing herself like that.

"Please go now," she told him.

Justin didn't argue. "Good night, Meghan," he said, and left.

Meghan went into her bedroom. She tried to feel nothing, tried to empty her mind completely. She unpacked, showered and put on her nightgown. She went to bed and put out the light. Then, suddenly, the tears came—all the tears she had bottled up for years. She wept with shuddering abandon for the hurt child she had been, for her mother's sadness, for her father's misspent life—and then for herself and what she may have lost.

CHAPTER FIFTEEN

MEGHAN'S TEARS HAD MELTED a hardness around her heart that she had held on to for years. But she felt vulnerable without it. She wasn't sure what role her father would play in her life now. That would have to evolve with time. Even considering this question was, she realized, a complete reversal.

She spoke to her uncle, her father's brother, who was happy to hear from her and offered to help in any way he could. He'd even volunteered to be the conduit for whatever funds she would send. His reason, Meghan guessed, was to try to keep the money from being squandered on drink. But Meghan couldn't make her father a prisoner of her largess. There would be no strings attached to her help. She fervently hoped he would use it well.

She had no time to go over to Midway on Wednesday, but Lil called that afternoon to tell her everything was going well. Over fifty people had accepted their invitations to the open house, Clarissa and Cookie were over the flu, and there was nothing left to do but enjoy their Thanksgiving holiday tomorrow.

"I almost forgot about Thanksgiving," Meghan said.

"How could you?"

"It's been a hectic week. I've a lot on my mind."

"You and Justin both. He's not with it lately."

"What do you mean?"

"It's like he's in another world sometimes. I suggested that he cancel tonight's meeting, but Justin says this is a crucial time. So I told him if it's crucial, he'd better be on the ball."

"What meeting?"

"With the men. I know you don't approve, Meghan, but things are happening there. He may prove you wrong."

"He keeps trying, doesn't he?"

"What?"

"Never mind," Meghan told her.

"What happened with you two in New York?"

"It's a long story."

"I'm listening."

"Some other time."

"Okay. Ida's planning dinner for five o'clock tomorrow, but come early so we can talk."

"I'll try."

After hanging up, Meghan wondered what her answer would be to Lil's question, *"What happened with you two in New York?"* Her meeting with her father was important, probably a milestone in her life, but what did it mean to Justin? *"With you two...with you two..."* The words kept drumming in her head. She had been grateful that Justin was with her in the hospital, even though she had known she had to play out that scene on her own. And afterward, he'd been careful not to intrude on her thoughts. An indication of sensitivity—or was it a desire to distance himself? She felt a flush of shame when she recalled how the evening had ended. She had practically begged Justin to take her to bed. His response had been an analysis of her real motives, and a rejection.

In his work, Justin had to maintain a balance between professional concern and personal involvement. It didn't always work. Maybe she had misread his interest in her. It was personal enough, and had been sexually passionate, but was there also the zeal of a do-gooder? He'd been convinced that she needed to break free from the past. Yesterday had been critical, but even before that, from the first day she had stepped into Midway House, Justin's influence had been pervasive. He had changed her life, just as he was trying to change the lives of the people he worked with. Did he consider her in the same category with the others, with the extra dimension, or complication, of sexual attraction thrown in? Now that his mission was accomplished, Justin might want to pull back.

The whole situation seemed so muddled now. Initially, she had looked upon Justin as a natural adversary. Intellectually they differed, but his humor, sensitivity and dedication began to compensate for their divergent views. At first, she tried to deny their mutual physical attraction, but Justin's tenderness and passion had won her over. Now, she wondered if she had surrendered too much—perhaps more than either of them wanted. Justin believed that each person had to make his own life. Did he want any further part in hers?

THANKSGIVING DINNER at Midway was a family affair. The four residents, along with Clarissa, Justin, Lil and Brian, had developed a bond closer than in many families. They had learned to get along, to disagree without fighting, to support without taking over and to accept advice and help without being submissive. Oh, there were lapses, regressions to old habits and defensive postures. They still had a long way to go, but, as Justin told them, the going could be mighty satisfying.

Meghan, however, felt a strange alienation. Did she belong here? Did Justin really want her here?

"Meghan, don't you like the turkey?" Ida asked. "You're not eating."

"It's delicious. I'm just taking my time," Meghan assured her. Not for the world would she hurt Ida's feelings. Ida had taken great pride in cooking up a traditional American dinner—turkey, oyster stuffing, giblet gravy and sweet potatoes. Meghan's compliment was truthful. The fault was with her appetite, not the food, but she made herself eat everything she was served. The dessert was pumpkin pie crowned with swirls of whipped cream. Meghan was relieved when Brian suggested that they wait awhile before having it.

"We should give our stomachs a rest so we can do justice to this superlatively delicious concoction," he said. The others agreed and started to get up. "Wait," Brian told them. "Everyone stay put for a minute. Lil and I have a momentous announcement." He stood and pulled Lil up beside him, then made a grand gesture to give her the floor.

"As you can see, Brian is prone to hyperbole," she said.

Clarissa shook her head. "What's that?"

"Is it catching?" Cookie asked.

"No," Lil answered with a happy laugh, "but I hope what we're feeling is."

"I know," Cookie guessed. "You've set the date."

Lil nodded. Brian beamed. "New Year's Eve," Lil told them. "We both decided that was the perfect way to usher in the New Year."

"Ach, I think I'm going to cry," Ida said, brushing her eyes with her napkin.

"Does this mean you're moving away?"

Grace's question voiced what was on Meghan's mind, too. She hadn't come early enough for a private talk with Lil so this announcement came as a surprise.

"No." Lil's smile was radiant. "Brian turned down the offer from the pros. He decided that we'd both be happier staying right here."

"Poorer," Brian agreed jauntily, "but happier."

"Boy, I bet Lil twisted your arm real good," Clarissa teased him.

"Funny thing is, it was when she stopped twisting that I made up my mind."

Lil looked in Justin's direction. "I took my cue from a master strategist. It worked."

Master strategist. A good description, Meghan thought.

In the living room, the conversation focused on the upcoming wedding. Lil had no close male relatives. "Who's giving the bride away?" Grace asked.

"No one's giving *this* bride away," Lil told them.

"I offered," Justin said with a teasing smile, "but Lil said she wasn't mine to give."

"My father cried when he took me down the aisle," Ida remembered wistfully. "So many years ago. I think it's a nice tradition."

"As long as it's not taken literally," Stella said. Meghan knew what her young client was thinking.

"Are you having a big wedding?" Stella asked.

"No. Nothing elaborate. Just relatives and close friends."

Cookie looked disappointed. "No bridal party?"

"Not if you mean bridesmaids in matching taffeta parading down the aisle," Lil said. "That's just not my style." She gave them a big smile. "If you're all there right in the first row, cheering us on, that's bridal party enough for me."

"How come it's *bridal* party?" Brian asked. "The bride gets all the attention in these things," he complained.

"Because *groomal* party sounds stupid, that's why." Lil's perky answer made them all laugh.

After a while, the conversation veered to Saturday's open house. "Everything's set," Justin told them. "You guys have done a fabulous job."

"Yeah, we did, didn't we?" Cookie agreed.

"I never expected to paint walls and actually enjoy the work," Grace admitted, "but then I'm doing a lot of things I never did before."

"It was good," said Stella. "Too bad it's over."

"You know, this isn't just a one-shot effort," Justin told them. "Getting community support for Midway has long-range benefits. Not just for you people, but for others to come."

"Yeah, well I'm not ready to give up my spot just yet," Cookie said.

"How about if Manny makes you an offer you can't refuse?" Brian teased.

Cookie grinned. "I dunno. We'll see."

Meghan felt out of tune. Lil, Cookie, Stella, perhaps the others, were reaching for the future. Meghan sensed no such forward thrust in her life. Justin had talked about becoming free of the past, but free to do what? This freedom held no promise.

Meghan took advantage of a pause in the conversation to excuse herself. "Tomorrow's a heavy workday for me, so I think I'll pack it in," she said. "It was great." She went over to Ida and gave her a hug. "That was a fabulous dinner."

"But you haven't had your dessert," Ida protested.

"I don't think I left any room. Brian," she called over, "you can have my share as a prenuptial present."

"I accept," he cried.

Lil poked him in the ribs. "Glutton."

Meghan felt ashamed of the sudden stab of envy she felt. A slang phrase, "getting it together," came to her mind. Lil and Brian had done just that, individually and as a couple.

It was something Meghan had never completely experienced—not even with Justin.

"There's two pies so there's plenty for Brian," Ida said. "Come." She took Meghan's hand. "You'll take yours home for later."

Not wanting to disappoint Ida, Meghan complied, saying good-night and following the older woman out to the kitchen. Ida was carefully wrapping a large piece of pie in tinfoil, muttering about ruining the cream topping, when Justin came in.

"Are you coming Saturday?" he asked.

The question annoyed her. "Of course. Did you think I wouldn't?"

"I wasn't sure."

"I've been in on the open house from the beginning. I always finish what I start."

"Finish?" He repeated the word, but didn't comment on it.

"Besides," she said attempting a light tone, "I want to hear your speech and see how you charm all the skeptics."

"Will you back me up if I don't?"

"You don't need a backup. You're the supreme master of manipulation."

For the first time, she looked at him directly, noting his frown and the troubled darkness of his eyes. Meghan was grateful for Ida's bustling interruption. Ida handed her the wrapped dessert with the warning, "Don't squash it."

"I won't."

"Tell her it would taste better if she ate it here," Ida told Justin.

Dutifully, he repeated Ida's words.

"I really can't," Meghan replied. "I'll see you Saturday. I'll come early to help set things up."

"Fine." Justin offered no further argument. "I'll walk you to your car," he said.

"You don't have to see me out. I know my way."

She left, and Justin stared after her. Under his breath, he muttered, "Do you really know your way?"

Ida was standing next to him. "What did you say?"

"Nothing important."

Puzzled, Ida said, "It's not that late. Why didn't she want to stay?"

"Meghan has her reasons."

"Maybe," Ida suggested, "she wanted you should coax her."

Justin remembered what Meghan had called him, the master of manipulation. That was not what he wanted to be—not with her. "I don't think so," he said to Ida. Meghan had been withdrawn all night, looking on rather than sharing. Justin understood her confusion, could guess some of what she was experiencing. Meghan had clung to her old rage and pain as a barrier against a recurrence. Her barrier had disintegrated and she didn't know what to do.

What Justin feared was that she would put up a new defense, that she wouldn't trust him, or herself, enough to do without it. If he came on strong right now, she might take it as another assault. And even if she didn't, he did not want her response to be one of giving in to his pressure. He knew she cared for him, but did the caring go deep enough? What he wanted was her love, freely recognized and freely offered. He would have to wait.

"Come on, Ida," he said with false heartiness. "It's time for dessert."

SATURDAY MORNING WAS GRAY and drizzly. "It's no catastrophe," Justin reassured everyone. "There's plenty of room inside. We're only expecting about fifty people."

"What if the rain gets worse and nobody comes?" Grace asked.

The weather had put a damper on their spirits—Meghan's too. From the time she had awakened that morning, her mood had reflected the grayness of the day. Suddenly she realized that she had to snap out of it. They all did. "Hey, that's negative thinking," she told Grace. "What's a little rain? It will make the inside look even cheerier. We want people to see what a job we've done on Midway House, and they will. Besides, the weather might clear by one o'clock."

Justin flashed her a grateful smile. "Now that's the right attitude."

Stella stood up resolutely. "No sense moping around."

Lil took up the cause. "Okay, let's get cracking."

People dispersed, each with a special chore. Justin caught Meghan's arm as she went to pass him. "Thanks for stepping in with the pep talk. You make a pretty good cheerleader."

It was casual praise but she flushed warmly. "Thanks, Coach."

"Do you have a minute to look over the press release I prepared?"

"Sure." She followed him into his office. Justin gave her a page with a short paragraph. She leaned against his desk to read, aware of his eyes on her. When she finished, she looked up.

"That's nice," he said.

"What?"

"What you're wearing…it's very nice." He reached and ran his fingers over the butter-soft suede of her burgundy top. It was a cross between a jacket and a blouse and a perfect counterpart for her wool challis circle skirt.

Through the heavy material, his touch was hardly an intimate one, but she felt a trembling response. This was the first time they had been alone since returning from New York. Meghan felt awkward, as if, somehow, they were starting all over again. But starting what? She held out the page, inserting it between them, and his hand dropped. "This is all right, but..."

"But?"

"It could be improved. Justin, it reads like a memo. There's not enough information."

"I couldn't describe the event before it happened. I figured whoever comes from the press would add to it."

"Sure, but you could expand a little, give them more to work with."

"For instance?"

"Something about yourself, your background and credentials. Don't make faces. You know that's important."

"This is about Midway House, not about me," Justin protested.

"Midway House wouldn't have gotten started without you. You should put in what makes it unique."

"That's covered in my talk."

"Why not include a little in your press release? It could make the difference between a four-line mention or a good write-up in the paper."

"You think it should be rewritten?"

"Yes."

"Are you volunteering?"

She had to laugh. "I should have guessed that was coming."

"You know the rules. When it's your idea, you're in charge. We can collaborate."

"You really don't need my help," Meghan said, but she moved around to the other side of the desk and sat down. Justin pulled up a chair next to her.

"You're wrong," he said, "very wrong."

Meghan gave him a searching look, but his face was impassive.

They worked together to revise and lengthen the press release. Then Justin showed her the short welcoming speech he had prepared. He wrote well, and with all his experience addressing groups, he didn't need anyone's help. The suggestions she made were minor ones. It was nice, however, to be working together like this. After today, there would be few occasions for collaborative efforts.

"It's a good speech," she told him, "friendly, informative, and not too long. You'll probably have to field a lot of questions, too."

"I expect that. It's okay. The more people know, the less suspicious they'll be. Midway's not a hideaway; it needs ties with the community. If we reach out, other people will, too."

Why did she keep suspecting personal undertones in such innocent comments? Perhaps it was because she hoped they were there, that he was telling her he wanted her to reach out for him. Yet when she'd wanted him to make love to her the other night, he had drawn back, questioning her motives. He wanted her—but on his terms. She was afraid to ask what those terms were, what he wanted from their relationship. Meghan wasn't ready for his answer.

What were the choices—a companionable friendship, a sexual affair, a combination of both...? Then there were the other two extremes, a complete break-up at one end, permanent commitment and marriage at the other. The first seemed unthinkable, the second, scary. Her mother had married for love, and the marriage had become a travesty.

Yet ending the marriage had offered only relief from abuse, not real happiness. Tim O'Brien had dominated his wife for so long that she couldn't establish a separate identity. Meghan was afraid that in her, as in her mother, was the propensity to love too much. Justin would never use a woman as Tim O'Brien had, but Meghan balked at giving any man power over her. Justin knew that.

She wondered if her reservations about their relationship had rubbed off on him. Perhaps he shared her ambivalence. If she couldn't declare herself, how could she expect a declaration from Justin?

Meghan roused herself, aware that Justin was studying her. Why did she think he could see into her mind? She stood up and said brusquely, "You're all set. All you need is your audience."

"Do you think people will come?" He walked over to the window and peered out between the blinds. "Grace has a point about the weather being a deterrent."

"Come on, think positive." Meghan joined him and raised the blinds. "I think the clouds are breaking up."

"Where?"

"That way." She pointed. Justin put a hand on her shoulder, and Meghan resisted the urge to lean against him. "See, there's some blue sky showing."

"So, there is."

"Didn't I say so?"

He swerved to face her. His hand tightened on her shoulder, and for a second, she thought he was going to kiss her. But instead he smiled and said, "Counselor, I like the way your predictions turn out."

"I also predict," she said, moving away from his touch, "that the open house is going to be a great success." She wanted it to be, for his sake.

"How about after today?" he asked. "What do you see for us in the future?"

The question was probably meant to tease her. The word *us* could mean anything. "Sorry," she said flippantly. "My power's limited to a twenty-four-hour period. I can't see beyond that."

"Too bad."

THE OPEN HOUSE was indeed a success. By one, the skies had cleared and a pale wintry sun had made an appearance. Most people had arrived by two o'clock, and when the mayor's party came, Justin made his welcoming speech. He explained the philosophy of Midway House, how it operated, and what it aimed to accomplish for those who sought help here.

"Misfortune should not be allowed to cripple people. The past doesn't have to be repeated, or allowed to govern the present. Each of us is capable of growth and change. That's what Midway is about. We're looking to make the future better, to use whatever good remains from the past, and to create the life we want for ourselves."

He introduced Lil and Meghan and praised their contributions. Then he referred to Midway's first clients and how much he had learned from them. "We can all learn from each other," he concluded. "That's why we invited you all here today. To encourage your input and support. We want Midway to be a part of the community. We intend to be a good neighbor, and we would like to have good neighbors. Thank you for coming."

He invited questions and got plenty. There were still suspicions and concerns, but Justin and Lil were forthright with their answers. There was no overt antagonism, and Meghan felt that the open house was accomplishing its purpose.

She made a point of seeking out Jesse and Martha Glendening, who had spearheaded the petition drive against Midway House. Mrs. Glendening had been won over. Her husband's approval was more grudging. "It could've been worse, I guess," was as far as he would go. But then he added, "I have to admit you've got this old place sparkling. I guess it's better than having a run-down eyesore next door."

Next door, Meghan knew, was over a mile down the road, but she didn't quarrel with his definition. She felt confident that the opposition to Midway House had been successfully diffused. Meghan excused herself and went over to talk to Rose Esposito.

Rose was at the buffet table, enjoying one of the desserts and complimenting Ida on her pastry. "Hi, there," she greeted Meghan. "How's it going?"

"Fine." Meghan glanced around. People were milling about, talking, reading the brochures they'd picked up. "I don't see any scowling expressions," she said. "I think we're a success."

"Just feed everyone enough of Ida's...what did you call this?" Rose asked as she took another big bite.

"Rugalach," Ida said, beaming. "My grandmother's recipe. Josef, he used to eat a dozen at a time."

"Who's Josef?" Rose asked.

"My husband."

"Oh." Rose threw Meghan a curious look but all Meghan knew was that Josef's name was coming up in Ida's conversation more often lately. "Well, the man's a damn fool," Rose asserted. "Abusing a wife's bad enough, but abusing a good cook is positively criminal."

Meghan was used to Rose's brash, outspoken humor, but she was surprised when Ida laughed. At one time, deep shame was her only reaction to any mention of her husband's treatment of her.

"You know, Ida," Rose continued, "Maybe I'll sign up for your cooking class. Think you can teach an Italian to cook Hungarian?"

"Sure."

"Good. And I'll teach you how to cook spaghetti Italian-style."

"All right." But when Rose wandered off, Ida whispered to Meghan, "Noodles are better for you than spaghetti."

Meghan laughed. Ida left to replenish her tray of *rugalach*. Meghan saw Lil beckoning and went to join her. "I think we're a hit," Lil said. "Midway House is slated for a long run."

"I hope so, for your sake."

"*My* sake? Honey, I'm not alone in this."

"I meant all of you."

"All of *us* is what you should be thinking. You're a big part of this project."

"Lil, the project is over."

"No way. Today is all that's over. There's a lot more coming. Justin's got big plans. You know that."

"That's his department. I've got a law practice to run."

"What's this message you're giving me, girl? Are you seceding or something?"

"Don't be so dramatic. I'm not abandoning Midway. I'll continue to take care of any legal work, though there shouldn't be much need, but no more garage sales or open houses."

"We won't need more, but," Lil said with a grin, "there'll be other things."

Meghan shook her head. "I didn't agree to a lifetime commitment."

"Are you sure about that?"

Meghan didn't answer. She was distracted by the sight of Barnaby Trask heading in their direction.

"Miss O'Brien," he said gruffly.

Meghan introduced Lil, then said, "I'm surprised to see you here, Mr. Trask."

"Why? You sent me an invitation."

"That wasn't my doing," said Meghan coolly. "Your daughter thought you should have a chance to learn something about Midway House. But after what happened last week . . ."

She was surprised at the change in his expression. "Yeah . . . well, that was a mistake. It didn't work out the way it was supposed to." He seemed uncomfortable. "Kids these days don't know what's good for them."

"And they'll never learn if you don't let them grow up," Lil told him with quiet authority. "Brad and Stella aren't kids, Mr. Trask."

He flashed Lil an angry look, started to say something, then changed his mind. He shook his head with frustration. "It wasn't like this before. Lately, whatever I do, whatever I say to Stella, she takes the wrong way."

"Maybe you're saying it the wrong way," Meghan told him.

"What does she want from me?"

"You're asking the wrong person. Ask your daughter."

"I will." He went off to find her.

"How can people who mean well do so many wrong things?" Lil asked rhetorically. "Do you think he's seen the light?"

"I hope so," Meghan answered. "This divorce isn't going to be easy for Stella. She can use some support."

"Justin thinks those two might have a chance if they got a fresh start."

"Justin gets his role confused sometimes," Meghan said sharply. "He's not a marriage counselor."

"Why so vehement? Did I hit a nerve?"

"I just don't understand his posture. He claims to be fostering independence, yet he seems to be maneuvering people."

"I don't see him that way at all."

"Your perspective is different from mine."

"That's true," Lil agreed, "but, if you'll excuse me for saying so, your perspective's more than a little foggy right now. Do you want to tell me what happened in New York?"

Lil was so obviously sincere in her concern that Meghan opened up. She told about Justin's having located her father and her decision to go to New York to confront the man she hadn't seen for more than ten years. "What I expected and what happened were totally different," Meghan said and described the scene in the hospital.

"That must've been rough," Lil said. "What are you going to do about your father? Are you going to see him again?"

"I don't know. I intend to help him, but whether we have anything else to give each other at this point in our lives, I don't know."

"Now for the jackpot question—what are you going to do about Justin?"

"What do you mean?"

"Are you in love with him?"

"I don't think I want to be in love with anyone right now."

"Meghan, I don't mean to get on your case," Lil said sympathetically. "This last week hasn't been easy for you. I just hate to see you jumping to the wrong conclusions."

"Which is why I'd better avoid jumping to *any* conclusions for a while."

"I guess you're right. Brian bet me a dollar that you two would follow our lead. That's a dollar I would sure love to lose."

"You and Brian are unique, Lil," Meghan told her. "Some of us have all that excess baggage from the past that we keep stumbling over."

"Baby, everyone's unique—and we all have stuff to deal with. Don't shake your head at me. You'll see. Come on." She linked her arm through Meghan's. "End of lecture. Let's circulate. Have you said hello to the mayor yet?"

"No."

"Come on, then. Who's that with him?"

Meghan recognized the honey-haired young woman smiling up at Mayor Holscomb. "Allison Bragg. She's a reporter on the *Sentinel*."

Allison greeted her effusively. "Meghan, love. How are you? I haven't seen you since that story I did about the Mendez case. You made quite a splash with that one, didn't she, Mayor?"

The mayor obviously didn't recall a thing about the case, but he smiled diplomatically. Meghan introduced Lil, and Holscomb immediately launched into a review of his administration's record on civil rights issues. Lil listened politely, but Allison pulled Meghan aside.

"What's your gig in all this?" she asked sweetly.

"Gig? I don't understand."

"I know you're their lawyer and all, but so much interest from such a busy person as you are . . . well, I was just wondering . . ."

"There's nothing to wonder about," said Meghan. "I've always been involved in women's issues."

"What about the *man* issue here?" Allison's shiny pink lips stretched into an appraising smile. Meghan followed her glance to see Justin coming toward them. "Now there's quite an attraction. I don't blame you one little bit." The smile turned provocative when Justin joined them. "Just the man I've been wanting to meet."

With a sidelong glance, Meghan caught Lil's raised-brow expression. She introduced Justin to Allison.

"I'm glad you could make it," Justin said amiably. "Did you get a copy of our press release?"

"Yes, but I'll need a lot more information. I thought I might get a real human interest piece here. You know, interviews from the women about what they've been through and—"

"That's not possible." His abruptness startled the reporter.

"Why? You can certainly count on me to be discreet in my questions."

"No questions." There was no doubting his determination. "That's something we all agreed. While they're here, the privacy of the residents at Midway House is protected. You can ask them about the program; you may not question them on their private lives."

Meghan silently applauded.

"Then I guess I'll just have to be satisfied with you," Allison said and linked her arm through Justin's. "That shouldn't be too hard. Let's find a little corner where we can talk."

Justin shrugged, smiled and let himself be led away.

"Allison Bragg's a go-getter when it comes to a story," Mayor Holscomb observed.

"Hmm," Lil agreed with a meaningful look at Meghan. "She does seem motivated, doesn't she?"

The mayor excused himself to greet some friends.

"I think that gal's after more than a story," Lil said to Meghan. "Don't you?"

"That's her business."

"Not yours? You're not jealous?"

"No." That was only partially true. Meghan didn't see Justin succumbing to such an obvious come-on, but if he did, she really had no right to be jealous. As she had told Lil once before, Justin was a free agent. There was nothing binding between them. Meghan remembered Lil's reply, that when you loved someone, free agent assumed a different meaning. What Meghan feared were the strictures that came with love. You weren't free anymore when another person controlled your happiness. But she had let it happen. Out of need? If so, her need was as dangerous as Justin's power. Little by little, Justin had extended his sphere of influence in her life. Meghan felt she had to pull away.

Would Justin object? Did she want him to?

CHAPTER SIXTEEN

DECEMBER STARTED OFF unusually cold. Christmas decorations were in all the store windows and restaurants, and the streets had bells and wreaths hanging from the lampposts. There was holiday spirit all around Meghan, but none inside her.

When Meghan's father was released from the hospital, he called her from his brother's. He had received the check she'd sent and would use it for the security and rent on an efficiency apartment his sister-in-law had found for him. "The rent's high," he had told her, "but that's the way it is in New York. There's not much left over to buy a few sticks of furniture," he hinted.

In the background, Meghan had heard her uncle's exasperated voice. "Timmy, can't you be thankin' the lass for what she's given before you start askin' for more?"

"I appreciate what you're doing," was the best he could do. It was enough. Meghan didn't want gratitude. Her uncle got on the phone and said that her father could get by with what was in the flat and pieces that relatives would donate. Still, that night, Meghan wrote out an extra check and sent it to the address he had given her. "An advance Christmas present," she had written, hoping that he would spend it on the furniture he said he needed. After all, it was the season for giving.

Usually, this preholiday season was a slow time at Meghan's law firm. This year was different for some rea-

son and she was very busy. Not so much from new clients.
Initiating litigation was usually put off until the start of the
new year. But many of her cases in progress were coming to
a climax, as if people wanted to get things settled before
Christmas. In addition, Lester Patterson was trying to get
away for a prolonged holiday with his family, and Meghan
volunteered to pick up some of his workload.

"You are a glutton for punishment," Stacy remarked
when she delivered several of Lester's files to Meghan.

"Work is not punishment," Meghan told her.

"When it takes all of your time, it is. Everyone needs a
break. You came in last Sunday, too, didn't you?"

"What of it? I don't mind."

"That's because you're numb. What's with you?"

"Nothing."

"Ain't that the truth. Nothing but work." Stacy didn't try
to hide her exasperation. "Look, you'll probably want to
tell me to butt out, but I think you're a fool for letting Justin go."

"You make it sound as though I had him on a leash or
something. He wasn't mine to 'let go,' as you put it. Besides, we still see each other." The pressure of work had
made it easy for Meghan to curtail her visits to Midway, but
she had no wish to break off the connection entirely. She
cared about the people there—all of them.

"Yeah, you see each other," Stacy said, "but it's not the
same."

"No, it's not the same." Meghan didn't resent her friend's
interest. It emanated from concern, not curiosity. "I
thought it better to put some emotional distance between
us . . . for the time being."

"What on earth for?"

"So I could get myself together."

"Emotional distance, huh?" Stacy shook her head skeptically. "Well, you'd better not take too long. That distance could turn into a chasm you won't be able to reach across."

"I'll just have to take that chance."

"If it were me, I'd forget about that distance stuff and thrash it all out together so I'd know where I stand with the guy. That's what I'd do," Stacy said and flounced out.

How can I do that, Meghan thought, *until I know where I stand with myself?*

Her emotional armor had flaked off like a dry crust, and she couldn't piece it back together. She wasn't sure she wanted to, but she wasn't sure she was ready to expose herself without it. It was the needs of this new self that she had to explore, but on her own—not influenced by Justin's powerful personality or her strong attraction to him.

It was as if their relationship had been put on hold. Neither wanted to end it, but neither was willing to venture forward. Meghan wondered if Justin had the same feeling that she did—that they were at a crucial point, and the road ahead skirted an abyss. They needed to be sure of their footing before taking any steps. For now, it was safer to stay put.

That's why Meghan had kept their recent contacts casual. Justin hadn't seemed to mind, and she took his tacit agreement as approval. Perhaps he welcomed the limits she was setting. He made no sexual overtures, and Meghan couldn't help wondering if he might be finding distraction elsewhere. She even considered allowing herself that freedom but couldn't picture herself being intimate with another man.

Meghan got back to work. She looked over the files of the cases she would be handling for Lester. Nothing problematic, but nothing particularly challenging, either.

Meghan was making some notes when the receptionist buzzed her. "Mr. Klarowitz called."

"Don't tell me he canceled again?" She had been trying to meet with Brad Cranshaw's attorney for the past two weeks. Justin had asked her not to move too quickly on Stella's divorce and, despite Meghan's efforts to the contrary, it was working out that way.

"No, but he said he was running late."

"That's an understatement. He was due here a half hour ago."

"He wants you to meet him at his office instead of his coming here."

"Is he on the phone?"

"No."

"Well, you call and tell him..." Meghan paused and controlled her irritation. What was the point?

"Tell him what?"

"Never mind," Meghan said.

"Are you going?"

"Yes."

STEVE KLAROWITZ WAS A SURPRISE. Knowing that he was also Barnaby Trask's lawyer, Meghan expected someone portly, gruff and smoking a cigar. Klarowitz was young and sharp with a polished surface affability. What he revealed was also a surprise. Meghan looked up from the folder he'd given her. It had not taken much time to read through the sparse contents.

"According to this, Bradley Cranshaw has no assets," she said.

"Not quite. There's his car, a sailboat in the Washington Marina and some household furniture."

"The house?"

"Belongs to Barnaby Trask."

"What about the business? Isn't Brad a partner?"

"No. Strictly an employee, and not even that anymore."

"Don't tell me Trask fired him."

"I'm not sure what happened. The point is that if your client's hoping for a juicy settlement, she's going to be sadly disappointed. In fact, I don't know how Brad's going to pay my fee."

"Stella's not out for a juicy settlement, just what's fair. It's going to take her a year to get her degree and become self-supporting."

"What's fair is one thing. What we're talking about here is what's possible. There are damn few assets to divvy up."

"We'll ask for alimony."

"Be my guest. But if the guy doesn't have a job..." Klarowitz made a helpless gesture.

"A rather convenient excuse at this particular juncture, don't you think?" Meghan asked coldly.

"If you're suggesting that it's contrived, I don't think so. Trask isn't particularly happy with his son-in-law right now."

"We intend to go ahead with the divorce."

"That's up to you."

"To Stella."

"That's what I meant. Brad doesn't want this divorce, you know."

"Is he going to contest it?"

"Not if that's what she wants. He could, you know. She was the one who walked out."

"Mr. Klarowitz," Meghan said with icy determination, "if you and your client should dare to go that route, I'll wipe up the courtroom with you both. My client did not *walk out*—she ran—because she was afraid he would hurt her again."

Klarowitz backed down. "I didn't say that was our intent. In fact, Brad is prepared to sign over whatever Stella requests. Unfortunately, his affluence doesn't match his generosity."

Meghan got up to leave. "Thank you, Mr. Klarowitz. You'll be hearing from me."

Meghan walked back to her office. It was dark now and people were hurrying home or into the restaurants along King Street. Market Square was alight with Christmas decorations. There was a gay ring to the voices she heard. Meghan felt anything but gay.

She should tell Stella about her meeting. After stopping at the office long enough to check her messages, Meghan drove out to Midway House.

She found Ida in the kitchen. "Welcome, stranger," Ida greeted her. "How are you?"

"Just fine."

Ida gave her a thorough scrutiny. "You don't look so fine to me. Are you losing weight?"

"I don't know. I haven't weighed myself."

"You are. I can tell. You're probably eating out of those microwave packages again." Ida's bustling concern was somehow warming and welcome. "At least you'll get a decent meal tonight. I've got a lasagna in the oven."

"Lasagna? Is there such a thing as Hungarian lasagna?" Meghan teased.

Ida smiled sheepishly. "It's Rose Esposito's recipe. She thought I should broaden my horizons."

"That sounds like Rose."

"Rose isn't a bad cook, for an Italian," Ida said and they both laughed. "Dinner's in about an hour."

"I'm not sure I can stay. I really came to talk to Stella."

"So you'll talk to Stella and then we'll all have dinner."

"I'll see."

"You have to eat. Why not here? What's the matter? You used to like my cooking."

"I still do." That much hadn't changed, but other things had.

"So it's settled. Stella's in the living room with the others." Ida turned away to preclude further argument.

An interesting sight greeted Meghan in the living room. With her usual raucous delivery, Clarissa was holding forth like a teacher, and Stella, Cookie and Grace sat around her, watching and listening. They had newspapers spread on the floor in front of them and mounds of evergreen branches and clippings.

"What's going on?" Meghan asked.

"Hi. Clarissa's showing us how to make Christmas wreaths," Stella replied.

"It'd be a lot easier to buy them," Cookie said.

Clarissa was indignant. "At the prices these guys charge . . . no way."

"Yeah, but look at our Band-Aid expense," said Cookie, holding up two bandaged fingers. "Some of this stuff's got thorns."

"So watch how you pick it up," said Clarissa, showing little sympathy.

"What's wrong with artificial ones? You can put 'em away and use them next year, too."

Grace sniffed at a fragrant pine cutting. "It's not the same," she said. "This makes it smell like Christmas."

"You can buy that smell in a bottle."

"No, you can't," Stella said. "Not like this."

"Do you want to make these things or don't you?" Clarissa growled.

"Okay, okay," Cookie agreed. "Just keep those Band-Aids handy. Boy, I'm glad my fortune's in my dancing feet and not my fingertips." The others laughed.

Meghan had heard this kind of good natured arguing before. Though it was without rancor, she had wondered why Justin didn't discourage it. He'd said that he didn't expect people to think alike all the time. Meghan came to realize that these bantering arguments served as an assertion of individuality, but that they usually ended in compromise.

"How 'bout you, Meghan?" Clarissa waved her scissors in a beckoning gesture.

"I don't think so. I'm not very good with my hands."

"You can make a spray for your front door. Sprays ain't hard to do."

"I don't have a front door. I live in an apartment."

"So? A door's a door. Gives it a Christmasy look."

"I'm not feeling very Christmasy."

"How come?"

Suddenly, Meghan became very self-conscious. The women were looking at her and she didn't know what to say. She mustered a smile. "It's still too early," was her lame reply. "Actually, I came here to talk to Stella. Can I steal you away for a few minutes?"

"Sure." Stella got up and followed Meghan out.

"Is anyone using the office?" Meghan asked.

"Justin."

"Oh." Why did just the sound of his name give her this inner jolt?

They went up to Stella's room. "Something's wrong, isn't it?" Stella asked.

Meghan explained what she had found out from Brad's lawyer and was surprised by Stella's apparent relief. "You're not upset?" she asked.

"I thought something really bad might have happened," Stella told her.

"Like what?"

"Someone being hurt, getting sick...something like that."

"This is bad enough. Stella, there aren't many assets. I thought you had joint ownership of the house at least, but it's in your father's name."

"I know. Dad likes to keep his gifts on a string."

"Could there be a bank account that they conveniently neglected to list?"

"No. Brad wouldn't hide anything. He's not like that. We just never saved. That was my fault as much as his."

"Then the only major assets are the two cars and the boat."

"All I want is the one car. I'll need transportation for going to school next semester."

"Stella, you can't afford to be magnanimous. How are you going to live?"

"I don't want alimony. I intend to make my own way."

"You may have to, if Brad doesn't get another job."

"What do you mean?"

"According to his lawyer, he's out of work."

Stella looked troubled. "I wonder what happened."

"What's going to happen to you is what interests me."

"Meghan, I'll be all right. There's that trust fund my mother left me. There's enough for tuition and to live on for a year when I leave here—if I'm careful."

"Your father could help. Maybe this time, he'd leave the strings off."

"I'd rather do it on my own."

"Good for you." Meghan was impressed with Stella's determination. The young woman had traded her submissiveness for self-reliance and was ready to test her independence. "Now that I know what the financial situation is, I'll draw up the papers for you to sign."

"Meghan, do you have to put in about his hitting me?"

"Lord, don't tell me you still want to protect him?"

"I would rather not have that said in court."

"But that's your grounds for divorce."

"Does it have to be?"

Meghan sighed. "Since he's not contesting, I guess not. I'll talk to Klarowitz and see what we can work out. Is this Justin's idea?"

"No," Stella answered, but Meghan knew how pervasive Justin's influence could be.

As they came downstairs, Justin was coming out of his office. He looked surprised to see her. Stella excused herself to get back to the wreath-making group and left them alone.

"I didn't know you were here," Justin said.

"I needed to talk to Stella."

"Is everything all right?"

"It could be better." Meghan told him about meeting with Klarowitz.

"So he really did it," Justin said when she had finished.

"Who?"

"Brad."

"What are you talking about?"

"He quit that job."

"I didn't say that. All Klarowitz knows is that he's out. Maybe he was fired, or maybe it's a contrivance so he can plead poverty."

Justin frowned. "You are one suspicious lady."

"That's part of my job."

"Not part of your life?"

"We weren't talking about my life."

"Sorry." He truly looked sorry and Meghan was disconcerted.

"Whether Brad Cranshaw quit or was fired doesn't really much matter," Meghan said, returning to the subject.

"On the contrary. It matters a great deal."

"Why?"

"Because he said that he wanted to quit, but he also said that he'd felt that way before and never had the guts to do it. This time he did." Justin looked gratified.

"You've been meeting with him?"

"In group sessions."

"After that business with Stella at Trask's house? How could you let him continue?"

"Because I thought that incident could turn out to be a turning point for him."

In frustration, Meghan cried, "Don't you ever give up?"

"Sure I do," he replied. "When the situation is hopeless."

His words sent a cold tremor through her.

At that moment, Lil and Brian came in the front door. "Brr, it's cold out there," Lil said. "Hi, you two. Are we interrupting something?"

"Nothing at all," Meghan was quick to answer.

"Then come upstairs and let me show you what I bought." Lil was holding a big box under one arm.

"It's your wedding dress," Meghan guessed.

Lil nodded, her eyes blazing with happy excitement. "Wait'll you see it. It's outrageous. Not you," she said, veering away from Brian. "You'll just have to eat your heart out in anticipation until December thirty-first."

"Come on, Brian," Justin said, "we're not wanted here."

"You know," Lil said as the two women ascended the stairs, "Justin may really believe that."

"Believe what?"

"That he's not wanted."

"Lil, please..."

"You don't want to talk?"

"Not about that. Let's talk about what a beautiful bride you're going to be."

"Another favorite topic of mine," Lil quipped.

In her room, Lil tried on the dress for Meghan to see. "What do you think?" she asked.

The only decoration on the cream-colored sheath was a vibrant flower pattern embroidered around the high neckline and down the front of the dress. Its very simplicity was perfect with Lil's striking, mahogany beauty.

"Outrageous," Meghan agreed.

"The saleswoman kept wanting me to try on bouffant, frilly stuff, but I told her that wasn't my style. This looks kind of African, don't you think?"

"A little. It also looks American, svelte and sophisticated. It's perfect for you."

Lil grinned happily. "You know, I thought I was going to be blasé about this whole wedding business . . . like why not just go to city hall or something."

"Obviously you changed your mind."

"I did." Lil's smile softened. "I like the idea of a ceremony in a church where Brian's uncle is the minister, and of having family and friends witness our vows. Brian says we can write our own words, but I'm not good at that sort of thing. I wouldn't know how to put what I feel. What would you say, Meghan?"

"I don't know. I've never thought about it."

"Great help, you are."

"Hey, this is your wedding," Meghan chided as she helped Lil take off the dress.

"Sure, but you could use the same vows when it was your turn. This way, you'd have a head start."

"Preparing for a wedding that may or may not ever take place isn't high on my list of priorities," Meghan said wryly.

"That's what I was afraid of."

"Just start with 'I pledge my troth,' and go on from there," Meghan suggested.

"What's a troth?"

"How do I know?"

Lil gave a whoop. "How can I pledge it if I don't know what it is? Maybe I don't even have it."

"It's probably an archaic word for loyalty or love or respect. You've got all those, don't you."

"Sure."

Suddenly serious, Meghan said, "Lil, you know what you should do. Pretend there are no words, no 'I pledge my troth' or any other precedent. Think only of what you are feeling, and what promises you want to make to Brian, and to yourself." Surprised at the emotion in her voice, Meghan gave an uneasy laugh.

Lil's eyes deepened with appreciation and affection. "That's good advice, friend," she said softly. "And not just for me."

When they went downstairs, Ida was ready to serve dinner.

"You're staying, aren't you?" Justin asked Meghan.

Ida answered for her. "Sure, she's staying."

Justin smiled. "That's good."

There would be no point arguing. She had missed the conviviality of this group. When everyone was seated, Ida brought in the huge tray of lasagna.

"It looks marvelous," Meghan said.

"Take advantage while you can," Lil told her with a teasing glance at Ida. "Our gourmet meals may be numbered."

"What's up?" Meghan asked.

"Ask Ida," was Lil's answer.

Ida looked flustered. "Eat," she commanded. "With your mouth full, you won't talk nonsense."

Meghan suspected that it wasn't nonsense.

After dinner, Justin walked Meghan to her car. "Is Josef Kremsky trying to get his wife back?" she asked pointedly.

"Josef's been trying from day one."

"Your first successful reconciliation? How nice," she said sarcastically.

His face hardened. "If there is a reconciliation, and that's not a certainty, it will not be *mine*. It will be theirs."

"You underestimate your influence."

"On the contrary. I take full credit for urging people to make their own choices."

"What if they're bad choices?"

"By whose standards?"

"Theirs, of course."

The frown lines around his mouth softened. "If you accept that, then we're not so far apart." Meghan wasn't ready to agree with him. "Ida has the right to take control of her life," he continued. "I don't think she'll want to surrender that control again."

"Isn't that what she'd be doing?"

"It doesn't have to be. Josef knows things can't be as they were before Ida left. Maybe they'll work it out together. But reconciliation's not something I'm pushing, Meghan. For some people, it would be destructive to stay together. If Grace went back to her husband, she'd be returning to the same horror that she fled from. Herb Canto has no intention of changing his ways. Grace has to develop the strength and confidence to make her own way. Hell," he said with a troubled shake of his head, "there's no guarantee, and I don't have a crystal ball. Sure, I hope that everyone who leaves Midway House meets only with success, but that's not likely."

"Aren't you taking terrible risks with people's lives?"

"I hope what I'm doing is helping them cope with the risks we all have to take. Meghan, you can't spend your whole life being afraid."

She stopped by her car and turned to confront him. Belligerently, she asked, "You think I'm a coward?"

"No." Her feistiness brought an ironic smile to his lips. "You're a fighter, Meghan O'Brien." He reached to touch her cheek, then let his fingers glide over her mouth. She pressed her lips tightly to control her trembling response. "But I do think," he concluded softly, "that you're fighting the wrong enemy."

"And what enemy is that?"

"Yourself."

He kissed her and she could not keep her lips from yielding tremulously. He held her only with the gentle touch of his hand against her cheek, but she felt gripped. It was a long, tenderly searching kiss that Meghan had no thought of ending. It was Justin who broke away. "Good night," he said, leaving her no choice but to get into her car and drive home.

He wanted her. Of that, she was sure. Meghan felt frustrated. They were both so tentative with each other right now. She'd never thought of Justin or herself as procrastinators, yet each seemed to be waiting for some kind of signal. Did he want an invitation from her to resume their sexual intimacy? When he accused her of fighting against herself, did he mean against her desire for him? Would he be satisfied with a sexual affair? Would she?

Meghan slept very little that night.

CHAPTER SEVENTEEN

AT THE END OF THE WEEK, when Meghan had the divorce papers prepared, she called and asked Stella to come to her office. "You'll have to sign forms, and there are matters we should discuss."

"Wouldn't you like to come over here?" Stella asked.

"Better not. This is business, and the atmosphere there gets turbulent sometimes." What Meghan didn't say was that her own emotions contributed to the turbulence. She had not seen Justin all week. She had waited to see if he would call her. He hadn't.

"All right," Stella agreed. "How about Monday morning?"

"I've got to be in court Monday. I thought tomorrow. Lil can probably give you a lift."

"I won't need one. I've got my car now."

"When did that happen?"

"Brad brought it over yesterday."

"Oh...well that's one less thing to haggle over." Meghan thought that, when they met, she would tell Stella it wasn't wise to have personal dealings with Brad at this point. "So, is tomorrow all right with you?" Meghan asked.

"It's Saturday. I don't want you to work on my account. The papers can wait."

"There's no reason they have to," Meghan said firmly. "I often come in for a few hours on Saturday morning. The office is quiet and I can get a lot done."

"I can't make it in the morning. We're having a meeting at ten."

"Surely you can miss one meeting."

"I'm sorry, I can't. Not this one." Stella was apologetic but firm.

Meghan agreed to a twelve noon appointment time. "I'll see you then," she said and hung up. With some irritation, Meghan wondered what was so sacrosanct about a group meeting of the residents. Was this one special?

ON SATURDAY MORNING, Meghan was surprised to see snowflakes when she opened her bedroom blinds. It wasn't even officially winter yet. Since she didn't have to rush to the office, she decided on a leisurely breakfast—but twenty minutes was the longest she could stretch out her toast and coffee menu. She'd have to remember to pick up some groceries this afternoon.

Hanging around the apartment had no appeal. She might as well go in and do other work while waiting for Stella. Since she had the time, she could walk to her office and enjoy the early snowfall. It wouldn't be lasting very long. Meghan hadn't been very diligent about working out lately, so the exercise and fresh air would do her good.

She dug out a white turtleneck sweater and corduroy pants. Where was her brown stadium coat? Meghan finally found it in the garment bag that still held most of her winter gear. Working on her closets was another thing she'd neglected. In the pockets of the coat were a white woolen hat and mittens. She was all set.

In the lobby, she met an elderly man coming in from walking his dachshund. The little dog wore a plaid coat that was encrusted with snow. "It looks like the snow's sticking," Meghan said.

"It stuck on Schatzie," he said with a friendly smile. "She's glad to get back inside. She doesn't like the snow."

"It's probably just a snow shower. The sun will melt it."

"I'm not so sure. Did you hear the weather report this morning?"

"No. Was it bad?"

"One of those 'iffy' ones. You know, *if* the wind changes or *if* this or that air mass does something or other, we could be in for trouble. Then again, maybe not." His derisive snort showed what he thought of "iffy" weather reports.

"I don't think we have anything to worry about. It's too early for a real storm."

"We'll see," he said.

Outside, Meghan noticed that snow coated the grassy areas, and the cars in the parking lot had a frosty film on them. She was glad she'd worn her heavy boots. The air was colder than she had expected and the pale yellow sun she had earlier seen from her window was gone. But the snowflakes falling on her face felt refreshing. Meghan liked snow in its early stages, before people mucked it all up.

To prolong her exhilarating walk, Meghan took the long way around to her office building. It was almost eleven when she reluctantly went in, took off her damp outer clothing and sat at her desk. The morning walk had been a good idea. By the time she left here, the snow would probably be nothing but a slippery residue.

Meghan got out her files and started to work. Her sexual harassment case was coming up on Monday, and the conflicting depositions were going to cause problems. She became engrossed, and a long time passed. Puzzling over whether to cite a particular precedent, Meghan swiveled in her chair and faced the window. It was still snowing.

She looked at her watch—almost twelve. Stella must be on her way. They'd get right down to business without wasting time. If the snow persisted, driving could get tricky.

When Stella hadn't arrived by twelve-thirty, Meghan decided to call. Maybe the morning meeting had dragged on. If so, she would tell Stella not to come. But Lil answered and said Stella wasn't there.

"What time did she leave?" Meghan asked.

"Well, the meeting broke up a little after eleven...."

"That was over an hour ago. She should have been here way before now."

"Calm down. She left to take a walk with Brad."

"Brad! What was he doing there?"

"This was a combined meeting, husbands and wives."

"Oh, Lord." So that's why it was special. Stella hadn't mentioned the reason—probably because she guessed that Meghan wouldn't approve.

"Don't sound so gloomy. It was a good meeting."

At the moment, Meghan was more concerned about Stella's whereabouts than arguing over the merits of Justin's meetings. "They can't still be out walking," she said worriedly.

"Maybe she's on her way over."

"Lil, please do me a favor. See if Stella's car is there."

It took but a minute for Lil to check. "It's parked outside. Maybe Brad's driving her to your office."

"Or someplace else."

"You're not suggesting he kidnapped her?"

"I wouldn't put it past him. He's against this divorce...maybe violently against it. Is Justin there?"

"No, but he should be back in about an hour. I'll have him call you."

"All right. I'm at my office."

"Don't worry."

It was advice that Meghan couldn't follow.

At one-thirty, she left the office. This time, she walked with a purpose, hardly noticing what had seemed so beautiful that morning. When she got to her building, she went straight to the garage to get her car. She couldn't just sit around and wait. Brad must have taken Stella to his home.

The heavy traffic on the roads irritated her, and driving to McLean took longer than it should have. When Meghan pulled up in front of the Cranshaw house, she noticed that there were no tire tracks leading to the garage. Could the snow have covered them already?

Meghan rang the front doorbell. The housekeeper she remembered from her first visit opened the door. "Yes?"

"May I see Mrs. Cranshaw, please?" The woman looked puzzled. "I'm her attorney."

"But she's not here. You know Mrs. Cranshaw left long ago. She ain't been here since."

"Then I'd like to speak to Mr. Cranshaw."

"He's gone."

"Did he say what time he'd be home?"

"I don't believe he's coming back."

"I don't understand."

"Mr. Cranshaw—he moved out."

"When?"

"Last week."

Meghan had a sinking feeling. "Do you know where he went?"

"He never said."

"Thank you." Meghan went back to her car.

What now? she wondered. Where could Brad have taken Stella? If Klarowitz was right and Brad was at odds with his father-in-law, he wouldn't go there. But where? Justin might have a clue. Brad had apparently confided in him enough to gain his trust. Misplaced trust—as this latest antic of Brad's proved. What was important now, however, was finding Stella.

"CALM DOWN," Justin told her.

"I don't understand your attitude," Meghan said. Her initial relief at seeing Justin was being crowded out by anger. "Don't you understand? Stella's gone—she's in danger."

"I know she's gone, but she's not in danger."

"She's probably with Brad."

"I don't doubt it."

"If you know that he's kidnapped her..." Meghan almost sputtered the words.

"I don't know that," he said firmly, "and neither do you. They went for a walk and then Stella left with him."

"Against her will."

"Meghan," Justin said patiently, "Brad was parked right here in front. Clarissa saw her get into the car."

"Then he tricked her."

"Cajoled is more like it."

"Were you aware that he was going to do this?"

"I knew he was going to ask her."

"Then you know where he is?"

"I think so."

"What are we waiting for? Let's go." Meghan was grateful that Justin didn't argue.

In his car, Justin turned on the radio and fiddled with the dial, but there was heavy static. "I can do without music," Meghan told him.

"I'm looking for a weather report. There's a storm watch alert." He finally got an audible station and they heard that the report had been changed to a storm warning. The snow was thickening and there were far fewer cars on the road now. Justin drove slowly. "They'd better get those plows out," he said. "I guess no one was expecting so much snow this early."

"You probably hate me for making you come out in this."

"I could never hate you. If you don't know that by now..." He paused, then changed the subject. "It's not that bad. I've got good traction."

Justin drove to Old Town and pulled up in front of a white brick town house in a row of old attached homes on South Columbus Street. "This is where Brad lives," he said. "He got a reduced price on the rent for managing the two adjoining houses for the owner."

"Quite a come-down from the McLean colonial," Meghan observed.

"Depends on your point of view. I think it's a step up for Brad. He's making a new start."

"Without a job?"

"He's got a job—general reporter for the *Alexandria Community News*, as of last Wednesday. He'll finally get to use his journalism degree. It's not much of a salary to start, but it'll pay his rent and living expenses."

"You think they're here."

"That's my guess. Brad was anxious for Stella to see the house. He hoped it would convince her that he was turning his life around, that he'd changed."

"Do you believe he's changed?"

"Yes."

"I'm not as trusting as you."

"I know."

"You didn't want to come here, did you?"

"That's not true," Justin said. "I have a responsibility to Stella . . . and to Brad. In fact, I tried calling earlier, but his phone's out. I think there's a line down because of the storm. I'm not against checking to see if they're all right."

There was no doorbell, just an old-fashioned brass knocker. Brad opened the door. His smile was welcoming, but nervous. "Hey, come on in." He ushered them into a small foyer. "What a coincidence!" he exclaimed. "We were just talking about finding a phone so we could call you two." He paused when he saw Stella at the top of the stairs. "Hey, isn't this something, Stell? Look who's here." She came flying down. "Weren't we just talking about getting to a phone to call? Isn't this some coincidence?"

Stella's excitement was more subdued but she certainly looked happy. When she came close, Brad went to take her hand, then hesitated, as if afraid she would pull away. It was obvious that they were still somewhat tentative with each other. It was also obvious, Meghan had to acknowledge, that Stella was there by choice.

"I should have called you. I'm sorry," Stella told Meghan.

"I can see that you had other things on your mind."

Her tone was more questioning than accusatory, but Brad broke in to defend his wife. "It was my fault. I didn't know about your appointment." Unconsciously, his hand reached out again, and Stella moved closer to take it. "I brought Stella over to see the house, and then we went out shopping. . . ."

Stella joined in explaining. "There's a big crack in the living room wall, so we got these straw mats to cover it...like the ones Cookie and I put up in our room at Midway. Well, they have them at Pier One, so we went out to buy a couple...."

"In the store...that's when Stell remembered."

"We drove right over to your office, but you'd gone. There was a phone booth on the corner, so I called your number at home and got your answering machine."

"I didn't think to check my messages," Meghan said. *I was too busy panicking and running around to rescue you,* she thought, feeling somewhat foolish and resentful.

Stella repeated her apology. "I'm sorry if you were worried, I know I shouldn't have forgotten, but so much was happening."

"I was anxious for Stella to see the place—and to like it," said Brad. He turned to her. "You *do* like it, don't you?"

"For the hundredth time, yes," Stella said with a smile. "It's going to be fun fixing it up."

Yes, thought Meghan, a great deal had been happening with Stella and Brad. They had apparently reached some kind of understanding. Confronted by the happiness and hope on their faces, Meghan's resentment began to fade. It gave way to a sympathy that surprised her. Not that her doubts were erased, but perhaps she had been wrong—at least about these two. She *wanted* to believe she'd been wrong.

"How about showing us around?" Justin suggested. Silent up until now, he apparently felt that some hurdle had been cleared.

Brad looked anxiously at Meghan, still unsure of her reaction. He was afraid she would oppose him. He didn't trust her.

It's okay, she thought to herself. *I don't trust you completely, either. But I'm willing to give you the benefit of the doubt, if that's what Stella wants.* "Might as well, as long as we're here," Meghan said. "I've always wanted to see the inside of one of these old houses."

"Well, come on," Brad said with relief.

The house was small, but the high ceilings and crown mouldings gave it an old-world charm. It was a far cry from the spacious opulence of the McLean house, but Brad and Stella didn't seem to care. Stella showed off the colorful wall decorations they had picked up. "Aren't they great looking? They were on sale, too. I've learned a lot about budget shopping from Cookie and Ida," Stella said. "With a few added touches, this place is going to be really nice."

"What about college?" Meghan reminded her. "You're still going back to school, aren't you?"

"Yes, but the new semester doesn't start until next month. And it's only about a twenty-minute drive from here."

"So, I gather you're staying?"

Stella nodded.

"Permanently?"

"I'm not sure. That remains to be seen. I'm not ready to rush into anything permanent—not yet."

Brad's look of apprehension returned, which was all right, Meghan thought. He shouldn't take anything for granted.

"Brad and I agreed to a trial reconciliation," Stella continued. "If we decide it's working—"

Brad interrupted. "It'll work," he said with determination. "I'm going to *make* it work."

"I hope you mean that," Meghan told him.

"I do."

"Then you're not coming back with us tonight?" Meghan asked Stella and realized it was a silly question when the young woman flushed rosily. She didn't wait for an answer. "I'll talk to you next week," she said. Meghan and Justin left.

Justin had to brush an inch of snow off his windshield. "Do you have another scraper?" she asked. "I'll do the back window."

"Don't bother. Get in the car and keep warm."

Meghan didn't obey. She used her mittened hands to clean the rear windows. The snow was wet and thick. In the car, she took off her damp mittens and blew on her fingers.

"I told you not to bother," Justin said.

"I'm stubborn."

"So I've noticed." His disarming smile took the sting out of his comment.

The storm was on full blast now, and the wind was causing drifting. On the radio came the news that six to nine inches had already fallen and the expected accumulation by morning was for a foot or more. There was practically no one on the road. Snow plows had finally made a pass at the main thoroughfares, but not the side roads. "It's not icy yet," Justin said. "If we don't get stuck, we'll be okay."

"We probably shouldn't be driving."

"What's the alternative?" Then he had a thought that made him smile. "Of course, we could have asked Brad and Stella to put us up for the night. I'm sure they'd have loved the company."

"You are evil."

Justin persisted. "Can you just picture Brad's face if I'd suggested we sleep over?" She could, and it made her join in his laughter.

The twenty-minute trip to Midway House took them an hour and a half. They got stuck once. Justin backed down the hill and made another charge up, taking a slightly different path. It worked. Meghan was surprised at her lack of apprehension. She was alert to the dangerous driving conditions, but had complete confidence in Justin's ability. She usually preferred being the driver instead of the passenger. Not this time.

At Midway House, Justin pulled up behind Meghan's parked car. When Meghan got out, she sank almost knee deep into the snow. Justin rushed around to steady her. "I'm all right," she said with a laugh, "but will you look at my car. The snow's over the hubcaps. I hope you have a shovel so I can dig out."

"You've got to be kidding. No digging out tonight. You can't drive in this."

"You made it through. So can I."

"Not while it's coming down like this. It's much heavier than before. Look, you've only been standing here for a couple of minutes, and you already have an inch of snow on your hat."

"I do not. Not even a quarter of an inch." She was judging by the snowflakes clinging to Justin's lashes and his hair. She watched, fascinated, as the flakes that touched his skin quickly melted, dappling and softening his face.

"It doesn't matter. You're not going anywhere while it's still snowing, and that's final."

"Whew . . . talk about stubborn."

He grinned. "I was being forceful. There's a difference."

"Really?"

"Yes, really." He took her arm and led her to the front door. "Forceful is pushing for something you know is right."

"And stubborn?"

"Clinging to an untenable position when you know you should let go."

His words had a deeper implication that Meghan didn't want to deal with right now. She stuck to the surface meaning. "Okay, I'll stay until it stops snowing."

BY ELEVEN O'CLOCK Meghan gave up the idea of leaving. The storm was abating, but wasn't yet over. It would be foolish to try to drive home. They had all sat around talking after dinner and then clustered in the living room to watch an old Sherlock Holmes movie. Perhaps it was the hot toddy that Ida had served, but Meghan was feeling mellow and warm, a feeling she didn't want to trade for going out into the cold night—alone.

"We can be roomies," Cookie said. "You can have Stella's bed. Of course, if you want to hold out for a better offer..."

"Cookie!" Ida said reprovingly.

"What'd I say?" Cookie was all innocence. "All I said was—"

"Never mind," Ida told her.

"Your offer's fine," Meghan said. "I accept."

She didn't resent Cookie's teasing her about Justin, but wondered if it had applicability any more. Was there anything left between her and Justin to warrant teasing? She wasn't sure what to make of the way he was acting toward her. During the evening, she often caught him studying her, his eyes glowing with a questioning intensity. When their eyes met, there was an instant connection as if each held the end of an invisible cord. But Justin made no move to pull on that cord. He seemed to be holding back ... waiting. Waiting for what?

"I wonder what Stella's doing now," Cookie said after putting out the light in the bedroom and getting into the twin bed next to Meghan's. Her imagination must have supplied her with an intriguing answer because she giggled appreciatively. "Stella and Brad—they never had no problems with sex—not like Manny and me. Of course Justin says the problem's not with sex. It's with people and how they treat each other...in bed or out. You know you can love someone and still hurt them?"

Meghan realized that Cookie's conversation was really a soliloquy. She didn't have to respond.

"And not just by beating on 'em," Cookie went on. "Manny says I made him feel like he wasn't a man when I pushed him away. But that was because he was actin' like an animal. If he'd acted like a real man, I wouldn't have pushed. But he can't make himself feel good by hitting me— not no more. He says now it didn't make him feel good. So why'd he do it? He swears never again. You think I should believe him?"

This time, Cookie waited for a reply.

"I don't know," Meghan said. "I used to think I had answers, but I don't. You have to decide for yourself."

"Yeah, I know. That's what Justin says. But he also says for me to take my time and see if Manny sticks with it. It's funny. Justin doesn't pull no punches with Manny. I mean the talking kind, not the fighting kind. But Manny doesn't get mad. He takes it from him. He likes the guy."

"Most people do."

"Including you?" Cookie asked.

"Why should I be different?"

"Do you love him?"

The directness of Cookie's question startled her.

"If you do, I'd get the news out, if I was you," Cookie said. "You're wasting a whole lot of time."

"Good night, Cookie," Meghan said pointedly.

"I can take a hint. Good night." Cookie turned onto her side and promptly fell asleep.

Meghan lay awake for a long time.

In the past, sleeplessness usually evoked memories of her childhood pain, memories that had obsessed her. Justin had helped her to shatter that obsession, but she felt in the throes of another. She had allowed Justin to become too important in her life. Indispensable perhaps? It was a troubling idea. She had always guarded her independence. Now that he had insinuated himself into her heart, into her life, into her very being, could she live without him? It depended on how she defined *living*. She could survive—as she always had—but it was a prospect that was captioned, "Color me Gray." Meghan sensed that what she'd always had would no longer satisfy. She wanted the color and vibrancy that Justin had put into her life.

She hadn't replied to Cookie's question, but Meghan could no longer deny the truth to herself. She loved Justin Forbes. It wasn't a sudden happening. Step by step, he had made inroads to her heart. Refusing to be intimidated by her initial coolness, he had captivated her with his humor and energy and compassion. He had drawn her into his life. Even when she differed with his ideas, she'd had to respond to his sincerity and his sensitivity with people. And when they made love... Meghan was filled with a surging warmth at the memory. Making love with Justin was a more consuming and fulfilling expression of mutual passion than she'd ever known. Meghan muffled her sigh against her pillow.

That was the plus side of loving—but what of the other side, her lingering fear of being trapped? There was a yielding factor that could be perverted into submission and surrender of self. She had seen it happen. Yet everything about Justin, the way he dealt with other people, suggested that he valued and encouraged independence—just as she did.

Or was it just as she did? Perhaps Justin had found a way to reconcile the need for love with the need to retain authority over one's life. Maybe she could learn his secret...if he was willing to teach her. This thought took over, soothing Meghan's troubled mind.

WHEN MEGHAN OPENED HER EYES, shafts of bright light from the half-opened window blinds stroked her face. In the other bed, Cookie slept soundly, curled into a child's sleeping posture. The clock on the night table said 7:15.

She lay back on her pillow for a moment and closed her eyes, savoring the palpable touch of the sunlight warming her skin. Her body felt rested—she must have slept deeply and well. A delicious smell crept into the room. *Hmm, coffee.* She wasn't the only one up.

Meghan stretched to throw off her languor, and the stretching felt good. She got out of bed and looked out of the window, blinking against the sharp sun-lit whiteness. The storm was over.

Meghan walked to the door and opened it a crack. The house was very quiet. The aroma of the coffee became more tantalizing. If she fussed about getting dressed, it would waken Cookie. She would just sneak downstairs and have a cup of coffee with whoever was in the kitchen, probably Ida or Clarissa.

But the figure holding the steaming mug of coffee and gazing out of the kitchen window was Justin. Meghan had padded down barefoot so he hadn't heard her approach. She stood in the doorway for a moment, gazing at his dark profile silhouetted against the brightness outside. He wore faded jeans and a white T-shirt. She saw the play of muscles under the stretched T-shirt as he lifted the mug to his mouth, and she noted the thrust of his lips reaching for the rim. He exuded a sensuous masculinity more powerful than surface handsomeness.

Meghan watched him for a long time. There was something so perfect in the picture. Justin looked self-contained and completely together—a man who knew himself and accepted what he was. He was decidedly not a man who needed a woman's submission to bolster his ego. In Meghan's mind, things started to fit into place.

She took a step forward at the very moment Justin turned to face her. Again that instantaneous connection.

"Good morning," he said with a smile brighter than the morning. "You look very fetching."

His sweeping glance reminded her that she was wearing a flannel, granny nightgown borrowed from Grace. "I expected Ida or Clarissa," she said and started to retreat.

"Hey, where are you going?"

"I'd better get dressed."

"Why?"

"I'm wearing a nightgown."

"Which, in case you haven't noticed, covers you from chin to ankle. A most prim and proper cover-up."

"Then how come you're looking at me like that?"

His laugh rang out. "Because I know what the cover-up covers up." He came closer. "Have I made you blush?"

"It's the light."

"Of course. Want some coffee?"

"That's what enticed me down here."

He poured her coffee while Meghan went to look out of the large window. When he handed her the coffee mug, she debated taking it upstairs, but found she had no desire to move. They stood together, close, but not touching. The sun was higher now and streamed upon them through the shadeless window. Meghan felt herself absorbing its rays; warmth and illumination spread through her body and filled a dark hollow deep inside her mind.

She was certain that Justin sensed her feelings. Surely, he would speak up now, knowing how she would welcome hearing him say that he loved her. This was the perfect moment.

The moment stretched, Meghan waited. Then Ida came into the room—and the moment was gone....

AFTER A HEARTY BREAKFAST, it was snow-shoveling time, a massive job that got them all involved. When Meghan put on her heavy clothes and first ventured out, she caught her breath at the impact of the scene that greeted her. The snow was crusted with a glaze that reflected the sunlight so brightly she had to close her eyes for a minute. The sky was innocently, serenely blue. Tree branches were heavy with snow, or else gleamed in crystal sheaths.

"It's almost too beautiful to disturb," Meghan said. Then she caught sight of her car, almost buried in the white stuff. "But disturb it we must," she said resolutely, "if I'm ever going to make it out of here."

"We'll dig your car out," Justin said, "but you'll still have to wait for the snowplow to clear the road."

A little while later, Brian arrived in a borrowed Jeep and confirmed what Justin had said. "You can't move out there without a four-wheel drive."

"I'm glad you got through, sugar," Lil said, giving him a kiss and then handing him a shovel.

Brian moaned. "I could have stayed in bed, you know."

"And waste such a gorgeous morning! How sinful," Lil scolded. "Besides, this if more fun."

She was right. The cooperative effort had the air of a winter festival. It took all morning to dig out the cars and clear the driveway. It wasn't so much the work as the frequent interruptions. There were the hot-chocolate breaks, impromptu snowball fights and general cavorting. Brian started building a snowman and everyone got into the act. When the figure was finished, Lil went into the house and emerged with a long string of blue beads and a colorful chiffon scarf.

"Hey, you can't put that stuff on him," Brian objected.

"Why not?"

"Because it's a snowman . . . get it . . . *man*?"

"It can also be a snowlady, wise guy," Lil said and tied the scarf around the head. "There's no genital proof either way."

"Well, I can fix that," said Brian, picking up a mound of snow and shaping it in his hands.

"Don't you dare," Lil warned.

"Why not?"

"We're apt to get an X-rating," Grace told him, and everybody laughed. The sound reverberated in the sharp, clear air.

Meghan's eyes kept seeking Justin. How dynamic and vivid he looked against the stark white backdrop. How alive! It was freezing, but Meghan suddenly realized that she had never felt so warm. Something hard and cold surrounding her heart was disappearing. It melted into a vapor that she exhaled in a sigh of happiness.

Her love for Justin Forbes engaged every part of her being, intellectual, emotional and sensual. What was new wasn't the feeling, but the fullness of her acceptance of it. She must have loved Justin for a long time, but had burdened this love with the pressure of her fears and doubts. Justin had challenged her belief that it was dangerous to trust any man, but her unwillingness to trust herself was a defense he couldn't attack. He had waited.

Her joyful laugh pierced the crystal air, reaching Justin and sending him to her side. He smiled and touched her face with a snowy, gloved hand. Meghan looked up at him, hoping he would read on her face the message that was in her heart. She felt so open—and so vulnerable. It was this vulnerability she had always shunned. Her protective barriers had given her immunity, an immunity she no longer needed or wanted. She was ready to trust Justin and herself, and their future together. Wasn't this what he wanted from her?

A lone cloud suddenly shielded the sun and cast a shadow over Justin's face. For a brief moment, Meghan tensed. What if she had misread Justin's feelings . . . if she was offering a love he didn't want?

IN THE AFTERNOON the snowplow finally cut a path through their street and Meghan started for home. The side streets were passable and the main roads practically clear as the sun melted what the plows had left behind. She kept glancing at Justin's car in her rearview mirror. She had made no argument when he insisted on following her home in case she got stuck. Instead she offered to reward him with dinner and he accepted.

Except for that brief interlude in the kitchen, she and Justin had had no time alone. They'd had a wonderful morning—shared with all the others. What Meghan now wanted—desperately wanted—was a moment of privacy for the two of them.

Stopping for a light, she searched for his image in the mirror, trying to read his expression. What was he thinking? Did he guess what was on her mind? She felt keyed up and unsure of herself. Had she waited too long? What if she reached for him and he moved away?

Suddenly Meghan became angry with herself. *To hell with that kind of thinking.* She was known for putting up a fight for her clients. It was time she did the same for herself. Whatever happened, she would handle it.

At her door, Meghan fumbled with her key and dropped it. Justin stooped to retrieve it, opened her door and, when they got inside, pressed the key into her hand. "Your fingers are cold."

He kept her hand covered with his and the contact sent her pulse into fast forward. "Does that mean my heart is warm?" she asked.

"That's what I'm hoping to find out."

"Don't you know?" she asked tremulously, abandoning her attempt at lightness. Meghan looked up at Justin and was startled by what she saw. He wanted this moment as desperately as she did.

"I want you to tell me," he said.

Meghan had planned on certain preliminaries—music, some brandy, sitting together on the couch, and then a gradual leading up to what she had to say. Not like this, standing in the foyer still dressed in her heavy, damp stadium coat. But she looked into Justin's eyes and saw tenderness and passion and understanding. Her heart opened up and the words just came. "I love you, Justin." Hearing herself say the words acted like a spur, pushing her on. She came close and reached to take his face in her hands. "I love you . . . I love you," she repeated.

His lips curved in the sweetest smile she had ever beheld. "Finally," he breathed softly and kissed her.

Justin was shaken by the most powerful emotion he'd ever known. He understood what Meghan had been through, how difficult it had been for her to break out of the walls she had put around herself. They were walls whose foundations he had questioned and tried to shake, but they could be toppled only by Meghan herself. And she had done so. It was her victory, but Justin exulted with her.

Meghan's kiss was sweet with promise and fiery with passion. Then she drew away and looked up at him. "You haven't said it yet."

He knew what she meant, but he asked teasingly, "Said what?"

"I love you. You made me say it three times."

He laughed. "I didn't *make* you say anything."

"You kept waiting."

"That's different," Justin told her. "I figured if I came on strong, you'd close the gates on me and I'd have to retreat."

"You did retreat."

"No way," he said softly. "All I did was step back."

"This morning . . . when we were alone in the kitchen . . . there was a moment there when things just came together. That's when I was sure it was right between us."

"I felt it, too."

"But you let the moment pass."

He smiled. "Because I was waiting for this one. I love you, Meghan O'Brien, completely and forever. Is that what you want to hear?"

"Oh, yes. You've never said it before."

"It wasn't true before." He saw her startled look and hastened to explain. "I've wanted to love you from the beginning, but you kept a part of yourself closed up. You denied me—and yourself—the woman you could be, the woman I wanted to love. I guess," he said with a tender smile, "I loved you in stages, knowing there was more, holding back until it was all there."

"And now?"

Justin gathered her into his arms. "Now, we've got it all."

Meghan knew it was true. She felt truly free for the first time, no longer bound by the past. No more constraints to stem this surging happiness. Meghan raised her face to his kiss and gave herself up to the love that filled her heart....

Harlequin Superromance

COMING NEXT MONTH

#314 BEYOND MERE WORDS • Jane Silverwood
Though Francy Rasera can't read a book or a newspaper,
she dreams of opening her own drapery shop. Maryland
attorney Adam Pearce offers his legal expertise—and his
love. But Francy knows their relationship won't succeed.
What man wants a wife who can't read?

#315 FAIR PLAY • Suzanne Ellison
Betsy Hanover and Geoffrey "Spence" Spencer are
pretending to be courtly lovers for the sake of Muskingum,
Ohio's Renaissance Faire, when they truly do fall in love.
But Betsy soon realizes that romance isn't what it used to
be and refuses to sign the premarital contract that Spence
presents her with....

#316 THE RIGHT PLACE TO BE • Barbara Kaye
Monica Jordan knows she should be thrilled to have
inherited a historic mansion in her hometown of Gillespie,
Oklahoma. But she's not. She considers the house a
monstrosity, and she has no idea how she'll ever get used to
living in it—until she discovers that her childhood
sweetheart, Drew Lacey, is back in town, too. Suddenly the
house seems less daunting and her future brighter. If only
she can find the truth behind Drew's return....

#317 RACE THE SUN • Lynda Ward
Despite the pain Brazilian industrialist Ruy Areias de
Fonseca has brought her and her family in the past, Dr.
Elaine Welles finds herself falling for him all over again.
Somehow she can't bring herself to believe that he's only
using her to wreak his revenge on the powerful Welles
family, that his passion isn't real....

Can you keep a secret?

You can keep this one plus 4 free novels

FREE BOOKS/GIFT COUPON

Mail to   **Harlequin Reader Service**®

In the U.S.   In Canada
901 Fuhrmann Blvd.   P.O. Box 609
P.O. Box 1394   Fort Erie, Ontario
Buffalo, N.Y. 14240-1394   L2A 5X3

YES! Please send me 4 free Harlequin Romance® novels and my free surprise gift. Then send me 8 brand-new novels every month as they come off the presses. Bill me at the low price of $1.99 each*—an 11% saving off the retail price. There are no shipping, handling or other hidden costs. There is no minimum number of books I must purchase. I can always return a shipment and cancel at any time. Even if I never buy another book from Harlequin, the 4 free novels and the surprise gift are mine to keep forever.   118 BPR BP7F

*$1.99 in Canada plus 89¢ postage and handling per shipment.

Name _____ (PLEASE PRINT)

Address _____ Apt. No. _____

City _____ State/Prov. _____ Zip/Postal Code _____

This offer is limited to one order per household and not valid to present subscribers. Price is subject to change.   MSR-SUB-1B

◈HARLEQUIN *Temptation*

Give in to Temptation! Harlequin Temptation

The story of a woman who knows her own mind, her own heart . . . and of the man who touches her, body and soul.

Intimate, sexy stories of today's woman—her troubles, her triumphs, her tears, her laughter.

And her ultimate commitment to love.

Four new titles each month—get 'em while they're hot.
Available wherever paperbacks are sold.   Temp-1

HARLEQUIN SIGNATURE EDITION

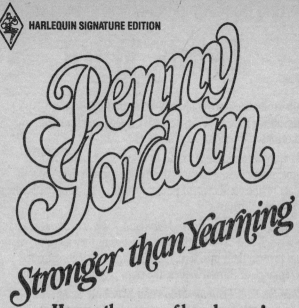

Penny Jordan

Stronger than Yearning

He was the man of her dreams!

The same dark hair, the same mocking eyes; it was as if the Regency rake of the portrait, the seducer of Jenna's dream, had come to life. Jenna, believing the last of the Deverils dead, was determined to buy the great old Yorkshire Hall—to claim it for her daughter, Lucy, and put to rest some of the painful memories of Lucy's birth. She had no way of knowing that a direct descendant of the black sheep Deveril even existed—or that James Allingham and his own powerful yearnings would disrupt her plan entirely.

Penny Jordan's first Harlequin Signature Edition *Love's Choices* was an outstanding success. Penny Jordan has written more than 40 best-selling titles—more than 4 million copies sold.

Now, be sure to buy her latest bestseller, *Stronger Than Yearning*. Available wherever paperbacks are sold—in June.

STRONG-1R

HARLEQUIN SUPERROMANCE BRINGS YOU...

Lynda Ward

Superromance readers already know that Lynda Ward possesses a unique ability to weave words into heartfelt emotions and exciting drama.

Now, Superromance is proud to bring you Lynda's tour de force: an ambitious saga of three sisters whose lives are torn apart by the conflicts and power struggles that come with being born into a dynasty.

In *Race the Sun, Leap the Moon* and *Touch the Stars*, readers will laugh and cry with the Welles sisters as they learn to live and love on their own terms, all the while struggling for the acceptance of Burton Welles, the stern patriarch of the clan.

Race the Sun, Leap the Moon and *Touch the Stars*...a dramatic trilogy you won't want to miss. Coming to you in July, August and September.

The Welles Family Trilogy

LYNDA-1A